# OCEAN DRIVE

# OCEAN DRIVE

A NOVEL

## SAM WIEBE

HARBOUR
PUBLISHING

*For Carly*

Harbour Publishing Co. Ltd.
P.O. Box 219, Madeira Park, BC, VON 2H0
www.harbourpublishing.com

Edited by Derek Fairbridge
Cover and text design by Libris Simas Ferraz / Onça Publishing
Cover photograph by Sam Wiebe
Map by Emilija Mihajlov
Printed and bound in Canada
Printed on 100% recycled paper

Harbour Publishing acknowledges the support of the Canada Council for the Arts,
the Government of Canada, and the Province of British Columbia through the
BC Arts Council.

Library and Archives Canada Cataloguing in Publication

Title: Ocean drive : a novel / Sam Wiebe.
Names: Wiebe, Sam, author.
Identifiers: Canadiana (print) 20240292952 | Canadiana (ebook) 20240292979 |
      ISBN 9781990776694 (softcover) | ISBN 9781990776700 (EPUB)
Subjects: LCGFT: Detective and mystery fiction. | LCGFT: Novels.
Classification: LCC PS8645.I3236 O24 2024 | DDC C813/.6—dc23

A new report about policing of Metro Vancouver port terminal facilities says there's "literally no downside" for organized criminals to set up shop.
—*The Canadian Press*, September 29, 2023

There's no rock bottom anymore, it's a grave.
—former outlaw biker

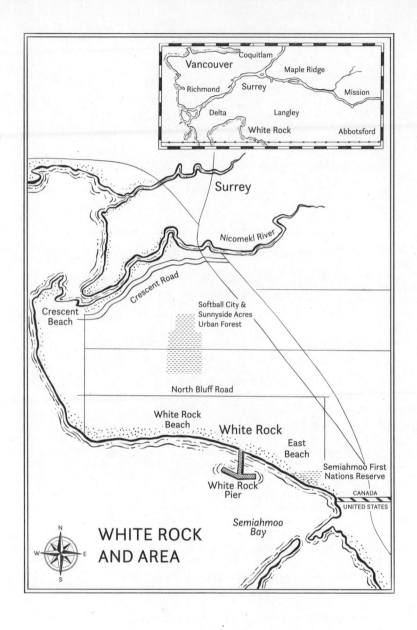

# ONE

He walked out of Kent on statutory release, with three years of parole to look forward to. Reading over the regulations, the timetable of visits with his PO, he thought about staying inside. Serve the full ten and come out clean, clear, beholden to no one.

This isn't freedom, thought Cameron Shaw, tucking the binder of paperwork into the brown grocery bag that held his toiletries and ID. This is just a slightly longer leash.

If Cam had learned anything, these seven lost years, it was that owing people, needing them, always proved dangerous.

It was raining lightly, and he'd turned down a ride. As he walked toward the bus stop, he breathed in the cold September air and found it a welcome change from the stale sweat and antiseptic smell of prison. He wasn't free yet, but this was no doubt better. And who knew what might happen?

Maybe the note wasn't entirely bullshit.

It had come to him through legal aid. His fourth case worker in seven years. Cam couldn't remember her name. Nice, eager, but clearly overworked, she'd recited the contents of the note to him the night before he was released.

"There's no name, and the lady who left it didn't leave one. It says, 'I'll be at the Home Diner in Langley the afternoon you're released. Our meeting will be worth your while. How much is up to you.'"

"Sounds like bullshit," Cam told the assistant. Ariel. Her name was Ariel.

"Could very well be," Ariel said. "The lady seemed on the level, but I wouldn't let it mess up your plans."

As if he had plans.

It was a little over an hour to Langley. A sheriff's van dropped him off. At the Willowbrook Mall, he bought a pair of black Rockports, blue Wranglers, a soft, blue checked flannel shirt. Changing in the food court restroom, he tossed his old clothes. The ratty Carhartts and D.O.A. hoodie didn't fit properly anymore. He'd slimmed down in prison, bulked up in the chest and shoulders.

The face in the mirror was gaunt, sun-deprived, fearful.

At noon he walked into the Home Diner, past a revolving display of pies and cakes that looked like a television idea of home. A woman at a booth in the far corner nodded to him.

Cam sat down across from her, set his new Arcteryx backpack between his feet.

"Zoe," she said.

"Cameron."

She was almost as tall as him, say five ten, and probably fifty pounds heavier. Her suit was a well-tailored metallic grey, expensive looking, and her watch was large and faceless. *Big shot*, thought Cam. Her face was pretty, her hazel eyes showing something warmer than contempt.

"Order whatever you'd like," she said.

"Steak and eggs, coffee."

"You tell the *waiter*." She smiled. "Been a while, hasn't it?"

Cam nodded.

"It passes. By tonight you'll barely remember the last seven years."

He shrugged, not fucking likely, but said nothing.

Zoe dangled the tea bag above her cup, letting the last few droplets fall. "I'm glad you decided to come."

"Your note said there'd be money involved."

"An opportunity for it, yes. Let's order first."

She flagged down a waiter and ordered one poached egg, dry toast, a fruit cup. Cam ordered his steak and eggs. The waiter set an ashtray full of plastic cream thimbles between them.

"Your breakfast is on me," Zoe said, once they were alone again, their voices safely beneath the general murmur of the restaurant. "I also have a cheque for you for a thousand dollars, plus a lead on some legitimate work."

"Legitimate," Cam repeated. "Meaning the rest of your proposition isn't?"

The bottom of her mouth tightened. "It's not illegal, I can tell you that. You'll want to hear it."

"You say so."

"Now, the cheque and the job lead are yours regardless. We want you to have those as a gesture of good faith. The proposition is both of ours to take or leave—meaning you have to agree and I have to think you're up to it. Disclosure in this case is a one-way street. I'll ask you some questions and I expect answers, full, frank and candid. You can ask me what you want, and I may or may not respond. That's how this will work."

Cam drank some coffee. Hotter than what was served in Kent. It scalded his throat.

3

"Are you a guilty man, Mr. Shaw?"

The question startled him, and for a moment he couldn't think of how to reply.

"I'm not speaking philosophically," Zoe said. "We're all sinners, if you believe certain sects. What we're interested in is, did you commit the crime you were imprisoned for?"

"I served time, didn't I?"

Zoe scowled. "Those are the kinds of answers you and I need to avoid if we want to develop a working relationship. No equivocations. No leaving things out. You committed the crime you were imprisoned for—yes or no?"

"Yeah," Cam said.

"Good," Zoe said, looking pleased. "Now tell me about it."


He'd been, what, twenty-two? A few months shy. A different person entirely. Cam had abandoned community college to work full-time with his uncle. Minor renovations and electrical, a lot of drywall, mostly hauling the stuff Uncle Pete couldn't, on account of his back.

In White Rock there were dozens of rich clients that relied on Pete to build their decks and garden sheds, restore the teak on their yachts, turn their basements into trophy rooms and man-caves. Soundproofing, flooring, clearing out gutters. Peter Shaw handled it all, and did so under the table, making him a popular man in the beachfront border town.

At twenty-two, Cam had wanted nothing more than the backroom of his uncle's place, enough money for booze and pot and cigarettes, and a beater to drive around on the weekends. College? Sell it to someone else.

The Garricks had been Pete's best customers. Roger and Elizabeth. A castle of a home near the White Rock promenade, a cottage in Point Roberts nearly the same size, and a new yacht in the marina seemingly every year.

Cam had been working at the Garricks' home that night, alone. He'd been drinking a little, had smoked a joint earlier that day. A freak storm had pierced the roof, soaked the kitchen wall and burnt out the circuitry. Pete had entrusted the job to Cam, thinking he was ready to work on his own.

The Garricks had come home later that night. Both had been drinking. Roger more so, crushing his wife's azaleas under the wheel of his Lexus.

They'd argued, he and Roger Garrick. Cam couldn't remember the words. But Roger had accused him of something, and the drunk man had picked up the stainless steel trim guard for painting.

Cam's first legal aid lawyer told him it was only provocation that saved him from a murder charge. If the defence could prove that Roger Garrick provoked him by word or deed, to the point where a normal person would lose control, then the jury must opt for manslaughter. Thankfully Roger Garrick's skin cells had been on the handle of the tool, Cam's blood on the blade.

Cam, five foot eleven and one seventy, felt the edge cut into the muscle of his shoulder.

He'd swatted the tool out of Roger Garrick's hand,
        taken up what was closest to him,
            a hammer,
                and beat the older man's head in while
                    his pregnant wife looked on.

The official cause of death was cardiac failure, though on the stand, the pathologist who'd done the autopsy impressed upon the jury that traumatic head wounds such as those Roger Garrick sustained could and very likely would have been lethal.

Most of what Cam remembered from that night was the aftermath: the shrieks of Elizabeth Garrick, his own stunned revelation at the blood on his hand, the small black wisps of hair still matted to the hammer's head. The pain in his shoulder and the rush of adrenaline, turning into panic, as the man coughed out his last breath.

The memories still triggered flashes of that night, the same feelings of power, helplessness. Just snapped, someone had claimed. It was more like a fizz, your brain like a shaken-up Pepsi bottle, overflowing—

—and then suddenly reduced, empty.


He'd left a few things out, but by the time Cam finished reciting the details of his arrest, Zoe was nodding, satisfied.

"What's the worst part of it to you?" she asked. "The one detail you'd change, if you could, knowing that everything else was bound to happen."

He thought about it while Zoe picked through her fruit cup, avoiding the watery-looking melon. Cam, busy talking, had only taken a corner off his steak.

Cam finished his second cup of coffee and pushed the mug to the edge of the table. "I wish Liz hadn't been in the room. She was pregnant, she didn't need to see all that."

"She testified against you."

"Yeah."

"If I recall, she underplayed her husband's attack on you."

"It was just the one cut," Cam said.

"Did it leave a scar?"

Cam nodded. He pulled down the collar of his shirt so she could see the ugly pink-white mark. He wasn't ashamed of it.

"And you wouldn't change that," Zoe said.

"If he hadn't've cut me, then I'd be in for murder, wouldn't I? Given who he was?"

Zoe smiled and nodded, like Cam had come up with a solution to a problem she didn't think he'd get.

"Very good point," she said. "You're not a dumb kid, are you?"

Her accordion-style case sat on the bench next to her. Zoe reached inside and brought out a folded cheque, which she smoothed out before passing it across to Cam. One thousand dollars, made out to cash from Prentice and Partners. He examined the name on the cheque.

"Are you Prentice or one of the partners?" he asked.

"Prentice," she said.

"So what's the proposition?"

Zoe Prentice took a moment to study him. Her gaze felt intense, and despite himself he looked down, away, toward the empty mug.

"I think," Zoe said, "your intention is to do your best to stay out of prison."

"I won't be going back," Cam said.

"Short of that, would you be willing to pretend to have, say, a bit more of a reckless streak than you in fact possess?"

"Just say it straight."

"Your conviction gives you credibility with certain people. We'd want you to associate with them, in order to feed us information."

"Which people?"

"The League of Nations," Zoe said.

Cam's mind flashed to B Block, weeks ago. A small group of shaved-headed soldiers gathered in a corner of the common room. Young men his age, mostly white and South Asian, tattoos on their arms in that gangster script: *Thrive or Die*. A tall, blond kid at their centre, nodding at Cam like an estate owner greeting a prospective yard worker.

"You've run into them before," Zoe said.

He nodded.

"They're a feeder group, street-level associates, of the Heaven's Exiles Motorcycle Club, who I'm sure you're also familiar with."

Again he thought back, this time to the activity room. Three middle-aged men, bearded, smaller up close than the aura they projected. Tattoo sleeves. A seeming army of young white boys fetching things for them.

"The League allegedly controls cross-border narcotics trafficking, kicking up to the Exiles. They have other interests, too. It's important for us to learn about these, get a sense of things on the street."

"Rat on the League of Nations," Cam said. "Yeah. No thanks."

"You'd be paid—better than any straight job. Plus you could keep some of what you'd earn in their employ."

"*Employ*," he said. "You're fucking kidding me."

"It would only be for a few months," Zoe said. "A year at most. Would you like to hear what you'd be paid?"

"Forget it," Cam said.

"Are you sure?"

"Dead fucking positive."

She nodded. "In that case, kiddo, I think it's for the best we don't waste more of each other's time."

"Who do you work for?" Cam asked. "Are you a fed?"

"Thanks so much for meeting me, Mr. Shaw. As agreed, this cheque is yours."

She extended her hand. Cam, baffled, took it.

"That's it?"

"I can't coerce you into something you're not willing to do. This *is* dangerous work, and you're probably right to turn it down. And for our part, we're looking for someone with a little bit more—" she canted her head, choosing the word with sardonic care. "Ambition, let's say."

Zoe Prentice stood up, dropping two twenties on the table. As an afterthought, she rummaged in her wallet and brought out a slip of paper.

"As I mentioned before, this is the address and number of a warehouse in Delta. They don't shy away from people with criminal records, as long as they have a good work ethic. Good luck, kiddo."


He went to a bar that night in Vancouver and got drunk. He couldn't remember registering at the motel, but he woke up atop clean sheets with a need to vomit. His only clear memory was buying a round for the five regulars at the bar. He'd talked to a woman at some point, but that hadn't gone anywhere.

Uncle Pete greeted him with a nod of the head and a handshake. He didn't ask Cam in. They stood on the sagging porch of Pete's house, the warped floorboards forming an idiot's grin. Despite his skills, Peter Shaw had never cared much about maintaining his own home.

Cam looked at the mossy roof, the grit-covered windows. The house had always been an eyesore. Now it was a dump. South Surrey was on the border of White Rock, but the difference in income, in class, was stark.

Pete spat off the porch and asked his nephew what he planned on doing, now that he was out.

"Was hoping to maybe pick up some work with you," Cam said.

"I look like I got work to spare?"

"Dunno. Place looks like it always did."

Pete fired another American Spirit and launched the butt of the last one into the dead flowerbed along the side of the property.

"I do some wiring for the school board when the cheap bastards'll cough up for it. The odd home reno." Pete spat again, adding, "Kinda hard to get referrals when your nephew kills your best client."

Cam nodded and took it. Roger Garrick had been a friend to Pete, or at least a friendly employer. Cam felt sorry, but knew an apology would be meaningless.

He said one anyway, then left, the presents he'd brought— the bottle of Crown and carton of cigarettes—forgotten in his backpack.

His parole officer was an overworked man in an off-white short-sleeved shirt, splotches of soy sauce and grease on his tie. They went through the checklist.

Address? Temporary, working on permanent.

Occupation? Applying later today.

No drugs? Watching your alcohol consumption? Check and check.

There were weekly meetings at first, then they'd assess. He'd need to show progress on the job front, as well as a permanent residence. Cam handed his cheap cellphone to his PO and watched the man write down the number. I expect you to answer when I call you, Mr. Shaw. If not you better have a damn good reason. Is there anything else you need from me? Good. Welcome back to civilization.

The Work-Flex offices had all the warmth of a DMV kiosk. Cam sat on the flimsy skeleton chair and filled in the application.

Skills: carpentry, light electrical.

Last employer: he wrote *government.*

Have you ever been convicted of a felony?

Cam checked the box and wrote in *manslaughter*, thinking how much worse the term looked on paper than *murder.*

He handed the sheets to the sunburnt man, watched his eyes narrow as he read the application.

"You put down carpenter and electrician," the clerk said.

"Right."

"You didn't write down what school."

"Self-taught. Well, my uncle taught me."

"I see, but that's not really a qualification."

"I can do the work."

"Yes, sir, but when Work-Flex contracts out, we need to ensure our clients they're getting accredited, certified trades-people. No disrespect to you or your uncle. It's just our policy."

The rest of the exchange ran by with Cam nodding, gripping the handle of his backpack so he wouldn't be tempted to reach for the man's throat.


Job hunt by day. Bars at night.

He was too tightly wound to attract women. When he managed to snag one's interest, his low tolerance for booze caused him to unspool too quickly.

At one Ladies' Night he was cornered by a woman who said he reminded her of an old boyfriend. They talked and drank. She asked him about jail. Even felt the scar on his chest and shoulder.

At the end of the night, he'd walked out with her number. When he phoned the next evening, she said her ex was in town. No, don't phone back, howzabout I call you once the craziness in my life has eased up a bit? It has nothing to do with what you told me. Swear.


His PO told him the job-skills course started next Wednesday, 9 a.m.

"What they do, they start by running a few tests to see what your personality type is. They give each one a colour—if you're, say, blue, they use that to figure out what you're good at, what you're gonna enjoy doing. Afternoons they workshop resumés and run practice interviews. Might be just the thing to help you find a job. Sound okay? Great."

Wednesday came. Turned out he was red.

"My name's Jingjing," the woman said. "It can be something else if you want. I go by Sasha sometimes."

He told her Jingjing was fine. She was around his age. Dressed in a pink sweater and dark black skirt, trailing a nylon baseball jacket, dropping a pom-pom toque on the table that he'd bought that morning from the Salvation Army.

"Usually I take the money up front. Since it's a GFE, and I'm here all weekend, let's say half now and half when I leave. Sound good? And I gotta see your ID first. Send a picture to my gal-pal, just in case."

He complied. When Jingjing asked what he wanted to do first, he shrugged. She suggested they watch TV. When they settled on a game show, she unzipped him and made short work of him.

"I don't know how this'll play out," he told her later as they moved to the bedroom again. "If I'll cry or, y'know, be rough."

"You can do what you like," she said. "Slaps are fine, long as it's light. Fuck my ass, okay too, but you gotta wear a condom, and listen, I say stop. Long as you don't break the rules, you're fine. That okay, boo? You like me call you boo?"

"I don't know."

She stayed all weekend. It cost him more than the apartment's deposit.

The next Monday, Cam dialed the warehouse office and told them, sure, he could start tomorrow night.

# TWO

White-grey coils of smoke carried over the shuttered store-fronts and restaurants of the White Rock promenade. The houses clinging to the hillside beyond Marine Drive would normally have a view of the beach and the water. The smoke from the fire had obliterated that view.

As she turned onto Magdalen, Meghan Quick saw the alternating flash of the fire truck lights. Thought, *Here we go.*

The fire truck was parked diagonally along Sunset Lane, backed up onto the curb. She recognized Emmet Nance under his visored helmet. He nodded briefly and kept relaying hose to the firefighters closer to the house.

"Almost out, Sarge," Emmet said.

"Here's hoping."

3457 Sunset Lane was a narrow three-storey Dutch Colonial, the roof mossy and in need of repair. Weathered paint-peeled wood, thankfully separated from its neighbours by a mulched but unplanted yard. The owners—was this the Reeds' place?—hadn't kept up its maintenance.

Smoke unfurled from the upper windows. Meghan parked her department-issue Ford Interceptor around the corner on Sunset Lane. She threw back a handful of acetaminophen, washing them down with cold coffee.

White Rock, BC, population just under twenty thousand, a great deal of them seniors or young families. "The newly wed and the almost dead," as the saying went. Trains slowed down when they rolled through White Rock, and the beachfront thoroughfare was mined with speed bumps. Nothing happened here that couldn't be blamed on rowdies from Surrey or Americans from the other side of Semiahmoo Bay.

Growing up in White Rock, Meghan ached to move away. And had, first for college, then training at Depot, followed by a series of posts around the country, from a rez in Manitoba to a security detail in Ottawa. After eleven years gone, now married and with Rhonda wanting to start a family, Meghan had seen a posting for White Rock and admitted to herself that going home would have its advantages.

That was twenty years ago. Now Staff Sergeant Meghan Quick was the detachment commander for the White Rock RCMP, a fearsome crime fighting squad comprised of two dozen officers and a few civilians. Divorced, mildly hungover, and wishing she was still in bed, Meghan swilled icy French roast and waited for the smoke to clear away.

Denny Fong was waiting at the foot of the steep drive. Her most junior officer had been blocking the street for nonexistent traffic. "Never seen a fire this close," Denny said as Meghan approached. "You think it was electrical?" Wanting to ask, without seeming eager, if it might be arson.

"We'll find out," Meghan said. "This was the Reeds' place, wasn't it?"

"Far's I know, still is."

The Reeds were one of those families that had received their entire allotment of tragedy within the briefest of windows. Emily Reed had fallen victim to a stroke, which caused her husband Richie to retire early to care for her. He'd been struck down by a speeding car three months later. Emily had held on almost a year before a second stroke claimed her. Meghan had been at both funerals, Emily's only a few weeks ago.

Meghan heard a crash from inside the house, a billowing of dust and smoke from the opened bay window. Emmet came down the drive, horked and spat. He adjusted the valve on the hydrant.

"It's out," he announced.

"Nicely done," Meghan said. Emmet was a few years older than her son, Trevor. He'd refereed Trevor's soccer games, what felt like a lifetime ago. "Neighbours okay?"

Emmet gestured beyond the hood of the truck, where a small group of robed and pyjamaed fortysomethings watched. Their mood was almost festive. Enjoying the entertainment provided by the burning house and flashing lights. Meghan thought they looked like a swinger's party, missing only the martinis and bowl of keys.

"Someone should call Alexa," Meghan said. The Reeds' daughter was probably back at college by now, thinking her family's troubles were over. Meghan didn't have the girl's number in Buffalo, but Elizabeth Garrick would. Liz and Emily Reed were cousins, and the widow was the girl's closest living family.

A rumble from inside the house, followed by shouting, stopped Meghan from dialing Liz's number. The door of the Reeds' house was kicked open. Dale Miller staggered down the drive. He shook off his helmet and ran a gloved hand over his blond hair, smudging it with ash. He sat and bent his head between his legs. When he looked up, his face sought Meghan's. Tears, from the smoke or something else.

"Body," Dale said.

Donning a mask, Meghan followed Emmet into the house. Her eyes watered instantly. Smoke hung in the foyer, and the carpet was wet, but the damage was on the top storey. Their boots squelched as they took the stairs.

The second floor was high-ceilinged and crammed with stacks of magazines, boxes of old receipts, damaged by water and fire-extinguishing chemicals. The windows had been forced open. Meghan felt herself shiver as a gust came off the bay, fluttering the tattered pages.

"In here," Emmet said. He led the way into a small bedroom away from the windows.

Here the walls were brownish-black and the smell of char was heavier. Meghan coughed and gripped the door as nausea crested and ebbed. The slender body, burned, lay next to the skeletal frame of a bed.

This would have been Alexa's room, Meghan realized. The guest room now. The body was turned on its side, legs wedged next to the dresser. Scorched beyond recognition, alternately red and black and earthy brown, skin cratered like coal.

Meghan had brought her camera. She documented the room, the position of the body. With Emmet's help, she shifted the dresser away and shot a better picture of the corpse.

"Likely female," she said, pointing to the unburnt fabric beneath the bottom leg. Paisley, a fragment of skirt. The arms were contracted, fists clenched, knees and back slightly bent. The extreme heat from the fire caused the muscles to contract in a classic pugilist's pose.

Meghan handed Emmet the camera and wiped a line of perspiration from her brow. "Let Dr. Varma know she's getting a body from us. She'll want it sent to Peace Arch. They have the facilities. After Greg's done, of course."

Greg Grewal, the arson investigator, had trailed them up the stairs. Balding, attired in a white Tyvek bunny suit, paper boots over his shoes, Grewal grimaced as Emmet spat on the floor.

"The locus was likely this room," he said. "If it's electrical it might be in the ceiling. Possibly the attic, but I doubt it. The heat came from here."

"Are we talking arson?" Meghan asked, knowing that Grewal was famous for his thoroughness. It drove Dale and the others crazy, waiting for his pronouncements.

"Could be, yeah, but I won't know for sure till we take a good look. Either way, hope this lady was asleep when it happened."

Meghan nodded. The fact that the body was on the floor, away from the mattress, gave her doubts. But like Grewal, she'd hold onto her opinions until all the evidence was in.

"Heard this happens in Seattle an awful lot," Emmet said. "Homeless break into a condemned place, smoke their crack or whatever, nod off, and—" He spread his hands in a gesture of growing conflagration. "*Poof.* Y'know?"

"Who was first inside?" Meghan asked.

"That'd be Dale. Me right behind him."

"Was the front door unlocked?"

"We had to kick it."

"Had to," Grewal said, "or you made the decision to?"

"Had." Emmet was facing away from Grewal and mouthed the word *asshole* to Meghan.

"You're sure it was locked?" Meghan asked him.

"Swear it was, yeah."

She left the room, took the stairs, pausing on the landing as Dale and another technician swept past her. On the ground floor she looked at the back windows, saw no glass on the floor. The back door was also locked.

The kitchen had been relatively untouched, though water dripped from a puncture in the ceiling. Meghan examined the fridge. Babybel cheeses and Diet Coke, a bag of shrivelled mushrooms. A half-finished carton of cream. The best-by date was next week.

She opened the cupboards beneath the sink, found a garbage bin mounted to the inside of one door. A yellow plastic bag from the Price-Low inside, along with a receipt dated six days ago.

Meghan's throat made a sound like disappointment. The house had been used as a home, by someone familiar with it. Odds were good that the body was Alexa's.

Alexa Reed, twenty-nine, a grad student at SUNY Buffalo, her whole life ahead of her.

She'd babysat Trevor a few times. Meghan remembered driving her home afterward, the girl excited to sit up front in a real-life cop car. Thirteen years, one divorce and several promotions ago for Meghan. She wondered what the years had held for Alexa, tried to remember if she'd spoken to her at the funeral.

What the hell was Alexa doing back here?

In the years following her husband's murder, Elizabeth Garrick had undergone a grand renaissance. She'd forged ahead, raising her son, Max, while keeping her husband's business afloat, even expanding it. The twenty-storey tower at Panorama Place was her idea, the first building over four storeys tall in White Rock history. She also chaired the Roger Garrick Foundation, sponsoring Little League and peewee hockey. This, too, was a way to keep Roger's name alive.

That was the public version, anyway. Meghan could admit there might even be some truth to it. She found Liz hard to read properly, knowing what an industrial-sized bitch the younger version had been, and was also aware of her own lingering envy.

Lizzie and Meg had been neighbourhood friends, thrust together by their parents often enough that they'd spent much of their childhoods in each other's company. That had changed in high school. Liz, a year older, had matured early, in that cigarette-smoking, black-makeup and jean-jacketed way. She'd quickly been accepted by the senior crowd. Meghan, tall, gangly and haltingly becoming aware of who she was, didn't move in the same circles. Liz had cooled on Meghan, eventually shutting her out.

Liz had married Roger Garrick, eleven years older than her and already wealthy. They made a good couple, seemed genuinely happy, and Meghan thought the gold-digger comments were unfair. Roger was, if not handsome, debonair, quick-witted and an excellent party host.

They'd seemed golden together.

Meghan hadn't crossed paths with them very often. When she did, it was always in the midst of a minor bylaw infraction—the Garricks and some other swells smoking a joint aboard one of Roger's yachts, or disregarding the noise restrictions to play music. She knew from Bob Sutter, the previous detachment commander, that policing White Rock was about issuing kindly reminders rather than filling the jails. The Garricks would wave to her and continue their good times elsewhere.

Secretly Meghan had thought, upon hearing of Roger's death: at last, the real world comes knocking on Lizzie Garrick's door.

When she arrived at the Garrick house, the porch lights were on, casting long silver rays past the pool room, down past the train tracks to a stretch of rocky beach. Liz stood near the water, smoking a cigarette, watching the first smear of dawn over the water. The dark surf rolled toward her, dying at her feet.

She turned, caught sight of Meghan, waved. Started back up the beach. Meghan met her at the edge of the lawn.

"Some bad news, Liz."

"I've heard. Should we go inside?"

She led Meghan through the screened-in porch, Liz slipping out of her sandals, discarding her jacket on an antique dresser. Meghan paused to stomp out of her boots.

They sat together in a rose-painted room that Meghan guessed would be called a parlour. Couches, a credenza, decanters of various liqueurs. Who had a parlour in this day and age? Liz sat with the ends of her black crocheted shawl tucked around her bare legs. Meghan asked if the widow needed anything.

"Nothing, no," Liz said. "Max is at Stacy's parents' place. They're not such good friends anymore, but her mother asked could he stay over for pizza and a movie. There aren't many kids in our social circle. I thought it would be good for him."

"He's doing all right?"

"Splendid. And Trevor?"

"Doing good. Enjoying college."

"And how is Rhonda?"

"Says she likes living in Chicago." Meghan thought her ex had met someone, but there were more pressing topics right now. "There's a chance the girl in the fire isn't her," she said. "Isn't Alexa, I mean. Do you have any idea what she might have been doing there?"

"Not the slightest," Liz said. "I purchased her flight home for Emily's funeral. It was round trip. I'm not sure of the date she was supposed to fly back to Buffalo, but I can look it up."

"I'd appreciate it."

Liz Garrick lit a cigarette, watched the smoke curl toward her ceiling. "I had to practically force her to attend. You imagine that, Meg—not going to your mother's funeral?"

"Grief hits people in different ways. 'Specially at that age."

"Of course," Liz said. "Here I am thinking of how it looked, ignoring what the poor girl was going through."

"How about you?" Meghan asked.

Liz swatted the air dismissively. "I imagine I'll cope. And who knows, Meg. Like you said, it might not even be her."

In daylight, with the first responders gone, Meghan went back through the Reeds' house, accompanying Greg Grewal. The arson investigator wanted to point out the source of the blaze. Meghan had a few things she wanted to look at herself.

"Point of origin's here," Grewal said, pointing to the junction of wall and floor in Alexa's bedroom. "Fire burned up and out from here. Accelerants were dumped, and then it caught the polyurethane stuffing in the mattress."

"What type of accelerant?"

"Kerosene," Grewal said.

"You're sure?"

"Won't be sure of anything till we spectrograph it, but sure smells like it."

A Greg Grewal eighty percent was more certain than most people's hundred. Meghan made a note, *kerosene*, on her pad.

"It has a higher flashpoint than ethanol," Grewal said. "Less likely to catch fire accidentally."

"Meaning it's unlikely this fire was accidental."

"I can't be certain of that, Sarge, but it's sure possible."

"Putting aside certainties," she said, "which I know for you is tough—are we looking for a professional arsonist?"

Grewal bent and peered at a section of carpet. "Hard to say."

"I know it is, Greg. Why else would I ask the fucking arson investigator?"

He looked up, flustered, then barked out a laugh. Typical response of a male in authority to anything other than lovingly gentle correction. "Jeez, Meghan, put me on the spot why don't you?"

"A pro, Greg? Or some kid with a camping stove?"

Grewal sighed and eased himself up to a standing position. Surveying the room, he said, "I'd be surprised if arson was the primary focus."

"Why?"

"Didn't burn enough, nor was it properly ventilated. A fire's got to be fed. You need to stoke it, 'specially at first. A pro would've smashed holes in the drywall to expose the wooden frame. This never really got going. Fact, if there'd been more of a breeze last night, it might've put it out for us before we got here."

"So an amateur."

"At starting fires, I'd say so."

"The doors were locked," Meghan said. "It's looking more and more like Alexa did this herself."

"The poor girl."

"Or someone targeted her, and wants to confuse things for us."

Downstairs, Meghan glanced around the kitchen, noticing nothing new save the boot tracks of firefighters and cops. Bare cupboards aside from two boxes of a hippie-looking cereal. The kind of thing Rhonda would insist on buying, only to eat a bowl or two, then leave it to go stale in their pantry.

In her own house, since Rhonda left, it had been nothing but Shreddies, generic corn flakes and the odd box of sugary shit for Trevor.

She wanted a cigarette. Meghan headed outside to see if she could cadge one from the officer guarding the scene.

Passing the hallway and shoe rack, she noticed the low, beige, particleboard shelf had been moved away from the wall. An umbrella had fallen behind it, a cane. And a thin piece of corrugated plastic.

Pulling it out, she saw what it was: a FOR SALE sign. Chung Realty, a glamour shot of a fifty-year-old bottle blond, and the slogan LET WINNIE WORK FOR YOU!

Carrying the sign, Meghan walked outside and down the driveway. On the corner of the property, near a deep furrow caused by a swipe from the fire truck's tire, was an L-shaped piece of white wood. The bottom was sharpened to a stake, dirty where it had been pitched in the lawn. The cross arm had been snapped off. The sign would have been posted here at one point.

She took a photo of the broken post, clutching the sign beneath her armpit to work the camera.

"Find something?" Greg Grewal said behind her.

Meghan showed him the sign.

"You think Alexa took it down?"

"Not sure, but looks that way, yeah."

He looked at the pieces of white picket on the lawn. "What was she doing back here?"

*Staying*, Meghan thought.


The girl in the fire was Alexa Reed.

Meghan herself brought the dental charts from the clinic to the pathologist and waited while Dr. Sonia Varma made the comparison. Varma was the opposite of Grewal—autopsies and chemical tests would take as long as they took, but she was willing to hypothesize an answer to any question Meghan put to her. The doctor was young, slender and had great hair. Meghan fought to keep her resentment in check.

"Not a suicide," Varma said. "Her neck is broken."

"I thought bones sometimes break due to heat."

"Sure do. But usually not before heat is applied."

Varma drew back the plastic sheeting, exposing Meghan once again to the featureless burnt face of Alexa Reed. The pathologist turned the corpse, prodding the skin at what would have been the nape.

"See the hematoma? You can kind of make it out beneath the burn—see?" Meghan noticed a dark discolouration but it looked less like a bruise than a blotch.

"Her neck was snapped," Varma said. "Probably with a weapon. Maybe a good shove into something with no give."

"Like a windowsill? Edge of the bed?"

Varma nodded. "Hard, though—you'd really have to work to cause a break this clean."

"Anything in her pockets?"

Varma set the body back down and craned her neck to read off her clipboard. "Haven't paid as much attention to the clothes, Sarge—you did ask me to hurry."

"But no metal," Meghan said, "no keys."

"No."

Meghan stared at the body. Stripped and opened and now sewn up, Alexa Reed resembled herself more than when Meghan had first seen her. Parts of her hadn't been touched by flame—a pale knee and thigh, a left ankle. That made the dark burns covering her face and torso that much more horrid. No mistaking this for the young woman Meghan had witnessed grow up, mature. Endure the pain of losing both parents. And all for this?

It didn't make sense.


A call to the SUNY registrar told Meghan that Alexa Reed was on academic suspension. She'd missed several appointments with her graduate supervisor, and her last round of exams had been dismal. Meghan thought that wasn't out of the ordinary, given what had happened to her parents. It had been a tough couple years for the Reeds.

Alexa's social media presence was a low-visibility simmer of rage and sarcasm. She had few friends, liked or reacted to little and rarely replied to comments.

Her last post was indicative of her public style:

*God, there's so much going on here that passes beneath people. Worse even than when I was a kid. LITERALLY no one cares. No one pays attention. You wouldn't believe it if you knew.*

*Believe what?* Others had commented below the post. Either Alexa hadn't had time to respond, or she'd chosen not to. "Vague-booking," Trevor called it.

Scrolling back farther, a year, she saw the inane, happy posts appropriate for a young woman with so much going for her.

*Last night's concert was the dopest! Nick C. touched my hand!!!*

*God, I can't believe what a homophobe this woman on Fox is. Gives blonds like me a bad name LOL.*

Meghan tried to pinpoint the switch, then thought back to when Alexa's father had passed. No, here she was sad, but eloquently so.

*My father was buried today by me and Mom and a few of his friends. If I don't respond to you guys right away it's just I'm dealing with this. Thanks for all the good wishes.*

A few months forward. There was nothing about her mother, only a short post about the terrible flight home. *God, can't they fucking see I am in NO shape for this fascist security gate bullshit!*

Meghan knew social media was at best a distorted version of someone's interior life. But something clearly had happened since her father's death that had driven Alexa Reed into despair. And maybe gotten her killed.

The toxicology report finally came through. Blood and urine samples tested positive for caffeine, theobromine, mirtazapine, hydrocodone, fentanyl and morphine. Antidepressants, stimulants and heroin.

Meghan stopped what she'd been working on, read through the report again and placed her glasses down atop her desk. She'd known the girl all her life, and she had no idea who Alexa Reed was. The girl's words came back to her.

*There's so much going on here that passes beneath people.*

*LITERALLY no one cares.*

*No one pays attention.*

"I am now," Meghan Quick said, surprising herself by saying the words out loud. Closing her office door, she added, in a murmur, "Sorry it took so long."

# THREE

To Cam's surprise he found he enjoyed the warehouse work. Liked the way his muscles ached at the end of the night. Liked speeding through the aisles of industrial shelving on the lift truck, dropping skids of dog treats, medical supplies, knockoff Red Bull. It was simple and hard and he was mostly left alone.

Doppler & Doppler Logistics was close enough to the port of Surrey that there was always work, as much as he wanted. Containers showed up and the receiving clerk assigned them to one of the twelve bay doors. Unloading them could take all night, sometimes into the morning. Pay was hourly, a dollar up from minimum wage.

No one cared that he didn't have his forklift ticket, that he rarely wore his helmet. There were no inspections from Workplace Safety at night. He'd drink coffee or a syrupy energy drink and blast through it, sweating, until five when the buses started to run. Then home, a meal of canned whatever was in the house, and bed.

The men he worked with were like him—unemployables, ranging from undocumented workers, to reformed crack- and meth-heads, to ex-cons. A few smoked weed on their breaks. There was little talk. Usually the radio was on, either classic rock or a Filipino station. You found out right away who would work and who would fuck the dog.

"You hustle like one of them," the skinny floor manager told him one day. Tyson Lee wore track pants and a ragged white T-shirt, had a salt and pepper goatee that sometimes melted into a playoff beard. He told Cam to slow down, no need to burn yourself out. He'd seen it happen to others.

Tyson and the designated forklift driver, Rashid Cole—Sheedy, Tyson called him—were close. Seniority gave them the pick of the cans. Sheedy had a bad back—scoliosis, he claimed—and regularly took pot breaks, using a vape pen unless Tyson rolled a joint. They were boisterous, loud, funny, and Cam didn't mind partnering with them. They appreciated someone willing to do the lifting.

Keep clean, Cam told himself. Live clean, piss clean, ride out these years. It's better than being back in Kent.

Two weeks in he noticed Tyson and Sheedy talking to one of the drivers in the yard. Something was slipped between them, the driver saluting as he climbed back into his rig. Cam thought nothing of it.

An hour later when he'd finished his container, Cam walked over to bay twelve and asked Tyson if he needed help.

"The fuck away from here," Tyson said. "I want help, bro? I'll ask."

"Whatever," Cam said.

Tyson shook his head and made a sharp, dismissive shushing sound. He walked back into the dark mouth of the container.

A few hours later, Cam was halfway through a can in bay four. Laptop parts. Sweat and Chinese-factory dust and the sound of zz Top from the warehouse floor. The rhythm of work. When he paused to string up the portable light at the mouth of the can, he noticed Sheedy, arms crossed, watching him.

"Need something?" Cam asked.

Sheedy stared at him. "Do *you* need something is the question."

Drinking the last of his piss-warm Sprite, Cam noticed the forklift sidle up, Tyson in its cage.

"Break time, my man," Tyson said. "Let's us three go smoke a bowl."

Cam didn't argue with them.

Outside, in the corner of the yard, by a wet stack of pallets, was a splintery lunch table, coffee cans around it full of drowned cigarette butts. Tyson sat on the tabletop, huffed deep on the vape pen and offered it to Cam.

"Can't," he said.

"Fuck not? It's legal."

"Dude, he's got to piss for someone," Sheedy told his friend. Smiling at Cam. "Been there. What'd you do?"

Cam told them.

"That shit's insane," Tyson said. "Goddamn. You're not fucking with us?" He said to Sheedy, "Dude here is a goddamn murderer."

"It's not like that," Cam said.

"We're not judging," Sheedy said. "We've all done shit. I'm sure you did what you had to."

One night he'd reached the end of a can and paused, voices heard through the metal. Tyson's, louder than normal, and Sheedy's, who never yelled unless he had to. And a third voice, louder still than the others.

Dropping his gloves, Cam walked outside. He saw Tyson and the driver standing chest to chest, arms out, goading the other to make a move. Sheedy off to the side, arms crossed. Tyson was yelling at the driver, who was backing slowly up toward his cab. "You cheap, trifling-ass piecesashit." To Sheedy, adding, "Soft boy here thinks we're gonna take this."

"Dumb motherfuckers, you think I make the rules? Price isn't fucking set by me."

"Sure," Sheedy said, "like that extra three hundred goes straight up the ladder, you don't see a piece of it." He was acting the more reasonable one, but both he and Tyson pressed closer to the driver.

"A *piece*," the driver said. "An extra seventy-five. And you're goddamn right, I'm the one on the fuckin' security cameras. I got a fuckin' union ticket to lose."

"Unlike us poor minimum-wage fucks, right?"

The driver put his hands out as Tyson tried to advance. "It's you and the fucking Hayes brothers gotta work this out. I'm just the goddamn driver."

"Not tonight, bitch," Tyson said.

He nodded at Cam, who was approaching slowly, waiting to see what would happen.

"Fuck does that—" The driver stopped himself as Tyson stepped onto the running board of his cab. "Get the hell off there."

"Ours now," Sheedy said.

Tyson swung the door open and leaned on it, looking ready to jump down onto the driver at the slightest provocation.

"That's my fucking truck! You can't take that, Tyson."

"Buy another with your extra seventy-five," Sheedy said. "Have it paid off in no time."

"My stuff's in there." The driver spoke this more quietly, seeing Cam approach and realizing there was no fighting all three of them.

Tyson reached in and threw a thermos onto the ground, a tan jacket. The driver bent cautiously and retrieved them. He started moving backward toward the gate.

"You know they won't let this end here," he said. "They'll come for the truck. And you too."

"Big fucking mouth on a guy walking away," Sheedy said.

"Just saying, not on me what happens."

Tyson jumped off the running board and sprinted across the yard. The driver took off at top speed. When they were close, Tyson halted abruptly, wound back, and threw something that hit the driver's shoulder as he dashed through the gate, losing his thermos, the jacket trailing across the ground.

Cam walked over to see what Tyson had thrown. He saw the plastic fragments of a novelty hula girl, the kind you suction cup to your dashboard. Tyson stomped on it again, crushing the girl's head with a pop.


They didn't discuss it that night. Cam went home and showered. He lay on his bed, thinking it over, his half-eaten bowl of mac and cheese abandoned on the floor next to the mattress.

He didn't care what was in the cans. It didn't take a creative mind to guess that it was illegal, which could mean bootleg smokes, or guns, but probably meant dope.

What bothered him was what the driver's response would be, and how Sheedy and Tyson would react to them. If this got ugly, if the police were involved—

Somehow he doubted they would be.

So much of his time in Kent had been spent looking the other way. A survivalist policy, and goddamn if he wouldn't have to adopt it again.

Nothing fucking changed. Inside, outside, there was no chance to drop your guard. Everyone had an angle.

What Cam needed to figure out was his own.


The next evening, he walked into the yard and noticed that the truck was gone.

Sheedy was off that day. Tyson, working the lift truck, gave him a chin-first nod and a terse "Sup, bro?" before dashing down one of the aisles with a skid of rattan chairs.

Cam wasn't going to get answers. That was fine.

Bays two through five were loaded with containers carrying truss connectors. Cam's least favourite cargo to unload. Plates of light-gauge galvanized steel, the teeth and edges on them could shred a leather jacket and draw blood. Cam had seen one carelessly wrapped skid topple, the plates slicing through a worker's leg.

Cam got to work. Drop a skid, stack a layer of plates so that the teeth faced down or inward. Set the second layer in a slightly different pattern to add stability. Like bricklaying with knives, he thought. Every three layers you stopped and shrink-wrapped the stack. When you finished twelve layers you had to drive the skid over to the shelving, and be heart-surgeon careful lifting it onto the shelf. Each skid took three times the plastic wrap and five times as long as any other cargo.

After that the holiday season started. Cam worked eleven days straight. On Thanksgiving, the Dopplers left them a flat of Coors for when they finished. Sheedy broke into it early, he and Cam the only ones who'd volunteered to work the holiday. Their last two hours were spent drinking and working in relative peace and comfort.

In the parking lot, Sheedy swung a six-pack into the bed of his Mazda pickup. "Lift, man?"

He'd never offered before. Cam climbed in and told him where he lived.

Delta was full of swaths of undeveloped meadowlands. Early mornings, he'd hear the sound of shotguns, duck hunters on the other side of the highway. The industrial areas—the warehouses and factories—bled into strip malls, which in turn bled into housing, so that the entire city was a mix of grass and asphalt, concrete and prefab.

Cam's apartment was on the other side of Scott Road in Surrey, a ground floor suite in a low-rise near a shopping centre. There was a franchise Irish bar, Diarmid O'Flanagan's or some shit, on the edge of the mall property. Sheedy pulled in and said he needed a drink.

In a Naugahyde booth, under a poster of the Celtic football team, they clinked glasses and dug into the Thanksgiving specials: turkey burger with provolone and cranberry aioli. They had the bar to themselves.

"Fucking holidays," Sheedy said. "Asshole colonizers patting themselves on the back. Fuck 'em."

"Fuck 'em," Cam said, finishing his pint.

"And it's just a prelude to fuckin' Christmas, which is the same shit times ten. People pretending to be all nice. Treat you like garbage the rest of the year, hold you down every chance they get. But come December? Then they're all Mister Rogers and shit."

Sheedy went on about commercialism, about phonies, about what dickless wonders the Dopplers turned out to be. They drank another pint, then another. Sheedy paid and they went to Cam's apartment, stood in the empty kitchen and drank the rest of the six pack.

It was coming. Cam felt it. This was all just a prelude.

"So hey," Sheedy said after a few seconds of silent mutual drinking. "You tell anyone about the truck?"

"No one asked."

"But say they did?"

"I'm on parole," Cam said, accepting the last can, drinking deep and passing it back to Sheedy. "Last thing I want is to be in the middle."

"I feel that, man. Last thing me or Tyson want for you."

There was that appraising look again. Cam waited, drank.

"Thing is," Sheedy said, "and you know better'n anybody, you can't get ahead on what you make clearing cans."

He gestured at the surroundings of the empty apartment, the lone Corning Ware bowl and spoon adrift in the scummy sink.

"Can't get ahead, can't even stay a-fucking-float. 'Specially not if you got family. Tyson's got two kids at home. I got alimony up the dirt chute, plus this bad back."

Cam nodded. "It's rough."

"And you, man, hard as you work, how much you bank, after groceries and shit? Motherfucking bus pass, forget keeping a car on the road."

It was true. The apartment had set him back, and the place was still bare bones. His mattress had been a thrift store special. Each time Cam tore his shirt on one of the truss connectors, he'd safety-pin it together, till it was more ragged than the garments worn by the homeless men he'd see around the SkyTrain station.

Compared to the alternative, though—

Cam finished the can, burped and tossed it into the sink.

"Here's the thing," he said. "Every few weeks I see this guy in his office, show him my pay stubs, piss in a cup for him. That's my life. He gets wind of anything—" He shrugged. "I mean, it's not like I was in for drunk driving, boosting a stereo. This guy, he's not even all that bad, but he'd send me back in a heartbeat."

Sheedy nodded. Sucking on his vape pen, expelling a cloud of pot smoke, he studied Cam's face.

"I feel that, completely" he said. "Something comes up that's no risk, though, you'd be interested?"

"No such thing," Cam said.

"I'm saying *if*."

"Can't, man."

Sheedy opened his wallet and shuffled through a wad of bills, counting out twenty, sixty, a hundred, two. "This is just for saying nothing."

"I'd do that for free."

Sheedy shook his head as if insulted. "Don't know how it works inside, but out here you never do shit for free, someone's willing to pay you." He added at the door, zipping up his jacket, "Happy Thanksgiving."

"You too, man."

After he left Cam looked at the money for a long time. He dug an empty soup tin out of the garbage, rinsed it off and dried it, folded the money and slipped it inside. He put the can at the back of his fridge, hiding it from view behind the Red Bull and the bag of coffee creamers he'd stolen from the break room at work.

The next Monday, he came in at five and saw Tyson standing outside, smoking with Scott Doppler, the owner's son.

"Hey buddy," Doppler said, patting his shoulder. "It's Cameron, right? Cam the Man? Tyson here says you're working out. One of our best guys."

Cam thank-you'd and said he was just here to help.

"Murray is taking some leave time, and Tyson here is moving to days. That means there's an opening for floor boss, nights. Interested? It's only for a couple weeks, but your pay goes up, and who knows? Murray might not come back."

Cam shook Doppler's hand, shook Tyson's. "Thanks. Thank you."

"Tyson'll show you the ropes. You handle receiving, double-check the orders when they go out. When it's dead you can still work cans. We'll try this out for a week and see how you do."

"I'm grateful," Cam said, coughing up a "sir" at the end, almost reflexively.

Scott Doppler saluted them and pulled out of the lot in his Lexus.

"Fucking choad," Tyson said.

Emptying cans, you shut your mind off. Floor manager demanded your full attention. Cam liked the responsibility. He liked jawing with the drivers, appreciated the way they could manoeuvre a fifty-foot container into a narrow slot almost effortlessly. He learned the paperwork of the various companies, could tell which cans held perishables and needed to go first. It beat the hell out of any work he'd done before.

Don't fuck this up, he told himself.

Thursday morning, 3 a.m. He was finishing shelving the last of the skids, humming along the aisles in the good lift truck, the gas-powered Toyota, when the men came in.

Three of them, the leader olive-skinned and bearded, standing in between two white guys, one small and blond, the other tall and thick with a shaved head. All three wore the same black shirt with glitter writing across the front, that scribbly gangster font like the tattoos he'd seen inside.

Cam brought the 'Yota to a halt near them and asked what they wanted.

"Tyson Lee," the big man said. "Rashid Cole. Where they at?"

"Not on nights," Cam said.

"Don't dick around, uh?"

"I said they're not here."

"Then call 'em."

He felt it in his stomach, had since they'd walked in. This was ending in a fight. The shirts were some sort of uniform. If Tyson wasn't here...

The paradox of his situation reared up faster than the growing sense of fear. Inside, if someone stepped to you like

39

they did, you fought. You had to. Otherwise you were a bitch, leaving yourself open for the next person.

But out here—if he won, he lost. If he ran, he lost.

Fucked.

"I'm calling the police," Cam said, slipping the 'Yota into reverse and creeping away from them.

The beard laughed and the blond rushed him. Cam swung the wheel hard and the 'Yota spun, the tines swiping their shins, knocking the beard down. The blond yowled, crawled away.

Cam booked it.

There was a back door behind the order-picking station at the south end. The 'Yota was fast—burning fuel, unlike the pallet jacks, which charged from a wall outlet. But, in his haste, he swung too tight and clipped the edge of the shelf on lane seven, making a steel-on-steel clang, burying the tines into a skid of cleaning products.

Cam reversed it, backed out and swung and cleared the tines, soap leaking down the shelf. He felt something snag the back of the lift, felt the extra weight on board.

The big man was holding onto the cage, reaching through.

Cam gunned it, feeling the man grab at his hair, his shoulder. He felt a fist pummel his neck. He hunkered forward, out of reach.

Now he floored the pedal, careening down the aisle, the 'Yota sliding, almost tipping. He leaned back and course-corrected, felt the fist grab his hair, tear it. Cam reached back, snagged the arm, forced it up, put pressure on the elbow till he heard a snap—

He was jolted forward, head hitting the front of the cage.

Felt the reverberations of the lift as it struck a pillar of shelving—

The man behind him screamed.

Cam looked up. Heard a ripping sound. Something slashed his eye.

The truss connectors.

Hundreds of razor-sharp teeth rained down on them.



The tattoos he'd seen inside.

The T-shirts. That same design.

*Thrive or Die.*



The 'Yota's cage had deflected the bulk of the plates. A few had forced their way inside. One had cut his right bicep, another raked his back. The worst had driven down the left side of his face, carving down his cheek close to his ear. Bad but superficial. Lucky.



Cam gave a statement to the police from his hospital bed. The big man being found in gang apparel, and Cam looking almost as wounded beneath his bandages, meant he was earmarked as the victim, despite his record. His answers were true, for the most part, and the codeine slur of his voice made his words sound pulled directly from his unconscious.

Do you know what the man wanted?

No, ma'am. They asked for someone, but I can't remember what name.

Did the man attack alone?

I think there was someone else with him.

One, two? Dressed the same?

Maybe, yeah, I think so.

Do you know anything about the League of Nations?

Not really, ma'am. To be honest, I'm pretty tired now.

All right. My card if you remember anything else.


Turned out the big man was in the same wing of Surrey Memorial. When he was mobile, Cam visited him. The man was being prepped for his fourth plastic surgery, most of his face still bandaged. One arm truncated at the elbow.

Flowers covered every surface of the man's room. One elaborate wreath was propped against the bed—purple and black roses in a yin-yang symbol. *Loyalty and love from Dalton and Cody Hayes.*

*League of Nations* along the top of the wreath. *Thrive or Die* along the bottom.


The taxi to his apartment was twenty-eight dollars, thirty-five with tip. He slipped the last of his money into the can at the back of the fridge.

There was still plenty of pain—fiery, dull, deep, unscratchable itches that threatened his sanity. Rolling his shoulders strained the stitches and brought out lingering tension in his muscles.

But pain was something that was manageable, that had answers. You could take a codeine and dull it, or a sleeping pill, or drink, or just gut it out. Pain could be known.

Things like rent, work—they had no answers. He could limp by for a week or two, but then what? Go back to containers? The doctors wouldn't approve, but then they weren't three weeks from losing their place.

He called his parole officer. It went to voicemail. He sank into the mattress, stirring up dust. Sneezing, tossing back pills, he closed his eyes.

The phone rang. He ignored it. It rang again, and he picked it up and shouted, "What?"

"Credibility," the voice on the other end said.

Zoe Prentice. Cam had no idea how she'd got his number.

"How are you feeling?" Zoe asked.

"Fan-fucking-tastic. Like you wouldn't believe."

"Clear your head. I'll be there in an hour."

"You know where I live?"

"Of course," she said. "We should revisit things, now that you've made contact. I think this time you're ready for my offer."

# FOUR

Alexa Reed's funeral was poorly attended. A few family friends, acquaintances from high school. Liz Garrick took a front pew with her son, nodding to Meghan from beneath a preposterous veil adorned with black crepe butterflies. The service was brief, non-religious, music-heavy.

Sometime between her mother's funeral and her own, Alexa Reed had decided to stay in White Rock. She'd taken down the FOR SALE sign on her parents' house, bought groceries, shot enough heroin and hydrocodone to appear on her tox report, had her neck broken and been set ablaze along with her family home.

Meghan guessed that Alexa wouldn't risk muling dope through airport security. She'd probably bought it from someone in town. That meant money, which meant the bank.

A few phone calls and Meghan found the branch where the Reeds did business. She met with their financial advisor, the vice president, Ernesto Marquez. The bank was small and glass-walled, already decorated with tinsel and plastic snow.

"Richie and Emily Reed were two of my first clients," Marquez said. He leaned over his desk while peeling a chocolate orange, banging the sphere on the corner of the desk to separate it. "Slice?"

"Thanks, no."

"I always make time for people like the Reeds. Salt of the earth types, y'know?"

Meghan asked if he'd talked much with Alexa.

"We had one meeting, yeah, after the funeral. She walked out with a couple thousand, what she said she needed to settle some stuff around town."

"Cash?"

Marquez nodded. "I wondered at that, but grief, y'know, tends to make a person want to simplify."

"What about the house?"

"Paid off ages ago," Marquez said.

"Who put it on the market?"

"No clue."

"But Alexa took it off."

"You'd have to ask her." Marquez caught his gaffe and grimaced. "You could talk to Winnie Chung about that. Think she was their realtor."

"The Reeds have any other debts, or money problems?" Meghan asked.

Marquez hesitated. "It's not that I don't want to tell you, ma'am."

"Staff Sergeant Quick. Just a general picture of their finances," Meghan said. "Stays between us, I promise."

"Sure. It's no secret they were limping by for a while, before they opened the second gas station. This was eight, nine years ago. I remember they begged and pleaded for a month's extension on their mortgage. Even drew up papers for a lien. But then they buckled down and righted the course, managed to set some savings aside. Never trusted mutual funds, which to me is downright lunacy, settling for a measly one or two percent—"

"So they were well off," Meghan said, hoping to skip the lecture. Her own finances were shambolic, would stay that way till Trevor finished college.

"Comfortable, is how I'd put it."

"Where'd the money come from?"

Marquez held up his index finger, a moment, please. He turned to his computer and clicked through several pages. Entered something on the keyboard. Another click, and then he reclined in his chair, chewing on his knuckle.

"Last time I talked with Richie was a year before he died," he said. "At that point he and Em had a hundred and seventy-nine thousand in their savings."

"Quite a turnaround." Meghan couldn't help but think of her own measly retirement plan, her accounts that she'd meant to fill up but just hadn't got around to it. Thank God her job paid reasonably well. "What's left of that?" she asked.

"As of right now, after Alexa's withdrawal, their balance is two hundred and eleven."

"Thousand?"

"Dollars," Marquez said. "The Reeds were basically broke."

He spun his monitor around, allowing Meghan to look at the account history. Three withdrawals a week, three thousand at a time, always during mornings and in person. This went back before Mr. Reed's accident and continued up to a week before Mrs. Reed's death.

"The money Alexa took was the last," Marquez said, sounding genuinely sorrowful for the state of the Reeds' finances.

"Truth be told I don't know what happened—I'd never counsel someone to eat into their savings like that."

Meghan thanked him and left, wondering if the withdrawals were connected to Alexa's death. Had it been spent trying to ward off an inevitable misfortune? And where had it come from in the first place?

Winnie Chung wore a look of distaste when the name Alexa Reed was mentioned. For a moment the stout blonde puttered in the break room of the real estate firm's office, adding tubs of fruit and a sheaf of wheatgrass to the concoction in her blender.

"That girl was the rudest thing," she said. "I'd talked with her mother ahead of time, and she'd even paid my commission. A remarkable woman, Emily Reed. Even in her last hours, she was thinking of others. Her daughter, though, was another thing entirely. Alexa called me a gold digger and a four-letter C-word I won't repeat."

"How did she look?"

"Like any of the kids we get in the summer, who bring one extra T-shirt and let themselves get grotty. I knew that girl—not knew-knew, but I saw her around when she was growing up. My kids were a few years behind her, but at swim meets or school events, we'd always say hi to the Reeds. How she ended up like that..."

She didn't finish the sentence, and Meghan certainly didn't have an answer for her.

"Did Alexa say what her plans were for the house?"

"Not that I remember," Winnie said. "Between the effing and jeffing she didn't make much sense. She did say—what was it?—right. That the place wasn't going anywhere till she got what was hers. I haven't the foggiest what that meant."

She wasn't alone.


On her day off Meghan made dinner for Trevor, a treat since she rarely saw her son. He was in his fourth semester at community college in Surrey, taking a hodgepodge of humanities and the less practical sciences. Over beer can chicken and a root vegetable medley, Meghan asked him about school, about the place he'd moved into last month—and finally about Alexa.

"What about her?" Trevor said.

"She was murdered."

"Shit, seriously?" A drumstick bone hung out of his mouth. "She was always a keener. I thought she was at some big-time uni."

"She was," Meghan said. "If I tell you something, will it stay between us?"

"Mom." His way of saying, you don't even have to ask.

Trevor had always been love/hate when it came to her job. When he was young, he'd been fascinated with police work. "Cop Mom," he'd called her, to differentiate Meghan from "Business Mom" Rhonda. In his high school rebellion phase, he'd enjoyed needling her, especially about drugs and the speed limit. The year he'd taken off to bum around had been the worst. It had tested her patience and her finances, strained Meghan's relationship with Rhonda. Her ex had found a gap year a totally normal thing for a nineteen-year-old to want.

"He needs space," Rhonda had told Meghan. "Time to think about who he wants to become. It's not like we can send him to Europe."

"Since when are we supposed to send him anywhere?" Meghan had replied. She'd had a full-time job at his age, done college around it. But a bootstraps lecture fell on two sets of deaf ears and only cemented the battle lines of her vs. them.

Rhonda had talked Trevor into giving college a try. Meghan would have been fine with her son living at home while in school, but Trevor had asked for his own place. To Meghan's dismay, Rhonda had agreed to cover his rent.

Her son listened as Meghan explained about the fire. He didn't stop eating but chewed slower, staring at the bones on his plate.

"The Reeds were pretty chill," he said. "It's insane, everything that happened to them."

"Very sad," Meghan concurred.

"What did you want to ask?"

"First, Trev, I'm not bringing this up for any other reason than I need to know what's going on in town."

"She was on drugs?" Trevor said. Immediately his posture had stiffened.

"If you have any idea where she might have scored, copped, whatever the hip term is now, I'd like to know."

Trevor sighed and let his fork clatter onto his plate. "Half of White Rock is old rich hippies," he said. "If it's pot or shrooms, who can nail it down?"

"What about heroin?" she said. "Hydrocodone?"

Trevor thought about it, resumed eating. With a mouthful of yam and potato he said, "At college there's a guy I know, we smoked up once."

"Pot?"

"Mom, you *just* said—"

"Reflex. Sorry. Go ahead."

"This guy does other stuff. We got to talking because I just like to party a little, but I was wondering about getting some coke for, well, I just want to try it. Don't say anything, please. So I ask him and he says he's got a League connect, and his guy can get anything I want."

"League," Meghan said. "That's League of Nations?"

"Yeah, I guess."

"You've never met them before, though."

"No. I've seen the T-shirt around the bus stops, though. Thrive or Die. That's sort of like their logo."

It troubled her that Trevor knew those people, would have to live alongside them. Meghan had assumed the town she'd grown up in was the same for her son. For Alexa, too. White Rock had never been the paradise it billed itself as, but she'd worked hard to keep the crime rate down. Now Meghan wondered if they didn't occupy two different cities, imprinted over each other like tracing paper on a map. A hidden world. Or at least one hidden from her.

Surrey PD agreed to send a rep from their Gang Unit to White Rock for a special briefing. Meghan and her department needed to know who they were up against. Inspector Nora Epstein spent a half-hour integrating her MacBook with the station's outdated projector. Finally she asked Meghan to dim the lights.

The first slide of her PowerPoint showed a map of the territory linking Washington State to the province of British Columbia.

"The world's longest undefended border," Epstein said. "Ironic, since it's vigorously defended by the gangs amongst each other. Border Services estimate they catch no more than twenty percent of what goes across, from contraband cigarettes to human cargo."

She tapped the corner of the map, where the beige land met the light blue of the Pacific Ocean. "This stretch of coastal real estate between Vancouver and Seattle, including the ports of Surrey and Delta, is valuable. White Rock is a small but not insignificant part of that turf."

"Lucky us," said Meghan.

Epstein continued. "Today's gangs are different. In the past, they cohered around ethnicity and poverty. Today it can be anyone. Any background."

Slides followed of various faces, various ethnicities.

"The border area is home to two main gangs: The Vipers and the League of Nations. Sometimes Nations is spelled with a Z. For the past decade, the Vipers were the dominant group. Lately, though, they've lost some ground. There have been some big defections to the League."

Another click. Another array of photos, these seemingly drawn from surveillance shots. White kids in sunglasses, a bearded South Asian in a hoodie. Kids with soft faces and empty eyes, some sickly grey from meth.

"The League of Nations was founded by the Hayes brothers, Dalton and Cody. They're at the top, along with Harvinder Singh and Tito DaSilva. Singh and DaSilva we don't know much about, other than they used to be Vipers."

"Why'd they change?" Meghan asked.

"Upward mobility. The League works for the Exiles biker gang, who in turn work for the Calabrians in Montreal. 'Ndrangheta. Better connections with Mexico, so coke, Fentanyl, some brown tar heroin. A truly global operation."

Epstein advanced through other slides. Dalton and Cody Hayes in high school and beyond. Dalton was slender and medium height, tattooed with a yin-yang on his right bicep. A white kid from the suburbs into karate and *The Art of War*, Dalton drove a Porsche Cayenne with bulletproof windows, the integrity of which had been tested. A shot of the car with punctures along the side panel, chips in the tinted glass.

Cody Hayes was the hulking younger brother, six foot four and Neanderthalic in stature. "Baby Godzilla" was his nickname, and he lived up to it. Epstein cited three instances where Cody had assaulted someone in public, with witnesses, and he still wasn't behind bars.

"The thing about the Hayeses," Epstein said, "is that they're strictly middle class. Their mom worked in a bank and their dad taught high school gym. They started out as wanksters—kids pretending to be thugs. But they've transcended that and put together a highly efficient crew. It's not an exaggeration to say the League pretty much controls the border. Any questions?"

Meghan had catered the presentation—coffee and a sandwich platter from the nearby Subway. Denny Fong was out on patrol, but three of the other officers were there. Amanpreet Brar had a notepad and pen ready. Katy Qiu occasionally looked up from her phone. The auxiliary officer, Ted Sommers, ate heartily from the spread and helped himself to a second cup of decaf.

"I remember reading something about signatures," Amanpreet Brar said. She was in her forties, had come to police work late. An academic with a master's in criminology, she sometimes taught first-year crim class at Trevor's college.

Epstein nodded. "The Vipers are known for using automatic weapons, and not being too accurate with them. With the League, because of the size and the variations in members, it's harder to pin down. But they started out with improvised weaponry: parents' shotguns and whatever they could steal during home invasions. And for a while they were modifying cheap Chinese SKS rifles to fire full auto. Now that they're in with the Exiles, you see everything from fifty-cal pistols to heavy artillery."

"What about fire?" Meghan said. "Any known arsonists?"

"It's not uncommon for the League to set a fire to cover their tracks. Destroys the evidence."

"What about house fires?"

"Nothing statistically significant. Why?"

As the expert drank her coffee and finished her sandwich, Meghan related the details of Alexa Reed's death, including the fire, the broken neck, the missing funds and Alexa's narcotics use.

"When it comes to drug-related property crimes," Epstein said, "there are a number of factors at play. Namely whether the arsonist themselves were involved in drug consumption, which can sometimes explain erratic behavior."

"The fire seemed set to obfuscate the crime," Meghan said. "Is that something you've seen the League of Nations do?"

"I'd have to do some research. Let's check back in a few days. Maybe we'll each know more."


"Christ," Meghan said when she was alone.

Most of the info in the lecture wasn't new. But it reinforced how complacent she'd become. Too focused on pleasing city council and the chamber of commerce. In the meantime the rot had spread, like the fire, till it had consumed Alexa Reed.

She made it known to her officers that she wanted to talk to anyone who had seen Alexa in White Rock. No matter how innocuous the conversation. If Alexa had bought milk, Meghan wanted to know about it.

When Denny returned from patrol he had a name for her: Michael May.

"They went to school together," Denny said, demolishing the leftover sandwiches. When his hands were free he tilted the cardboard coffee urn, draining the lees into his travel cup. "Michael works at the Price-Low on Buena Vista. He says she was in there a couple of times. They talked for a second while he bagged her groceries, not about anything important."

Meghan stood, adjusting her gear belt up toward her navel. The damn thing felt heavier with each passing month. "Is May still at work?"

"Yeah. Why, I miss something?" Denny said.

"Just feel like talking to him myself." Meghan smiled and nudged his shoulder. Denny was the most determined cop she'd ever seen, and also the most neurotic. If an act or word could be perceived as a criticism of his law enforcement prowess, he would choose to perceive it that way. Meghan gave him an attaboy before starting the walk up the hill toward the Price-Low.


It wasn't that she didn't trust Denny. Part of it was in the interests of investigative thoroughness. Mostly it related to her feelings of shame for overlooking the world Alexa had found herself in.

She hadn't shopped at the Price-Low in years. Its dirty yellow awning, dusty-looking produce and unfriendly staff gave it the feel of a store that had outlived its glory days and coasted along on proximity. Located near the middle of the steep hill that led from the beach up to the town centre, in the area known as Five Corners, the Price-Low shared a strip mall with a Liquor Quicker and the Just Friends Café.

White Rock had been built around strip malls like these and around the people who frequented them. That world was slipping away, metamorphosising into towers and franchises. Meghan felt she had ignored the change.

The grocery store was nearly empty. Two bored men sat on till. She asked the younger-looking one if he was Michael May.

"Yeah," he said, and rolled his eyes. "I just used my smoke break to talk to your buddy, so if you want me, you gotta ask Nico if I can get off till."

She did, knocking on the door of the manager's office, peeking in and talking to a sweaty man buried behind a mound of invoices and binders. He made a big deal out of clambering out from behind the mess and relieving his subordinate.

Out beyond the loading bay in the break area, May lit a cigarette and slumped down on a yellow milk crate. He was rail-thin, late twenties, already losing his hair. Tattoos on his arms—barbed wire and skulls and the Pantera logo.

"From the top, right?" May gave a listless shake of the head. "Alexa and me went to school together, up till grade eleven. We weren't close but we were lab partners and both smoked, so we got along pretty good. She's on my Instagram feed, but we didn't really keep in touch."

"Until she came in two weeks ago," Meghan said.

"That's right. She bought milk and some overpriced granola. The ten-buck shit with chia. I bagged her stuff."

"What did you say to each other?"

"Y'know, hi, how are things, that shit."

"You talk about her mother?"

"Nuh-uh." May drew smoke in and coughed. "Shit, that's right, forgot her mom died. I should've said something."

The smell of the cigarette was getting to her. Meghan crossed her arms and cocked her head in her best don't-bullshit-me-kid pose.

"Does Price-Low have surveillance cameras?"

"Yeah but she didn't steal anything. Alexa's not the type."

"Your conversation with her will be on tape, I check Nico's office, right?"

"Guess so. Why?"

"Because I think you said more to each other than just hello." Meghan was playing a hunch. "I think if I look at that tape, it'll show you two talking at length."

"Maybe we did. Just catching up. So what?"

"So, she's fucking dead," Meghan said, louder than need be.

May dropped his smoke and put his hands up defensively.

"Alexa burned to a crisp in that house, Michael. If I get the sense you're impeding my finding out who did it, you'll look back on your days as a bag boy with fond fucking remembrance."

"Okay. Jesus, okay." May hunkered down and retrieved his smoke, making a quick look for permission up at Meghan. She nodded. He wiped off the filter, inhaled, collected himself.

"All she said was she was gonna be in town for a while, and did I know anyone she could score from."

"Score what, Michael?"

56

"I don't know exactly." Meghan glared and May quickly added, "Okay, I asked if it was coke, 'cause I sometimes have, I mean my roommate has, some extra. And she said she was thinking harder."

"And?"

"And I said, 'Oh, someone's looking to party, ha ha ha, right?' And she made a face and said she didn't want company and just wanted to take the edges off. Said school was a bitch and she just needed a few days to unplug."

"Heroin?" Meghan asked.

"I thought she meant Oxy, 'cause that shit's everywhere."

"What name'd you give her?" Meghan said.

"Christ, I can't."

"What name, Michael."

Playing the irritable cop had rocketed up her heart rate. Meghan felt ready to strike him.

"You can't let them know I said, okay?"

She made no promises, continued the glare. Michael May's shoulders drooped.

"I know this girl, Sukhi, her brother's in the League. I put Alexa in touch with her."

A minute later Meghan left, with Sukhi Kaur's address and particulars. May only knew her brother by his nickname. Tequila.


Sukhi wasn't at her parents' home, and her phone went straight to message. A popular girl's throaty, slightly bitchy voice. Her message came out almost as a sigh of boredom, with a kissy lilt at the end. *Hi this is Sukhi, you know what to do, I'll hit you back when I can, mm-kay? Buh-bye.*

For the next few days Meghan remained in her office, catching up on the paperwork that had accumulated during the Reed investigation.

Denny and Amanpreet had both applied for a forensic conference on blood-spatter analysis. Her budget allowed one. Meghan spent a day wrangling with the city for a few extra dollars, then with a heavy heart flipped a coin. Heads, so Denny got to go. He would get more out of it, as a vote of confidence if nothing else. Meghan would have to make it up to Amanpreet some other way.

Bulletins from Surrey, Vancouver, Seattle, the interior of the province. A sex offender had been released in the Coquitlam area. If you see this pudgy moustached Caucasian around schools—

Meghan tacked the photo to the staff room wall.

A few BOLOS for stolen goods. Jewellery, mostly. Most big departments didn't bother with impersonal items like electronics or cars, but they'd make an effort if the pilfered goods were sentimental in nature. She hoped Beverly Chan, seventy-three, got her engagement ring and mother's brooch back.

One of the sheets on the bottom stopped her cold. Meghan cursed herself for not seeing it sooner and cursed her staff for not bringing it to her attention.

The photo was of a stone-faced, dark-haired man, twenty-nine years old. No tattoos or piercings, one thirteen-centimetre scar along his left shoulder. SHAW, CAMERON NMI. Paroled on condition and living now in Surrey.

The man who'd killed Roger Garrick had been released from Kent Institution five days before Alexa's death.

# FIVE

Three workers with shovels hurriedly scraped snow and ice from the warehouse yard. Cam didn't recognize the new faces. Despite the snow, all twelve bays held containers. Two semi rigs purred outside the gates.

He found Tyson Lee in bay six, shrink-wrapping a pallet of dog treats.

"*Dude.*"

Tyson dropped the roll and bear-hugged Cam. A jagged screaming pain shot through his shoulder. Cam slapped Tyson on the back and grinned.

"Fuckers couldn't keep Cam the Man down, could they?"

They headed back outside to talk. Snow was still falling, the sky the colour of a burnt-out light bulb. They lit cigarettes, huddled near the side of the building. When Tyson brought out his vaporizer, Cam held out his hand.

"Look who's broadening his fucking horizons," Tyson said.

Cam shrugged. "Found someone to piss for me." He drew in the harsh, sweet smoke, held back a cough as he exhaled. "Compared to the shit the doctors put me on, this is nothing."

Tyson offered his apologies, saying he wished he'd been there so he and Cam could've fucked those guys up, but thank fucking Christ you're all right.

"Hurt bad for a while," Cam said. It still did, but he'd practised not showing it.

"Not as bad as the other guy, right?" Tyson laughed. He banged on the side of the container in bay seven. "Sheedy, guess who's back?"

The three of them took a shift with the shovels, clearing a path for one of the rigs to remove the empty can. Cam told them how the three men had come looking for Tyson, how Cam had told them nothing. They'd attacked anyway. Cam made it clear he'd like very much to know who they were and where he could find them.

"Unfinished business," he said.

"Yeah," said Tyson sheepishly. "Here's the thing, bro. Sheedy told me about your conversation with him, how he explained we need the money. It's even truer now what with Christmas crawling up our ass."

"You cut a deal with them," Cam said.

"It's not like that, I mean we had to."

Cam held up his hand. "I don't give a shit about that. I'm not looking to bust heads. Just want to know where I can find them."

Tyson didn't answer right away. He spoke about what had happened at the warehouse in Cam's absence. The Dopplers had brought in some college kid to be the day manager, the kind of guy who you just fucking *know* will be out of here the second his daddy finds him something better. Till then, Tyson and Sheedy were back working nights—hence the need to

make peace with the League and get back to supplementing their income.

They moved inside, drank coffee in the break room. The same dirty mugs in the sink, same rain-warped George R. R. Martin paperback on top of the fridge.

"Glad you're coming back," Sheedy said. "We got more Filipinos, a few Vietnamese. They're good workers, but don't expect them to bust ass on any of the tough cans. Tyson and me picked up a lot of slack."

"Bullshit," Cam said, grinning at his friends.

"Serious, man. We're working twice as hard, getting half as far. You feeling up to starting tonight?"

It had been almost four weeks, and Cam still felt diminished. Bouts of wooziness hit him at least once a day. He'd see an explosion of shimmering stars, his vision would swim, and he'd have to gulp back nausea. He wondered if the pot would help with that.

"I'm not coming back," he told his friends. "Like you said, all work got me was this." He indicated the scar across his left brow and cheek. "I don't want work. What I want is to make money."

Two days before his return to the warehouse, he'd met Zoe at her office in Delta.

Prentice and Partners had a second-floor cubbyhole above a Baskin Robbins in a strip mall. Cam didn't see any signs, nor was there much in the way of office furniture. No books, only a few home and garden–type magazines. The interior looked more like a dentist's waiting room than a lawyer's workspace.

"You'll approach your friends Lee and Cole and tell them you want their League connection," Zoe said. "We already know who it is, but it's better if you get it from them."

"By better you mean more work," Cam said.

"In the short run. Anything I tell you, we'd have to figure out how you came by the info. That casts suspicion, and creates problems down the line."

"How far down the line are we talking?"

Zoe's desk still had the clear plastic veneer over it. She smoothed down the corner, took a sip from her takeout cup.

"This is a long-term operation. Years have gone into it, before you and I even spoke. I expect it'll take several months longer, four to six at the very least."

Cam thought about it. "How would I square any of this with my PO?"

"You'll have some help with that—but I'll stress the word *some*. It's on you to keep off his radar. We'll arrange for the drug testing to reflect positively, and we'll help you find a day job. Something inane that he won't look twice at."

"If I get pinched?"

"Then you get pinched," Zoe said.

Cam, seated on an Ikea chair, looked through the Venetian blinds at the parking lot. The mall included a dentist's office and not much else. No traffic on a Sunday afternoon. The only cars were in the employee slots for the ice cream parlour below.

"I'm not stupid, okay?" Cam said. "Things happen, shit you can't plan for. I could get stopped for a tail light."

"You don't have a car."

"But you get what I'm saying."

Zoe stood and moved around the room, pacing, working something out.

"If something were to happen," she finally said, "some minor thing—I'm talking very minor—we could most likely work around it."

"Meaning what?"

"You'd be provided with an attorney who'd present some documentation you're cooperating with authorities."

"Which is true, right?"

Zoe didn't answer.

The silence between them lasted almost a minute. Cam realized she'd made her offer. He nodded. That would have to be good enough.

"What do I do once I get the connect?"

"You talk to this person. Tell them you're available, should anything arise."

"And what exactly you think is gonna arise?"

The corner of her mouth twitched. Zoe seemed to be holding back a smile.

"Oh, in that business, things have a way of popping up."


Tyson listened as Cam laid out his plan, his face showing fear and incredulity.

"You took out one of their guys," he said. "Fucked with the League."

"In self-defence." Cam helped himself to an energy drink, hoping it would combat the marijuana fuzz in his brain. "So they're down a man, and they know I didn't say shit to the cops."

"You're looking for what outta this?" Sheedy said.

"Workman's comp."

They laughed.

"I'm serious," Cam said. "They need people and I need some way of catching up what I lost, then getting out ahead. If they've got work, I'm here." He added, smirking, "You guys know I've got the fuckin' resumé."

The name he received from them was Tito, who lived—fuck—on North Bluff Road. White Rock.

Every street sign seemed designed to trigger memories. There was a Roger Garrick Drive, now, for Christ's sake. A Garrick Park, maintained by The Garrick Foundation. Like the dead man had spread himself across the town, becoming less a ghost than the haunted place itself.

As the bus pulled off the highway, he noticed the new construction. Townhouses where forest had been. Half-finished developments along Duprez Ravine. He saw the top of a crane, rising above the city centre. Another tower going in.

It was unfair that Uncle Pete wouldn't see a piece of that work. For years the old man had built and fixed and consulted on every structure within the city limits. Cam decided, when this was over, he'd make peace with his uncle, share with him some of the payoff.

Tito's address was a house in a collection of grassy cul-de-sacs near Centennial Park. Cam had worked inside some of these houses with his uncle. Seven years hadn't changed the area much. The houses were a little bigger. No view of the water, but good schools, driveways holding high-end suvs, classic Porches, cutting edge electrics.

Cam's feet stepped in slush, soaking his runners and the cuffs of his jeans. He found Tito's house. It was smaller than its neighbours. A gravel yard, cyclone fencing, two Range Rovers blocking the drive.

Cam knocked, listened as whatever noise inside went silent. He knocked again.

The door was opened by the blond man whose shins he'd swiped with the lift truck. The blond's eyes bugged out and he yelled for someone else in the house, *oh fuck, you guys.* Worried, making to close the door.

Cam blocked the door with his boot.

Behind the blond came the bearded man, wearing a black wife beater, a chrome automatic shoved into the front of his jeans. League tattoos on his arms and throat. Someone else behind him, hanging back.

"Want to see Tito," Cam said.

"And we just let you in?"

"Why not? Scared of me?"

He was allowed inside then shoved left, ending up in a tastefully furnished living room. The bearded man followed him in, the blond behind them. Two green leather couches faced each other, a matching loveseat in the corner. Cam took the loveseat. If he was in for a beating, he'd at least see where it was coming from.

"You dumb motherfucker," the beard said.

Cam shrugged. "Self-defence."

"Devvy might not walk again."

"Then he's not much fucking good to you, is he? Meantime I'm here and I need work."

The beard shook his head at Cam's audacity. "Who the fuck are you?"

"Cameron Shaw. Recently out of Kent. Where you been?"

The name of the prison registered. Cam sat still and waited.

"Ivan," the beard said, naming himself. He tilted his head toward the blond. "Brad."

"Good to meet you, Ivan and Brad. I'd like to talk to Tito. He around?"

Cam placed his hands on his knees expectantly. If the beating was coming, it was coming now.

"Pretty fucking bold, brother," a voice said from another room.

The man moved into the doorway, hands pressed to the ceiling. He was at least six three and maybe taller, scarecrow thin, with a gaunt, almost sickly face. His hair was the permanent black of cheap dye, and his skin had a greyish tinge. Everything about him seemed washed out.

"My cousin's up in Kent." The man rocked forward and back on his heels, as if preparing to launch himself forward. "Know Marco DaSilva?"

"By rep only," Cam said.

The man smiled. "I'm Tito. What kinda work you looking for?"

"Kind that pays."

"But what are you good at, is the question."

Tito sprang forward into the room, pivoted and without warning went limp, slumped and fell lengthwise onto one of the couches, bouncing once, sitting up so he could look at Cam.

"What am I good at?" Cam looked upward as if pondering it. "I keep my mouth shut. I can get a job done that needs doing. Smart. Good at planning. And I don't like being fucked with." He smiled in the direction of Ivan and Brad. "Ask them."

"Oh, they told me about you." Tito patted down the pockets of his camouflage pants, finding his cigarettes in the pouch on his left calf. He had to sit up to retrieve it. "You sure fucked up Devvy."

"He fucked himself up. Who jumps on a moving forklift?"

"Way these two told me, you were running away."

"'Cause I wasn't who they were looking for, was I?"

Tito giggled as he lit his smoke, letting the lighter drop to the floor. Cam noticed the scars in the wood grain laminate. Stains, rubber scuff marks from boot soles dragged across the floor.

"It's true," Tito said. "I sent three guys to handle one. Not only did they not do what they were s'posed to, they attack the wrong guy. That's on me. Shoulda done it myself."

"Or pick somebody better." Before Ivan could say anything, Cam added, "These two at least weren't as dumb as the other one. If it'd been me and them instead, it would've gotten done."

"Got done anyway."

"'Cause the warehouse guys need the money," Cam said. "Not 'cause they're afraid."

Tito shrugged while inhaling, which caused him to cough and spill ash over his shirt. He brushed it off and jabbed the smoke into the floor. He sat up, coughing.

Brad had disappeared, and returned carrying a sports bottle with the lid off. He handed it to Tito, who drank it empty in one go.

Taking a few steadying breaths, Tito slouched back on the couch. Smiled at Cam. Drummed his fingers on his knees.

"So this is like your job interview?" he said. "You got a resumé? Got references?"

"Ask around," Cam said.

"Maybe." Tito's good humour slipped off his face, replaced by a jailhouse stare. Cam matched it. "What exactly are you looking for?"

"Take what I can get," Cam said. "Least to start with."

He heard nothing from them for four days. In that time Cam applied for another warehouse job, was told to leave his C.V. and three personal references with the office manager. Friday he took a Work-Flex job at the convention centre in Vancouver, rolling out carpeting and setting up booths for some food product trade show. Sunday night he bused back downtown and worked till seven the next morning, tearing it all down.

Work and exhaustion kept the doubts from overwhelming him. There was no guarantee this would work the way Zoe had outlined. They could ignore him, come after him, work it so he'd end up back in prison. That was the risk.

The crew chief at the trade show left two hours before the rest of them, after loading up his station wagon with every free sample the conventioneers had left behind. Boxes of granola bars, cookies, one-serving packets of cereal. Never offering any to the men and women busting their ass to do his work for him.

That said it all, didn't it? How rigged the whole goddamn set-up was. It wasn't enough for the guy to make triple what they did while doing one fifth of the work. No, he'd leave early, too, with whatever spoils he could.

The crew members were either early twenties or early fifties. Like looking at one of those evolution charts with a monkey ancestor on one end and a naked man with a spear on the other. Only this was the progress of one life—from too dumb to know you were being fucked over, to too broken to fight back.

Cam didn't think of himself as angry. Yet something seemed to be waking up. Only as it came back to him, that feeling of deep resentment, did he recognize it as familiar. He'd felt that way at twenty-two, working in houses he'd never afford. He'd felt that way the night he killed Roger Garrick.

And hadn't felt that way since, for a long time, until now.

"You prefer Cameron or Cam? Or how bout Shitbag?"

The voice was Tito's, a laugh accompanying the last suggestion. Cam sat up in bed, checking the time displayed on the phone. Twelve fifteen. He told Tito he didn't care about the name. What was up?

"Ivan'll be by your place in twenty minutes. You got a bat?"

"Like for softball?"

More laughing. "For softball, yeah. That's good. Our team plays a lot of night games."

Cam was out of bed and dressed, guzzled an energy drink, dumped the ID out of his wallet. He waited ten minutes, thinking where he could get a baseball bat at two in the morning.

He swept everything off his kitchen table, dumping the mess in his sink. Flipped the table, ignoring the banging on the floor from his neighbour downstairs. The legs were attached with wobbly screws. Cam worked one around till the leg pulled free. He tested its heft, took a few practice swings.

Wrapping it in a garbage bag, he left his apartment and walked to the corner just as Ivan pulled up. The car was an ancient Hyundai, rust red under the street lights. Brad sat shotgun, and told Cam to climb in the back.

The car was much too small for his knees, and the engine sounded like a go-kart that hadn't been maintained.

They drove south on the highway, past the turnoff for White Rock. That was a relief. Then east, into an area Cam didn't recognize. Long flat stretches of farmland, marked only by airplane warning lights and hulking farm equipment.

"Zero Avenue," Brad said, pointing at a dark crossroads up ahead.

"Yeah I see it." Ivan turned left and they continued on.

Cam knew he was supposed to ask where they were going; most people in his situation would. And he knew the answer would be to shut up and see. He gripped the bag holding the table leg, let it sit on his knees, which were pushed up nearly to his chest.

"Turn here," Brad said. His face was lit up from his cellphone screen. Following directions. Ivan cut his headlights and they drifted along Zero Avenue in darkness, feeling the asphalt turn to hardpacked dirt and finally tamped-down grass.

"Stop. This is us."

They parked up close to a barn, Ivan nearly scraping the side. Cam had to clamber out the other door. The bag with his table leg made rustling sounds. Brad shushed him, took the leg from him and quietly removed the bag, letting it fall into the mud. He handed it back, then made a point of shutting off his cellphone.

"What's the time?" Ivan said.

"Ask me just as I turn it off."

It was cold, but most of the snow had melted. Everything near them was muddy. They waited. Cam watched his breathing, keeping it measured compared to the quick wheeze of Brad's, or the nasal rumble of Ivan's. Neither of the others had visible weapons. Both were wearing dark hoodies, dark jeans. Cam zipped up his jacket, tucked his mouth into the collar.

Lights bounded over the hill from the opposite end of the road they'd come. The others ducked and Cam followed suit. A Jeep passed by, roofless, two shadows up front. Cam thought he glimpsed the barrel of a rifle or shotgun.

The Jeep didn't slow as it passed the barn. Maybe a hundred yards beyond, it stopped. Cam turned his head and saw that a separate set of lights had begun to make its way over the road. A sedan, sleek, its headlamps a cold white fluorescent stare.

"Wait," Ivan said.

The two vehicles met at the point where the road levelled out after dropping down from Zero Avenue. The people in the Jeep climbed out, one of them approaching the sedan, leaning down to conduct some kind of business.

The driver's door of the sedan opened. Ivan and Brad pulled the hoods of their jackets up, as if that was the cue. Cam did the same.

The driver stood in front of the Jeep's headlights. Monstrous. Taller than Tito, but stooped over like an ogre in a fantasy novel. Cam heard feet pounding grass. One of the Jeep's occupants was sprinting away from the cars, directly toward where they waited.

As he neared the barn Ivan reached out and snagged him, tossing the running man to the ground. The man flailed and broke away, collided with Brad. Panicking, he spun and ran right into Cam, who nudged him with the table leg out of reflex. The man took it in the chest and fell to the mud. Cam watched dumbly as Ivan and Brad kicked at the man's back, legs, shoulder.

"Get a hold of him," Ivan said. "Bring him back to Cody."

The man was frightened and dazed. A trail of bloody snot coated his upper lip. Cam took hold of his shoulder and pulled him forward. Brad seized the other arm and together they dragged the man on his knees toward the headlights.

The driver of the sedan looked at them with small eyes set deep in a caveman's face. His hair was blond, shaved on the sides. He was wearing a black vest, the words *Thrive or Die* glittering on the fabric in the headlight glare. He smiled as the man was dragged closer, thrown at his feet.

The other occupant of the Jeep was a woman who was sobbing as she saw the state of the grounded man. "Don't," she said. "We won't, we weren't trying to, I swear."

She looked to be in her forties. Grey hair with some sort of pink-purple streak. Nose rings and lip piercings, black eye makeup running down her face. The man on the ground looked a similar age, his leather jacket now pasted with mud and dead leaves.

"It's always fuckin' more." The ogre's voice was surprisingly high-pitched. "No matter how much we give you."

"Cody, man, it was extra," the woman said. "You were gonna get yours, and we were gonna give you a piece of the rest."

"Course you fucking were."

"Please, man, please. How can we make this right?"

Cody leaned on the hood of the sedan, causing it to bounce and squeal. Whoever was in the passenger seat shut the door. Cody crossed his arms and stared at them.

"How," the woman said. "Anything you say. How can we make this right?"

"Don't know it can," Cody said.

"You could, you could keep the product, no charge."

"Very fuckin' generous."

"Money?"

Cody glowered, silent.

"I'll—" the woman paused. "I'll suck you off. A-all of you." Looking at them with terror.

"And give us the plague?" Cody spat on the man on the ground. The man was sobbing.

"What?" the woman said through sobs. "Just—what? Please."

"It was his idea, wasn't it?" Cody said to her, pointing at the man.

"No, it was mine, swear."

"But he went along with it." Standing up and starting forward, Cody stopped and nodded at Ivan and Brad and Cam. "What d'you guys think? You caught him."

"Bullet," Ivan said solemnly. Cam was sure it was an act. But a good one. The couple looked terrified.

"Please," the man on the ground said. "Please, Cody."

"It won't happen again," the woman said.

"Damn right," Cody said to her. "You tell me what of his to break."

"What?"

"What parts."

"What?"

"Or I start with the neck."

"Wh—please."

"Break his neck," Cody said to Ivan.

"Finger," the woman said, spinning her head from the man on the ground to Cody.

"Sorry?" Cody said.

"Finger," she said. "H-hand."

"What else?"

"Foot. Left foot."

"And?"

"Please."

"Fucking *and*, bitch. And?"

"Arm," she said, adding "I'm sorry" to the man on the ground.

"Hand, foot and arm," Cody said, directing Cam and the others. He noticed the table leg in Cam's hand. "What the blue fuck is that?"

"Table leg."

"Yeah I know, idiot, but why?"

"Tito said bring a bat. I don't play baseball."

Cody looked at Cam with an anger and disgust that Cam hoped was for the benefit of the audience.

"Does it work?" Cody asked.

Meaning, *show me*.

Cam stepped into the light, holding the table leg in two hands, and swung at the man's ribcage. It connected, the nub of the screw on the end catching on the man's clothes and flesh. He howled and the woman covered her eyes.

"Guess it works," Cody said, taking it from Cam. He swung it one-handed, straight down like a club, onto the man's leg. Repeating it. And again, faster. Speaking over the couple's sobs. "Do. Not. Fuck. With. Us. Do. You. Un. Der. Stand? Do you?"

Crying, eyes closed, the woman nodded.

Cody swung the club at her, knocking her into the mud with the man. He tossed the leg back to Cam and walked toward the car.

This isn't me, he thought, pulling the man's arm from its socket with a pop of tearing cartilage.

After, they searched the Jeep and found two courier bags. Ivan took both and stowed them in the back seat of the Hyundai. Another car was approaching. Cam looked to Ivan for a cue, whether to run.

The car was a taxi, muddied from the trip down from the highway. It pulled up and a dark-skinned man exited from the back.

"Doc," Ivan said.

The doctor was dressed in a polo shirt, beige slacks and sandals. A thick gold watch on his wrist. He carried a plastic Safeway bag and a jug of purified water. He looked at the couple in the mud and shivered.

"Bring them into the barn," he said.

Brad and Cam dragged the unconscious man into the structure and laid him on a long bench near the door. Ivan lit a Coleman lantern, hanging it from a loose nail on a roof beam. They brought the woman and put her next to him. The doctor asked one of them to stay while he worked. Ivan and Cam stepped outside.

"You're better than Devvy," Ivan said. "That stuff we got— probably pretty good, if it's like what they make for us. You want, our guy can move your share. Save you trying to move it yourself."

"Thanks. Sure." Cam was still in shock.

"Should be five, ten grand a piece's worth. He'll take half and I'll need a piece, seeing as Tequila doesn't know you. Fifteen is the usual. So maybe two thousand to you?"

"Fine," Cam said.

"Great." Ivan lit a cigarette. "Guess you're used to this, huh?"

Cam accepted a smoke and didn't answer. They heard a howl from inside, swirling into a throaty whimper.

"You do not want to piss off Cody Hayes," Ivan said.


He spent a day in his apartment dealing with what he'd done, finishing off a bottle of Jim Beam and watching nothing on the television. He snapped the other legs off the table and snuck them to the building's dumpster, taking the top in sections. It took three trips.

The next day he left to buy food. On his way home he stopped at an internet café and checked if the incident had made the news. There was no mention of Zero Avenue, of Cody Hayes. He wondered who'd been in the passenger's seat of the sedan.

A week later he took the bus back to Tito's address in White Rock. He was met with back slaps and attaboys and given seventeen hundred dollars.

"Pretty slick," Tito said. "You up for more if it comes along?"

"If it pays," Cam said.

Tito giggled and offered him a brownish blunt, which they passed between them. "Ivan said you didn't even puke."

"I don't get the stuff with the doctor," Cam said. "They that valuable that Cody wants them fixed up?"

"Oh fuck no," Tito said, tittering at the thought. "Those two're just half-assed cooks. Probably fry themselves, sooner or later. We got better, if you want that shit."

"I just don't get it," Cam said.

"You don't have to get it."

"No, guess not."

Finishing the joint and tossing the roach on the floor, Tito said, "It's not like the old days. You put someone in the hospital, there's a paper trail. Cops are gonna want to know what happened. Becomes a big fucking deal. This way it stays between friends, y'know?"

He laughed himself into a coughing fit.


Part-time work, another convention, this one something to do with comics. Wolverines and Darth Whatevers walking around having the time of their stupid lives, while he straightened carpet, connected curtain rods.

With the money he made from the convention job, Cam leased a ten-year-old Civic and replaced his kitchen table with a dining set from the Goodwill.

He kept waiting for sirens and lights, some form of incrimination. A note from his parole officer telling him to come in, there's a lineup we want you to stand for. Something. The idea crimes went unpunished, naive as it was, held novelty for him.

Tito phoned twenty days after the beating and said there might be something else. How'd he get along with the dickheads at the warehouse?

"Fine," he said. "They're good at what they do."

"You say so."

"What's the job?"

"Tell you once we work it out."


He was due to see his parole officer Wednesday, but Saturday he got a call asking if he could come in Monday morning. Sure, of course, but why?

"There's a matter the police would like your help with," his PO said. "You know that a condition of your release is cooperation."

"No problem," Cam said. "Is it—can you tell me what it's about?"

"She didn't say, but she's coming from White Rock. Some questions about a fire."

# SIX

Meghan hadn't been working the night of Roger Garrick's murder. She'd heard about it the next day from Bob Sutter, then-commander of the White Rock detachment. Bob told her it was brutal, the ugliest he'd ever seen. That the Shaw kid had been caught stealing and had bludgeoned Roger to death while a pregnant Liz looked on.

The kid denied the robbery angle. He'd gone there to finish some repair job his uncle had assigned him. THC was present in the kid's system, and open beer cans littered the space near his tools. The kid said having a drink or a spliff during night work wasn't out of the ordinary.

Liz couldn't say what started the row. She'd stayed in the car at first, then gone in to see what was taking Roger so long. She'd seen him and Cam clenched together, struggling. Seen Roger swing the trim guard at him, the kid strike back hard. She remembered screaming.

The kid had spent the night in their cells. Meghan remembered checking on him in the morning. Cam had seemed almost infantile. Sitting on his cot, his shoulders slumped, staring at the end of his existence.

What she knew of Cameron Shaw before that was little. Pete Shaw, his uncle, had done some drywalling for Meghan and Rhonda when they'd first moved into the little rancher near Five Corners. Later he'd replaced their fuse box. She remembered Pete had smoked indoors despite Rhonda's instructions not to, and the man had sworn constantly as he worked, almost as a rhythmic accompaniment to his hammering or painting.

He'd brought his nephew along a few times. Meghan remembered the kid steadying the ladder for his uncle, staring up almost stupidly. When Pete had asked for wire strippers or a fresh screw, Cam had darted to the truck to retrieve it, rushing back as if the ladder would topple if he strayed too long.

A good worker. Shy, polite. Meghan had a hard time squaring her impressions with the killing.

What had seven years done to him—or undone?

Homicide, in her experience, was mostly done by people for whom the day of the killing was the worst of their lives. A man snaps at his wife after too many insults. A woman strikes her willful child, not taking into account how close they are to the top of the stairs. Gang killings were another thing, but for the average person, killing was trauma to them—not as much as to their victims, but trauma all the same.

Cam was an example of that. He'd been near-catatonic that morning in the cell. When Bob interviewed him, Cam waived counsel and admitted a half-dozen points that would damn him in the coming trial. It wasn't Bob's fault—in fact it was his job—and the kid was definitely culpable. But Meghan had felt uncomfortable watching a twenty-two-year-old tie his own noose.

Now, Liz Garrick's cousin once removed was dead, less than a week after her husband's murderer was paroled. Had Cam attacked Alexa Reed? Meghan couldn't see the angle.

She had officers looking for Tequila, real name Nik Narwal. So far they hadn't found him. His sister, Sukhi, was due back in town in a week from a skiing trip. Meghan had demanded a promise from Sukhi to come talk to the police once her vacation was over.

Alexa had asked Michael May for hard drugs. Yet she'd also tossed the realtor's sign, and set up home in her parents' empty house. Meghan wondered what Alexa had been planning. What did the girl hope to get out of this?

And who exactly had dashed those hopes?


Monday morning at eight, Meghan stopped by the Garrick house, parking along the curb, walking through the gates and up the long, slanted oval of driveway. There hadn't been much snow since the first flurry, but Meghan saw three yellow sacks of road salt propped against the brick pedestals flanking the front door. Stone lions grinned at her, perched atop the brick.

A note had been taped to the door, Liz Garrick's professional, slightly sloppy script. *Let yourself in, Meg. Around back in the pool.*

Must be important, Meghan thought, if she's interrupting her swimming. The pool room was a long glass rectangle lit by a combination of skylights and underwater lamps. Green waves shimmered on the windows. There was a steam room, too, Meghan had been told.

Liz was alone in the long strip of bubbling green water, doing laps. Naked from the looks of it. As Meghan approached,

Liz burst from the water. She gave a shake of her silver-black mane and smiled.

"I was hoping to finish before you got here," she said, laughing with only slight embarrassment. "Do you happen to see my robe?"

The woman was the picture of middle-aged beauty— stomach still taut, breasts staving off the tug of gravity, the nipples lightly scarred and puckered. She scampered toward the door at the end of the hall, returning with her body and hair wrapped in a series of towels.

"Apologies for the display," Liz said. "Usually once Max is at school, I'm alone until the maid gets here at noon. I hate the way bathing suits reek of chlorine after wearing. In the past, Roger and I simply didn't chlorinate it—the younger, stupider Lizzie didn't care about water usage."

"We all have to do our part," Meghan said.

Liz's smile involved a crinkling of the eyes and a slightly self-recriminating expression. "I know it's the height of First World problems," she said. "Some girls buy cars or jewellery. I like a clean pool."

They sat down in easy chairs in the solarium, a tea table laid out with orange juice, sparkling wine and ice. "Tempt you with an early morning mimosa?" Liz asked.

Meghan shook her head. "It'll have to be virgin," she said. "Lots to do today."

"You're doing your best, I'm sure," Liz said.

"I wish I had better news."

Meghan explained about the Reed family fortune that had disappeared through attrition, three thousand at a time. Liz frowned, perturbed, and ran a thumb along her chin and bottom lip.

"Roger and I helped them out from time to time," she said. "But the most we ever lent them was a few thousand. I've tried to help them out in other ways."

"Before her death, did Emily talk to you about any problems they might have been having?"

"Not financial," Liz said. "Our last real tête-à-tête was a few months after her stroke, maybe two weeks before Richie's accident. She was very upbeat, which I know sounds crazy given everything that happened. But she said that the weeks Richie was looking out for her, helped refocus them both. Caring for Em brought out a tenderness in Richie, and Emily, I think, fell in love with him all over again."

"Makes what happened worse," Meghan said.

"Much worse, yes."

"What about Alexa?"

"Lost in the shuffle, I assume. She flew back after the stroke, then returned to school. Back for her father's funeral, again, only for a few days. Maybe a week or so. And then her mother's."

"Did you talk to her? How did she act?"

Liz tilted her glass and emptied it, and built another. "I should've told you before, Meg, but I hoped it wouldn't be necessary. Alexa and I had something of a falling out."

"Over what?"

"I can't say." Liz drank and sighed in satisfaction. "I think, in some way, Alexa felt I was to blame for her parents' misfortune."

As Liz explained, the morning of the funeral Alexa had left the house early, borrowing Liz's car.

The funeral was at one. Alexa didn't return until quarter past twelve. When Liz mentioned that she might want to spend some time cleaning up, Alexa slammed the guest room door. She ignored her during the funeral, nodding sullenly to the expressions of condolences.

Liz had interpreted it as filial grief, though looking back she could see the girl had been troubled.

The next afternoon, Liz had knocked on her door and been told to go away. She'd pressed the issue, telling Alexa it was all right to have a full complement of feelings, some less than savoury. It was natural. She'd gone through the same when Roger died—

"You don't give a shit about anyone," Alexa had told her. "Definitely not Mom. She *told* me, y'know."

Liz had no idea what the girl was talking about, and hadn't replied.

"You ruined our lives," Alexa had said. "You and your rich friends. Don't pretend you have a fucking clue what I'm feeling."

Liz had let the matter drop. The next day Alexa had moved out. She was supposed to fly home that night.

"If Emily was broke," Liz said, "I would've helped her, no matter the circumstances. And Emily knew that. I'm sure she did."

"So am I," Meghan said. "Aside from Alexa's emotional state, did you notice anything wrong with her—any signs of drug use?"

"Nothing," Liz said. "I keep pot around the house, and sedatives. If some were missing, it wasn't noticeable."

"Nothing harder than that?"

Liz smiled. "You're not serious."

"Heroin and hydrocodone."

Surprise registered on the widow's face. "No, nothing like that."

"All right," Meghan said. "What was it you wanted to see me about?"

"A favour," Liz said, happy for the change of topic. She adjusted one of the towels. "Your year-end report to city council is coming up on January 7th. Some of Roger's friends and I are bringing a proposal for a gaming resort."

"A casino?" Meghan asked.

Liz nodded. "We're seeking a partnership with the Semiahmoo Nation. We're hoping to build where the band shell is now. We'd appreciate if you'd include an assessment in your report to council, independent of our proposal."

"I'm not sure I follow," Meghan said.

"The median age of White Rock residents is fifty-nine. You and I are youngsters compared to most of our population. If this place is going to have a future, it can't coast along on summer tourism. Wildfires are only getting worse. We must have an economic engine independent of weather and everything else."

"Crime would go up," Meghan said.

"Studies show drug offenses and property crimes take a slight upturn. But there's no reason to think expansion would raise crime substantially, or affect our standard of living."

If they were moving ahead with their pitch to city council in the new year, that didn't leave Meghan a lot of time to consider her position. This was a request that should have come in six, eight months ahead of time. Why hadn't it?

Maybe, she thought, Liz counted on their friendship.

Or maybe, like a lot of people, she'd had a shit year, and too much to deal with.

"No promises, but I'll do what I can," Meghan said.

"All I ask, darling," the widow said.

Meghan bought a chicken torta from the new Mexican place on the beach, ate lunch at her desk while reading through the file on Cameron Shaw.

There was an incident report from the Surrey PD dated two weeks ago. An industrial accident involving Shaw and another man, Devin Reese. Shaw sustained a few deep lacerations. Reese lost an arm. It was unclear what was going on between them before the accident, but Reese was wearing a League of Nations T-shirt.

Neither would say why Reese was in the warehouse. Meghan could hazard a guess. A warehouse so close to the port, there was probably something being smuggled in. The ports around Vancouver handled millions of shipping containers each year, less than one percent of which were inspected. An open invitation for smugglers.

Her sandwich was long gone. Still hungry, Meghan picked at scraps of cabbage and globs of cheese left on the waxed paper. She couldn't say if Cam deserved the benefit of the doubt. He was claiming partial amnesia for the episode. In any case, the kid seemed to attract trouble.


Amanpreet Brar had been acting slightly distant toward Meghan for the last few days, but when she knocked on Meghan's office door, she was grinning broadly.

"Sukhi never went on vacation," Amanpreet said.

She'd been at home the entire time. Amanpreet had stopped by to ask her parents if they knew the whereabouts of their son, Tequila. Sukhi had opened the door, then screamed, realizing her faux pas.

"She tried to tell me how her trip was cancelled," Amanpreet said, standing at attention in front of Meghan's desk. "That she'd only got back that morning. Her dress and mannerisms led me to believe that was a lie. I reiterated the importance of our getting in touch with her brother, and she assured me she didn't know where he was. She's waiting in the staff room."

Sukhi was short, pretty, overly made up and tucked into an enormous Gore-Tex jacket, which hung over the arms of her chair. She looked up at Meghan with hostility.

"I don't know shit about where my brother is, 'kay?"

Meghan smiled. "Okay."

"Why'm I here? You always ask me about my brother and I never know. We're not close or anything."

"So why lie to us?"

"Because," she said, her voice reaching a whine. "You always ask me and I'm tired of it."

"We always do?" Meghan said.

"Cops. You think everyone's got this super close family. One's a criminal, we all got to be criminals, right?"

"Is your brother a criminal, Sukhi?"

"I don't know anything."

Meghan doubted that, but the girl's tone was grating on her. Without any hard evidence to present her with, all they had was her deception.

"Where are your parents?" she asked.

"Wintering in Mexico." The young woman smirked. "Where are yours?"

"Do you know Alexa Reed? Someone said she contacted you, maybe looking for drugs."

"No way," Sukhi said. She pointed at Amanpreet. "Like I told that one, I don't know Tequila's number. If she asked, I didn't have anything to tell her."

"So Alexa did ask?"

"I don't remember."

Lying. Meghan checked the clock: time for her to make the drive to Surrey.

"All right, you can go," Meghan said.

The coat billowed upward. Meghan stopped Sukhi from rising out of her chair.

"Before you do, understand something. Your brother might know about the murder of Alexa Reed, a girl who's not much older than you. Which means sooner or later we'll be having words with him, and probably with you again."

The girl's feet kicked the legs of the chair petulantly. *What a fucking brat*, Meghan thought.

"If you want to save both of you some grief, tell him to get in touch. Understand?"

"Can I go now?"

Meghan shrugged and nodded at Amanpreet to drive her home.


She wasn't in the best of moods for her meeting with Cameron Shaw. Added to the mysteries of Alexa's death were why a girl who professed blind ignorance to her brother's criminal connections would lie to the police; what Alexa had found out about her parents and Liz Garrick; and, off-topic but another piece on the shit pile, this business with the casino.

Being detachment commander was a Sisyphean shoveling at said shit pile, with negligible results. Isn't that what Bob Sutter had always said?

The parole officer worked in a building a five-minute drive from King George Boulevard. Amazing how different Surrey was from White Rock. Colourless and industrial, clogged with traffic. Even the weather seemed worse. Greyer, somehow. Meghan had little cause to leave White Rock these days, and was thankful for it.

What impact would a casino have? Would it turn the town into a sleazy weekend jaunt for Seattleites? Who would live there?

The parole officer showed her into his office, a beige cubbyhole, and dropped Cam's file in front of her. In the months he'd been out, Cam had found work at a warehouse and then as a day labourer. His employer described him as hard-working. He pissed clean consistently.

So, no drugs, work physically but not mentally demanding. What did Cam spend his time on?

"Do you prefer if I'm present?" the PO asked. "During your interview. As an added authority figure."

Meghan told him she'd be fine.

Cam entered and sat down in the PO's computer chair. He shook her hand. She noticed the scar on his face, a dark purple furrow down the cheek. Otherwise a nondescript white guy in his twenties, slightly baby-faced, only a few years older than her son. Cam kept his eye returning to the door.

"What happened there?" she asked, gesturing at the scar.

"Workplace accident."

"I heard you were attacked."

"From who?"

"You know why I'm here?" Meghan said.

"No."

"Do you remember Alexa Reed?"

She watched his brow furrow, considering the name. "You mean like the Reeds that ran the gas station on Buena Vista?"

"Their daughter," Meghan said.

"I probably saw her around."

"When was this?"

"Back in the day."

"Before you went to prison for killing Roger Garrick."

Cam looked up at her, suddenly cagey. Studying her eyes the way she'd been studying his.

"That's right," he said. "Before that."

"Were you aware Mrs. Reed and Mrs. Garrick were cousins?"

"Nope."

"So in your mind there's no connection between what happened to Roger Garrick and what happened to Alexa."

"You haven't told me what happened," he said.

"Her parents' house was set on fire. With her in it."

"Really sucks," he said. "But I didn't know her."

"It happened the week you got out of prison," Meghan said. "Can you account for your whereabouts?"

"For the whole week?"

"That's the cooperation I'm looking for, Cam." Implying that failing to cooperate would be a strike against his parole—see how he holds up to that.

"Let me think," he said. "I got a place, I went for some job interviews."

"Were you in White Rock?"

90

"No."

"Not even to visit your uncle?"

Cam said sheepishly, "For about twenty minutes. He wasn't all that glad to see me."

"You murdered his friend and client, hard to wonder why."

"Manslaughter," Cam said.

"Right. You slaughtered his friend and client."

Cam sighed. His hands were clasped together, and he took a moment of staring at them before saying, "I'm aware what I did, ma'am."

"Staff Sergeant Quick. Do you know where the Reeds live?"

"Not an address, but if I saw the place I might recognize it."

"Have you been in there before?"

"I don't know."

"Recently?"

"No."

"Did you purchase drugs for Alexa Reed?"

"No."

"Did you break her neck, Cameron?"

"No."

"Set her body on fire to cover up your crime?"

"No, I didn't, Staff Sergeant Quick."

"How well do you know the League of Nations?"

"I—no."

That pause. Something there, she thought.

"Tell me about the warehouse attack," Meghan said.

"Not much to say. I didn't know the guy. He chased me. Climbed on the cage of the forklift. My memory's still blurry."

"Sure it is," she said. Leaning forward, playing nice now. "If you got mixed up with something, maybe starting while you were inside—"

"No."

"I don't believe you've never heard of the League of Nations. Not coming from where you did."

Cameron shrugged. "It's like have I heard of the mafia or the Exiles? I mean, sure. But that doesn't mean I know any."

"You were imprisoned with some."

"I saw some League crew inside, yeah, but so what? Not like we hung out. They keep to themselves."

"And who do you keep to?"

"What do you mean?"

"I mean, Cam, who have you been associating with since you got out?"

The question seemed to stump him. Meghan waited, letting him formulate whatever bullshit answer he felt like. The more elaborate, the easier it would be to disassemble when she came back at him. And she *would* come back. There'd definitely be a follow-up to this.

After at least a minute of thoughts and glances around the room, Cam said, "I'm mostly on my own these days."

"Poor little murderer—sorry, manslaughterer."

"You know who I see, Staff Sergeant Quick? People like you. People who don't see people like me."

"And what does that mean?"

Meghan stared at him. Cam's words seemed familiar in some way. Maybe it was the sense of resentment. It somehow echoed Alexa's post about the blindness of the people around her. Coming from Cam it seemed more of a challenge.

Her pocket shook. She removed her phone. A text from Denny Fong.

DP *East Beach. Likely homicide.* And following quickly after: *Arson, looks like.*

As she drove toward East Beach, Meghan's stomach flared with indigestion. The idea that she was facing another unsolved—maybe unsolvable—homicide was unsettling. Her talk with Cam hadn't improved things.

She parked and popped a Tums. Took a moment to compose herself. Then left the car, approaching the outcropping of beach where Denny and Greg Grewal were waiting.

Something lay covered in a green blanket behind them. A few gawkers stood in the grassy area between the parking lot and the beach, swiveling to take Meghan's photo.

At the far end the beach turned to rock. Gravel first, then larger pieces, which Meghan carefully leapt across.

"It would have to be the start of high tide," Grewal said, shaking his head.

"Means the techs better hurry. What do we have, Greg?"

"Nothing definite yet, but it's consistent with an execution."

Grewal pulled back the blanket like a magician unimpressed with his own trick. The body was curled in the same boxer's pose. Skin a purplish black, face melted into a featureless mannequin's mask. Looking down, Meghan could see what looked like the exit wound of a high-calibre bullet blooming from the trachea. The smell was sweet and excruciating. Thankfully the wind was blowing the worst of it down the beach.

"Shell casing, Sarge," Denny pointed to a rock a couple metres behind the head. "Haven't picked it up but looks like a .45 or maybe a .44 mag."

"Shot and then burned," she said. "Can we match the fuel?"

"Possibly, if it's from the same container."

The corpse's shoes were worn, white, off-brand runners. *A Kmart kid*, Meghan thought. The body male, adult, yet something young about it. She reached into a pocket, found keys and something else. A nametag. WELCOME TO PRICE-LOW. MY NAME IS MIKE.

"Michael May," she said.


The Mays lived up the hill and beyond the town centre. Here the properties were older, larger, less well maintained. The house had once backed onto a forest, but was now cut off by a row of townhouses. Mrs. May let Meghan in while her husband thumped up the stairs from the basement. He handed his wife a can of Old Milwaukee. The two sat down on the blasted sofa, Mr. May lighting a cigarette.

"What's this about Michael?" he said.

These were people from an older White Rock, the community Meghan had grown up in. They probably didn't get down to the beach much anymore, since the parking meters went in. Meghan had seen true, grim poverty, and this wasn't that. Instead it was what used to be called "getting by."

*The million ways this job breaks your fucking heart,* Meghan thought.

Bob Sutter had been good at delivering this kind of news, starting off folksy and banal, and feathering in to the catastrophe like a small plane landing in a deserted air field. Meghan found it more manageable to drop the load straight away.

"It's bad news, I'm afraid. A body was found on the beach. We believe it's Michael's."

"You're dicking around with us," Mrs. May said. "This is some sort of—no. You're wrong."

"We'll need a formal identification, but his nametag was found near his body."

94

"Maybe he got robbed."

"I'm afraid not, Mrs. May."

Her husband made a sharp, high-pitched sound, summoned out of his fleshy abdomen. Meghan realized it was a sob. He leaned forward, his hands flying to his mouth as if to smother the sound.

"He was just here last weekend," Mrs. May said. "We did chicken. I wrapped up the leftovers to send home with him. He still has my Tupperware."

Meghan comforted them as best she could, walking Mrs. May to the point of acceptance, and comforting the husband, who now wept silently, his hands pulling ropes of mucus from his nostrils.

Bob would have known what to say. We'll catch the bastard that did this, or something they could hang onto in their grief.

But she had nothing for them.



May's apartment was a ten-minute walk from Five Corners. The three-storey low-rise looked out on the back alley of the Price-Low, its view of the water now obscured by the skeleton of Panorama Tower.

Meghan huffed up the stairs, passing dumb graffiti tags, JOZ LIX AZZ, FUK PIGS and the like. Grey steel boxes of rat poison placed on each landing. She keyed the lock of apartment 311, finding it swung open to her touch.

Stepping inside, she saw the flash of an arm—felt something strike her head—

Then she was sprawled on the vinyl floor of the kitchenette.

Someone in black kicked her and tried to move past. Meghan reached out, her circumstances coming back to her. Cinched her arms around the fleeing leg and twisted.

Her attacker landed on the floor in front of her. She felt boots kick out at her. A heel smacked into her eye. Her vision watered. She heard crawling toward the door.

Meghan's sidearm was trapped under her. She freed her ASP, the expandible baton, and swung at the figure aiming for his head.

The attacker turned over and she saw his face. Frightened eyes, a goatee and sideburns with dark blood matting the hair. Tequila Narwal.

He kicked again and her wrist snapped back, going numb. The ASP fell. Tequila crawled forward and Meghan lunged, landing on top of him, striking at his nose and eyes.

His hand shoved against her neck. Tequila was slender but wiry, motivated by desperation. She reached to pull his fingers away from her throat and his other hand shoved her off-balance, tipping her off him, sending her head hard into the bifold door of the closet.

A blink of darkness. Meghan held her numb arm close to her body, keeping her sidearm secure.

She heard feet patter across carpet. A door gently click shut. Then she was alone.

# SEVEN

The basement of Tito DaSilva's house was an unfinished room. Tufts of fibreglass insulation poked out from rips in the kraft paper. Empty ammunition crates, rusty knives, beer cans overflowing with ash. Tito called it The War Room.

Cam was led downstairs by Ivan. He'd already prepared a story in case they'd somehow heard about his interview by the White Rock cop. Easy enough to play dumb about the murder she'd been asking about—he *was* dumb. He'd known Alexa Reed from around town, from a distance. That was it.

The cop sensed something was amiss, though. Meghan Quick was smart. More tuned in than the Surrey officers who'd questioned him after the warehouse attack. He'd have to be more cautious next time.

Down the stairs he saw Brad and Tito seated on over-turned crates. Tito looked anxious, shifting around on his seat. Cam soon saw why: a man and woman that he didn't recognize stood in the far corner, spreading papers on a work bench.

Both were South Asian. The woman was maybe twenty-four, short, pretty and scowling in response to her surroundings. A thick quilted Gore-Tex coat that must have been hers was folded on a nearby crate. Her T-shirt, black with the glitter League of Nations logo, was thin enough to show the nubs of her nipples through the fabric.

The man was dressed like the manager at a car stereo store—white sleeveless dress shirt, red tie, black pants blemished with War Room dust. Handsome, hair swept back and gelled in place. His beard extended his chin to a fierce point. He smoked and fiddled with a gold-plated Ronson lighter. A bundle wrapped in black plastic sat on the floor near the bench.

"This is the guy we told you about," Ivan said. "Cam Shaw. This is Harv and that's Sukhi."

Cam nodded. Sukhi eyed him with no particular emotion. Harv didn't look up from the paperwork on the desk.

"If that's everyone," Harv said, making no attempt to hide his impatience. "We've got a situation at the docks. There's a container that's been there since last week, that customs thinks has something in it."

"Which it does," Tito said. Trying to add to Harv's speech, play the good lieutenant. Harv winced and then ignored him. Cam saw who was in charge.

"There's a risk involved," Harv said, "but anyone that helps will be looked after."

"I'm bored," Sukhi said.

"In a minute, babe. Now, you'll need to know the container number, which is"—Harv shuffled papers—"AKSKA 9938. The first eight rows of shoeboxes are just that—there's shoes inside. After that you'll find what we're looking for."

"So what's our plan?" Tito asked.

"That's up to you," Harv said. "Because it's being watched, I'd suggest going in quick. You could probably get ten or twelve boxes out of there before security gets smart."

"You mean take it right off the dock?" Brad asked.

"Well the container isn't going anywhere, so you tell me," Harv said.

"Pull up alongside, break in, hand-bomb it off and zip out," Tito said, nodding. He turned to Cam. "Up for that?"

"What is it exactly?"

"You don't need to know that," Harv said.

"Can we go now, Harv? Chilly as shit in here." Sukhi shivered and sat on a bottom stair, crossing her arms.

"I *do* need to know," Cam said.

Harv held a finger up toward Sukhi and turned to Cam, scowling. "No, you fucking don't. You don't need to know anything. Just that there's cash involved if you want it."

Cam picked up the jacket and walked it over to Sukhi, who nodded thanks but didn't reach for it. Instead she leaned forward. Prompting him to drape it over her shoulders. He did.

"Merry fucking gentleman," Tito muttered.

"I don't care what the shit is," Cam said to Harv. "Only how it's packed, how heavy, that sort of thing. Can we carry it? Is it flammable? Does it smell? If it's in ten-foot boxes or gallon drums, that changes things. We want to do this right, don't we?" He looked around the room. "Because if we're gonna half-ass it, no way. I'm not *ever* going back inside."

Harv's face went from deepening anger to puzzlement, and finally to a shrug. He looked at Cam as if Cam had just entered the room. Evaluating him anew.

"P2P," Harv finally said. "Phenyl propanone. It's packed in jugs, each jug packed inside a box."

"How heavy?"

"Twenty-two kilograms each."

"How much is that in pounds?" Ivan asked. Seeing how

Cam's question impressed Harv, he was trying for the same thing. Could get jealous, Cam thought. Have to watch out for Ivan.

"Just under fifty pounds," Harv said. "There's a hundred and fifty boxes of it."

"Marked any special way?"

"No," he said. "But they'll be behind the first eight rows."

"Any clue about what kind of surveillance?"

Harv unwrapped the black plastic bag, producing a mobile phone and what looked like a clip-on ID tag. He turned the phone on, showed them the screen. Photos of the dockyard. A video, someone walking through endless aisles of shipping containers. Cans were something Cam understood.

"We've got a friend who works there," Harv said. "There'll be a couple of guards on that night who'll check the other lanes. But there are cameras up, maybe one aimed at the container." He shrugged. "That's what we know so far."

"Total fucking heat score," Brad said.

Cam was studying the video. "No chance they'd let us drive right in? Take the whole can?"

"A rig would never fit down those lanes," Harv said. "You'd need to operate the crane and move it."

"And the can is on the ground?"

"Where the fuck else would it be?"

"They stack them," Cam said. "If it's up ten cans high, no chance of us getting to it."

Harv nodded. "It'll be on the bottom."

"If it is," Cam said, "there's no reason we can't get all hundred and fifty."

Harv's last comment bothered him. How did he know it was on the bottom? Maybe the League had a crane operator in their pocket. But if so, why not have that person move the can and ship it out entirely?

*Total fucking heat score.*

The other possibility was the one that bothered him. That it had been deliberately put on the ground by customs, knowing there was a chance the League would try something like this.

Cam turned the idea over in his head. Ivan and Tito would call him, coming up with suggestions. Take it away in boats. Paint over the code number and hope the can got lost. Tito's suggestion was to take the place over by force. "Captive labour to do the lifting," he said.

Two nights later Cam had it.

He called Tito and said he needed to see Harv. Tito phoned back twenty minutes later saying okay, someone would swing by for Cam in about half an hour.

Cam was waiting outside, not expecting to see a Porsche suv with Sukhi behind the wheel, Harv himself in the passenger seat. He rolled down his window and beckoned Cam to approach.

"I need linesman's gear," Cam said. He'd written out a list of the materials.

"You can use all this?"

"Used to work for my uncle."

Harv nodded, took the list and handed it to Sukhi, who drummed impatiently on the steering wheel. "When are you planning to do this?"

"Soon as I get the tools."

"That case, we'll see what we can do."

The next morning the gear was left on his doorstop. Climbing tools, impact socket, side cutters, demolition driver. Even a tool belt, the worn leather looking oddly familiar.

Cam carried it all inside. He held up the tool belt and ran his hand over the underside, looking for the owner's initials.

PS. His uncle's.


They'd need as many hours of darkness as possible. The port workers usually went home at dinner. Cam waited until ten, watching the place, the three orange cranes like the necks of skeletal dinosaurs, sitting above the high black gate, beyond the rows of containers.

He walked past the place, the fenced-in parking lot. The road itself was empty save for one van with tinted windows, no hubcaps on its wheels. A surveillance car.

Dressed in overalls, with the lineman's belt cinched around his waist, Cam walked into the parking lot. At the far end it bordered the water itself, a barnacled outcropping of coast leading straight down to black water. He chose a segment of fence and, working quickly, cut his way inside the yard.

Flood lights burned above the cans, leaving the lanes under odd shadows. Cam walked past calmly, confidently. He belonged here, was attending to something. The decal on his hard hat read BC HYDRO. Clipped to his overalls was a decent-looking approximation of an ID card. He'd hated to use his own photo, but it had seemed the only way.

He passed a security guard, nodding at her. Then when she was three metres or so away, he turned around and coughed.

"Got myself lost," he said sheepishly. "Where's the electrical room?"

She pointed, swiping her finger left. "Around the corner. Late, huh?"

"This rate I won't get home till midnight."

"That'd be early for me," she said. "I'm on till four."

"Oh, nice. Enjoy that."

"Fuck yourself."

He continued on, following her directions, spotting the shed with the door marked with a lightning bolt shooting through the outline of a man. KEEP OUT.

The door was locked. Cam brought the key ring out from his pocket and flipped through, finding the one Harv had made for him.

Inside, he looked around and found the one-line diagram. Traced it to locate the panels for the lights, for security and for the gate. Once the gate was retracted, he switched off the panels, shutting off power to the yard.

Blackness. He worked quickly, turning on his headlamp, fumbling a little with gloved hands. Unspooling the red cord of the breaker lockouts. Attaching the teeth to one side of a panel, stretching the cord across and padlocking it in place. To turn the power back on, someone would have to cut the locks.

The security cameras would have battery backup, but without the lights, hopefully the picture would be blurry and no good. A chance he was taking.

He felt his way to the door and outside. Sprayed the key with contact cement and inserted it, locked the door. Struck the end with the demolition driver until it broke off in the lock.

Clouds obscured the moon, and the street light only carried to just inside the gate. Cam felt along the side of the containers, following the map he'd memorized. Lane C, spot four, bottom can.

There. He flipped open the burner cellphone he bought and told Ivan to drive in.

He'd hated to bring Tito along, since the man seemed erratic. He was likely to bolt or give up halfway through. But it was Tito's crew, not his. Not yet.

When he outlined the plan, he sold Tito on the role of driver. Tito liked that, envisioning a quick getaway. Dreams of movie car chases. Cam let him dream. It would keep him cool.

If the plan went off, they'd be able to saunter out at their own pace.

Cam heard them enter through the gate, the white van with BC HYDRO on its side. They'd painted it to resemble the work trucks, but inside the seats and cage had been ripped out, leaving nothing but a handcart.

He located the right staging area and examined the container ID, then bit the knuckle of his gloved hand. Wrong numbers. Searching around, he double-checked that he was in the right lane, the right spot. No AKSKA 9938.

A fucking set-up.

Who—

And then he looked up and bit down harder. Their can was second on a stack of three. The dolly would be useless.

The purr of the van down the wrong lane. Of all the fucking things. Cam waved them over, waited as Tito backed the van up to the edge of the lane.

Cam opened the back door and let out Brad, who carried the bolt cutters. "Let's do 'er," Brad said.

"Where's Ivan?"

"Something came up."

Cam took a breath, wondering if it was better not to just say fuck it now and walk away.

Which would leave him where? Another leg breaker, no closer to what Zoe wanted from him, nothing going for himself but a cop looking to pin a woman's murder on him.

You need this.

Be honest with yourself. You want this, too.

"Boost me," he said.

Clambering on top of the van with the bolt cutters, Cam clipped the seal off the door handle. The lip of their container overhung the bottom can by a few centimetres. A lucky break. Wrenching the handle down, he pried the opposite door open, feeling the stack wobble. Just his luck if the whole fucking thing came down on him. At least he wouldn't feel much.

Inside, the shoeboxes had been stacked side to side, but with about a half-metre along the top. Cam heaved out boxes, hearing them fall to the concrete. Between that and the creak of the door, he was already making more noise than he'd planned. But that couldn't be helped.

Climbing in, shoving the boxes aside, he counted the rows, six, seven, and came to a wall of merchandise that wouldn't shift when he touched it. He lifted one of the larger boxes, heard it rattle. A jug of some sort inside.

Carrying it out, he kicked more of the shoeboxes away, then crouched and passed the larger box to Brad.

"Fucker's heavy," Brad said.

Cam was already crawling back, thinking, *only one hundred forty-nine to go.*

It was slow, and Brad was as liable to drop them as Cam was to fumble the pass. He worked as quickly, as accurately as he could. Passing them down one at a time. Cam reached thirty-seven when he heard the car.

Stopping, he moved to the edge and looked down at Brad, who stared up at him, equally clueless. They waited in silence.

High beams played over the lanes. A truck of some kind.

Below, Tito started the van's engine. The running lights peeped on. Idiot, Cam thought, don't give away where we are.

In a pinch he could make a run down the aisle, sneak out the way he'd got in. Race for the break in the fence. If the road was blocked he could hazard the water. He hadn't swum in years, had no idea where he'd go or how cold the water was in mid-December—

A white truck passed along the far end of the lane. The path of the light wasn't interrupted. Cam relaxed. It was Hydro, the actual electricians, come to restore power.

Good luck. They'd need at least an hour just to hook things up, let alone repairing the gauges. And that was if they could get in.

Cam scrambled back into the can and began hauling out the boxes.

Once the van was three-quarters full, Cam told Brad to strip off the cardboard and jam the jugs anywhere there was space. They filled up the passenger's seat, and he ordered Tito to move his seat forward. By now the van sagged, overburdened, but by Cam's count they'd rescued one hundred and seventeen of the jugs.

Chemistry was beyond him, but that much would make a fuck-ton of something.

He debated sealing up the container, replacing the scattered boxes. But by then his own nerves were almost done. He closed the van's back door and told Tito to go.

"What about us?" Brad said.

Cam led him down the aisles, keeping a safe distance from the lanes in case of another vehicle. They passed by the Hydro shed just as the lights flickered on.

"Hello?" someone called out.

They ran for the fence, pushing their way through to the parking lot, gunning the borrowed Focus that had been left there the night before. Shooting onto River Road, Brad gave a loud wail of happiness. And Cam gave one, too.

They ditched the car in a mall parking lot, taking Brad's stupid luxury pickup back to the house. Tito was there, already deep in celebration.

"No one else could've pulled that off 'cept us," he said. "We are the fuckin' League, us three."

Still no sign of Ivan.

There was booze and cocaine and pot, and Cam was forced to indulge in all three. In truth he was as exhilarated as the others. His plan. His execution. Despite all the obstacles thrown in their way, they'd pulled it off. Goddamn right it was cause to celebrate.

Harv and Sukhi showed up later and congratulated them. Harv was beaming. Slightly uncomfortable in their company, like a slumming college kid in a bar full of night shift janitors, he nevertheless cracked a beer and saluted them, drinking it in one gulp.

"Way to fucking go," he said, pronouncing *fucking* as if the word were new to him. "Honestly, I thought if you were lucky you might get a few cases. But you got almost the whole thing." He handed out envelopes, their first initials pencilled in the corner.

"A present," he said. "From Dalton Hayes."

*The head of the League knows who I am,* Cam thought.

"He also wanted you to have this."

Harv passed him an object wrapped in a garbage bag that looked to Cam like the shape of a rifle. Opening it, Cam grabbed a taped and tapered handle, saw wood grain and a signature. Vladimir Guerrero Jr.

"The proper tool for the proper job," Harv said.

Cam took a practice swing with the bat. "Tell him thanks."

Even Sukhi seemed impressed. She followed Harv back up the stairs, pausing briefly to wave to Cam, the gold tips of her fingers sticking out beneath the cuff of her coat. Cam nodded back, thinking this was already better than the warehouse.

It made the local news. A headline read, BLACKOUT BANDITS STEAL MILLIONS IN METH CHEMICALS FROM PORT. The reporters had some of the details right. No witnesses, no statement from police other than they were investigating thoroughly.

He was surprised when they estimated the chemicals taken to be worth in the range of seven million dollars. His envelope had contained five thousand. Of course that was just the bonus, not the payoff itself. Harv had said they'd be taken care of.

The day after, Cam drove out to South Surrey, to the area of older, smaller houses near the Nicomekl River where his uncle lived. He knocked on the door, and when Uncle Pete opened it, he handed him a milk crate with his lineman's gear inside.

"Figured you'd want that back," Cam said. He had a roll of money in his pocket, but seeing his uncle's expression, left it there.

"That's you on the news, huh?" Uncle Pete said.

Cam said nothing, turned and stepped off the porch. After a morning of icy rain, it was turning into a nice day.

Pete followed him down the steps, his clawed yellow feet padding on the cement.

"I spent a lot of time defending you to people, saying you weren't bad, just did a wrong thing. Guess you had me fooled."

"Guess so," Cam said.

"The hell are you thinking, Cam? Think these people are gonna care for you? These are scum."

"Gave them your fucking tools, though."

"Think I had a choice?"

Cam turned, shaking his head, smiling. "No one has a choice in anything. 'Cept me, right? According to you, I got unlimited options in life."

"All right, Christ." Pete sighed. "We're both hypocrites. That your point?"

"No point," Cam said. "You told that cop you saw me."

"Not much Meghan Quick couldn't find out on her own," his uncle said. "And I worry about you."

"Keep worrying," Cam said. "Makes a real big difference in the world."

He drove back to Surrey to get ready. The *real* celebration was tonight.

They'd rented the private room of a strip club in Surrey, catered it with stacks of joints dipped in hash oil, lines of coke. Women circulated in silver heels, nipples pasted over with sparkling tassels. He was taken into a booth with a leather couch and red wallpaper, given a lap dance and then told anything else he wanted had been paid for ahead of time.

*Anything you want,* he'd hear again and again that night.

At one point two women pretended to fight over the privilege of servicing him. Sitting on the couch with his pants around his ankles, Cam thought the whole thing was silly. Phony. Over the top. He chose the one who seemed more comfortable, or maybe the better actor, and closed his eyes, and thought of Elizabeth Garrick.


There was no more money coming to them. Tito told him this a few days after the party, when Cam called about getting an advance. He'd spent two thousand at the party, tipping lavishly despite the League footing the bill. After repairing an oil leak in the Civic, there was only twenty-five hundred left.

It seemed impossible, after all that work, that kind of street value—seven million—that this was the sum total of his payoff.

"I know," Tito said. "I asked about it and Harv said the stuff wasn't as good as they'd thought."

"Took no less effort to get it."

"I fucking know, man. What can you do? He also said ditch our phones and change up our routines."

Routine, Cam thought. Looking for work, waiting around his half-empty apartment. He couldn't afford routines.

"Let me have his number," Cam said.

In the midst of dialing, a thought hit him—that he was so in character he forgot he was playing a role. He'd be paid later, by Zoe Prentice, once he established himself a bit further. What did it matter if the person he was playing was ripped off a bit?

It mattered. It was more than a role. For once, he deserved to be compensated fairly for his work.

"Go ahead," the female voice on the phone said. Sukhi. Suddenly polite, maybe flirtatious. "Oh hey, Cam."

"Is Harv there? I'd like to talk about getting paid."

"Would you," she said. "Did you enjoy the party?"

"It was fine. I still need some money."

"How 'bout you and I speak?" Sukhi said. "There's a fish and chips place by my house. Moby Dick's. You know White Rock?"


At first he worried about being recognized. People pointing at him, whispering. There goes Roger Garrick's killer. He'd worn shades and a Jays cap, let his facial hair grow.

It hadn't been necessary. This was White Rock, after all. Everybody had money, and problems of their own, and barely looked twice at a guy in cheap clothes.

Entering Moby Dick's, Cam spotted Sukhi at a side table, drinking a massive cup of soda with two straws. Her gold fingernails drummed the counter.

"You have a better chance of getting a blow job from the First Lady than getting your money," was the first thing she said.

Cam seated himself, took off the baseball cap, then decided it was better to leave it on. "Yeah?"

"Best to move on, you ask me. Harv will tell you the chemicals are weak, not worth that much."

"Papers said that stuff was valued at—"

"Millions." Sukhi rolled her eyes. "But that's after processing, wholesale, cutting it. Street value is bullshit. Plus there's the Exiles, who take a big piece. We just get the crumbs."

Cam was surprised, partly at Sukhi's knowledge of the business, more from her interest. She spoke like someone sick of the arrangement.

"Doesn't seem fair," he said.

"It's totally not. But that's the way it's set up."

The waitress came by and they ordered two-piece meals, a basket of fries to split. Sukhi refilled her soda from the machine in the corner, brought him back one.

"Harv's super smart," she said. "He's totally impressed by what you did."

"Impressed but not willing to pay."

She smiled. "That's how we do."

"If I'd known it was only that much—"

"Think about it like an investment," she said. "You don't know how big it'll pay off yet."

"Why're you telling me this?"

"Because you're smart," she said. "You got it done when even Harv said it couldn't. He only sent Tito because he figured he could spare him."

"And us."

"Yeah. And you."

The cola was flat and syrupy. Cam put the drink aside.

"Like everything else," he said. "The people that do the work end up with nothing."

"Doesn't have to be like that forever," Sukhi said. "Harv has plans. So do I."

So that was it. Cam crossed his arms.

Sukhi reached over and ran her nail along the scar above his eye, down to his cheek. "I like it," she said. "Makes you look badass."

He didn't feel badass. Powerless, yeah. And used. And about to be used again.

"Look, Harv knows you're better than what you're doing now. And I'll put in a word with him, and with Cody if I see him."

"Thanks."

"But I need something."

"Course you do."

"Oh quit it," Sukhi said, flashing anger and then hiding it, smiling. "I have to be around them and pretend to be a fucking ditz. Think I like that? Think I don't know Harv has bitches on the side? He gets more white pussy than a Bond villain. And I put up with that, in order to make moves of my own."

The food came and she picked up a giant steaming battered flank of fish, bit into it; spoke while she chewed.

"There's lots going on you don't know about. Harv wants things to change much as we do. More League independence, a better rate for the risks we take. He used to be with the Vipers, but he thought Dalton Hayes was better connected. That's why he jumped over. Harv says they could be partners, League and the Vipers, push out the Exiles and deal direct with the cartel. He says it'd be like that if Dalton had a bigger set of balls."

She spoke passionately, jamming food in during the breaks between sentences. Cam ate his meal and listened.

"This town is right along the border and totally open," she said. "That's why Harv moved his people out here. Get a foothold. You know what's coming?"

He shook his head.

"A fucking casino. And there'll be thousands more people here. More opportunities. It'll be this big resort 'tween Seattle and Vancouver, get all the tourist traffic. All we got to do is be patient and keep things moving our way."

"And what's our way?" Cam said.

"A little more slack from the Exiles, a bit more turf from the Vipers. Make White Rock League territory exclusive. We do that, when the casino comes in, we're running things."

She smiled, dabbed ketchup onto the last morsel of fish. "What do you think?"

"Sounds great," he said.

"I know."

"I'm still broke though."

"God, you are *so* fucking small time." Without asking, she broke off the corner of one of Cam's untouched pieces of fish. "You need money so much, I got something I need done. Only you can't tell Harv or the others."

"Sounds like I'm being put in a real good position."

"Shut up and listen," Sukhi said. "My brother Tequila. You met him?"

"No. He's their dealer isn't he?"

"He slings a little, yeah. He disappeared about a week ago. Hiding out. I need you to find him for me. You do that, there's another five grand in it for you."

"What's he done?"

"Don't have a fucking clue," Sukhi said. "After that Alexa bitch turned up in the fire, Tequila started acting weird. Two grand if you find him."

"Thought you said five?"

"It's two now, plus I'll see you again. Are you going to finish those?"

Cam pushed the basket toward her. "Tell me where I should start looking."

# EIGHT

**D**enny offered to run out and get her an iced coffee, or anything else. Katy Qiu smiled and held her chair for her. Even Amanpreet Brar nodded and asked if there were duties she needed done.

*I must look like trampled shit*, Meghan thought.

Bruises on the side of her face, what felt like a small tear on the outside of her left nostril. Thankfully her wrist was only sprained. The doctor had wrapped a tensor bandage around it and told her not to overtax herself for the rest of the week.

There was too much to be done. She read over the statements taken from the people at the beach, along with the notes Greg Grewal supplied her from the arson scene. The autopsy would be tomorrow, but "gunshot death, fire postmortem" seemed inevitable.

The accelerant used in both fires was kerosene, dyed red and several years old. The fuel was highly sulphuric, hence the smell, and sludgy from years of sitting around gathering bacteria. Grewal guessed that it was leftover camp stove fuel.

A jogger on the beach had smelled smoke during her morning run, sometime between 5:15 and 5:25. At that time Michael May was still ablaze. The human body could burn at most for seven hours; Grewal would hopefully be able to narrow the time frame further.

When she'd caught up, Meghan opened the Alexa Reed file and went over it, looking for connections. The Reeds' banking information, too. It seemed a constellation of strange, ill-fitting facts. She tried plotting them on a timeline to see if that would jog something loose.

The Reeds begin withdrawing their savings, three thousand at a time. Around then, Emily Reed has her first stroke.

What happened next? Richie Reed is struck down by a hit and run.

Two months ago, Emily Reed suffers another stroke, this one fatal. Alexa flies home from college to attend the funeral, has a spat with her mom's rich cousin, Liz Garrick, and doesn't make her flight back to Buffalo.

Instead, she stays at her parents' home, removing the FOR SALE sign.

Alexa asks Michael May, a former classmate, for a connection for heroin. He puts her in touch with Sukhi Kaur, whose brother, Tequila Narwal, deals for the League of Nations.

May then turns up dead, and Tequila turns up in May's apartment. Meghan had surprised him there and got her bell rung for her efforts.

Meghan stood up, worked the kinks in her neck and shoulder. She downed a pair of extra-strength Advil, chasing them with water. Then opened her desk drawer and pulled out the bottle of Laphroaig she kept for emergencies.

*Whisky and pills*, she thought. This heady concoction was believed by superstitious middle-aged divorced lesbian police officers to contain miraculous curative properties. Often paired with cigarettes and reasonably fresh coffee...

The others had gone home, leaving only the night patrol officers and the desk clerk in the station. Meghan turned off the lights in the offices except those in her own.

*Okay, brain, you've had your fill of stimulants. Let's try for a connection.*

First, the fire. Both Alexa Reed and Michael May were set ablaze with kerosene. Most likely May was burned post-mortem, as was Alexa.

That means the fires are ancillary. They're done to cover up or obscure something. Murder? Hard to disguise a bullet wound, and the newspapers had trumpeted the fact that Alexa's neck had been broken.

Robbery, maybe? Was this where the Reeds' missing money came into play?

Had the killer slept with Alexa, or Michael, or both? Maybe the fire was an attempt to remove DNA.

Or was this meant to disfigure, to desecrate. We'll show you who you're fucking with.

Or the killing itself was the message.

May being set on fire at the beach would draw unwanted attention, unless it was done for that very reason. As a message to someone still out there that this would continue.

Meghan sighed. As theories went, it wasn't awful, but didn't exactly lead her anywhere. Just back to the same few instances of seemingly random horrors.


Richie Reed's hit and run had occurred on 24th Avenue in South Surrey, near the turnoff for the highway. Meghan pulled up the report. Reed was crossing the street in front of his office. There was a Coffee Hut nearby, and Reed was known to dash across in the early afternoons, not bothering to walk down to the intersection. No witnesses. Neck broken on impact.

Accidental. Or not. But if not, it didn't provide much to go on.

Why would someone target the owner of a gas station?

There was more to this. Meghan crumpled her timeline and went through again, stopping only for another drink and another pair of pills.

Her eyes blurred. The murders, the arson, the money, the house, it was all getting muddy. She should stop. Go home. Throw together some sort of dinner. Phone Trevor and say hi, Cop Mom had a bit of a run-in this week, but she's fine, and she loves you very much.

She stood and leaned against the desk until the dizziness of the alcohol and painkillers wore off. She called for a cab. The taxi dispatcher laughed when she told him the address.

"Someone in trouble?" he asked. The joy of small towns, Meghan thought.

Closing up the files, shutting down her computer, her gaze lingering over a picture of the Reed house before the fire. The white L of the sign picket on the lawn—

Meghan dialed Chung Realty's office, and when it went to voice mail, she looked up Winnie Chung's home number.

"Better be a 'mergency," a slurred voice said.

"Meghan Quick here.

Immediate sobriety and polite solicitation. "Sorry, ma'am. What can I do for you?"

"Emily Reed told you to put the house on the market?"

"Hunh? Oh. Yes. We talked about it a few weeks before her death."

"And drew up a contract?"

"Of course."

"Can I see it?"

"Pardon me, ma'am, but what's this about?"

"It's about your story sounding like bullshit, Winnie."

A pause on the line. "Ma'am, no disrespect intended, but are you drunk?"

"No."

"You sound like you've been drinking."

"That's not the same as drunk, is it?"

Another pause. "Why don't we talk about this in the morning."

"You told me Mrs. Reed paid your commission up front."

"That's right."

"What's the going commission on a house—three or four percent? On a house worth mid-seven figures?"

"I wouldn't take money from someone in Emily's condition."

"I've seen her bank statements, Winnie. The Reeds didn't have the money to give you."

Meghan counted the seconds. She thought Winnie might hang up. A long sigh whooshed over the line, and the realtor said, "I've done nothing wrong."

"'Cept lie to the police."

"She had power of attorney. She paid. She told me it was Emily's wish, and why would she lie?"

"Why would *who* lie, Winnie?"

"Elizabeth Garrick," the realtor said.

Home, and sleep, and a breakfast of toast and peanut butter. Meghan felt hungry again as soon as she left the house. She stopped for a Sausage McMuffin before approaching Liz.

Not bothering with the front entrance, she went around the side of the property and knocked on the glass door of the pool room, startling the occupants. Liz was seated on the edge of the pool, her pale back to the door. She turned and frowned at the intrusion, then smiled when she saw who it was.

Below her, in the pool, a head bobbed in the water, ducking down immediately. She saw a face, tanned skin with a dark mustache, an orange blur springing out of the water, dashing toward the steam room.

Liz had left her robe atop the diving board. Wrapping it around herself, taking her time tucking the ends. Finally Liz opened the side door, timing it so that Meghan could only enter once the blurred figure was in the next room.

"If this is a bad time," Meghan began.

"No such thing." Liz smiled warmly. "Bob and I were just taking a break from our discussions."


Less than a year after his retirement as detachment commander, Bob Sutter had started showing up at city council meetings. He'd told Meghan it was to stave off boredom.

"Cop's hours don't exactly lend themselves to cultivating hobbies, Meg, and there's only so much golf a red-blooded man can put up with."

He'd run for council the next year, won handily. He was a personable, thoughtful, well-spoken man, with a wife who'd worked thirty years as a nurse. Community pillars with enough clout to impress upon long-term residents that Bob Sutter had their interests at heart.

Bob re-entered Liz Garrick's pool room in his typical slacks and polo shirt, strapping on his wristwatch. A bashful smile to Meghan and an unsolicited explanation: "Looks worse than it is," he said. "I'm afraid I let Lizzie talk me into a dip, even though I didn't bring a suit. A man of my age shouldn't try new things, should he?"

Meghan didn't have a response for him, but smiled and said it was none of her business.

"Actually we were just talking about you," Liz said. "We heard about the boy on the beach yesterday. Bob was saying he was glad you were on it."

"What I actually said was, I'm glad that I'm not." Bob Sutter flashed his grin. "My bad shit gallery is full up, and the May kid deserves someone with better brains."

"Before that we were discussing the casino," Liz said.

"I won't take up more time than necessary."

Meghan wondered if she should ask Bob to step outside, then thought she couldn't do that without permanently spoiling their friendship. Assuming it lasted beyond this. She didn't buy the "we were working and just needed a nude swim to blow off steam" story. You're a cop for fuck's sake, Bob, she thought. If you're going to cheat on your wife, at least come up with a better alibi.

"Winnie Chung told me you authorized the sale of Emily's house. Paid her commission in advance."

"That's right," Liz said.

"Before she admitted that, she was claiming Emily asked her to handle it."

"The fact is," Liz said, "near the end, Emily's finances were shambolic. I begged Winnie not to say anything about my involvement. Plus I wanted Alexa to receive the total of the sale, rather than have to pay the fees out of her inheritance."

"Nice of you," Meghan said.

"Em was my cousin. And I have enough."

"So the fight you had with Alexa the day after her mother's funeral, it was about the house?"

Liz nodded, pursing her lips in regret. "There was no other option but to put it on the market. Alexa didn't see that, or willfully wouldn't see it. She felt I should in effect buy it for her and allow her to stay there indefinitely, covering all taxes and fees."

"And you shot that down."

"Of course," Liz said sharply. "What kind of solution would that be—to subsidize Alexa dropping out of school and lying around the house alone in grief?"

"Like you said, you could afford it."

"Then it was a choice, and one I'd happily make again." Liz smoothed her hair with both hands, treating Meghan to a glimpse of armpit stubble. "Meg, there are a million things Alexa could've asked for which I would have gladly done. Who do you think paid her tuition these last years?"

"Wouldn't she be happy, that place selling and her coming into that money? Real estate what it is, the place must be worth a million. More."

"A rational person would be satisfied with that," Liz agreed. "But once Alexa saw the appraisal, then it became her evil relative's plan to cheat her out of the fortune she felt entitled to."

"Fortune?"

"I'm just saying what seemed to be in her head." Liz's eyes swam. "I don't know why she took such a dislike to me. She could have lived here, for heaven's sake."

"Not your fault," Bob said, comforting her.

Liz tucked her head onto his shoulder, drew her mouth into a taut fearless line. Meghan had seen him do the same for his wife, and, to be fair, to grieving women and men after delivering bad news. Standing there in his bare feet, though, with his arm around her robe, the gesture took on another meaning.

"Did Alexa know your plans for the casino?" Meghan asked.

"I didn't hide them from her, though she didn't seem all that interested. Why?"

"Nothing," Meghan said. But thought: If my aunt was planning to grow the city, and insisted on selling my parents' home immediately, I might think I was being cheated. Alexa would lose both the house and the much higher price it would fetch in Liz Garrick's new White Rock. It was a thought, anyway.

Before Meghan could escape the awkward scene, Liz brought up the casino once again.

"I know how very much you have going on right now, Meg, so I understand it's not a priority. But if you could find time to evaluate our proposal, I'd be grateful."

"Couldn't hurt to take a look, Meg," Bob said, as if he was neutral and making the only fair suggestion. Meghan couldn't help but feel disappointed.

"Sure, I'll look," she said. "But I want you both to think of something. This case, Alexa's death, Michael May's—these are kids in their twenties."

"Late twenties, and hardly children," Liz said.

"My point is, whatever's going on, it's harming young people like them. None of us even knew there was something wrong with Alexa. Or with Michael May. That this is going on under our noses, and no one seems to have seen it—"

"Well, that's your department," Bob said. "Literally." He smirked, dampening it when he realized she wasn't reciprocating. "You'll catch them, Meg. I have total confidence."

"If these kids are in trouble, should our priorities be on gambling, is what I'm saying."

"Understood," Liz said. "Of course that's reasonable, and it's commendable that you bring it up. Please look at the information, and take everything into account. I think you'll see the benefits vastly outweigh the negatives." Smiling, letting Bob's arm slip off her shoulder, she said, "I'd truly hate for us to be on opposite sides of this, Meg."


When people let you down, thank Christ there was always work to focus on. Meghan arrived at Peace Arch Hospital and quickly dressed in a gown and mask. The morgue was in the basement.

She watched Dr. Varma weigh out the organs of Michael May's body. It was an atrocious sight, even more than autopsies usually were. The mottled purple-red skin, the features melted. Clothing fused to flesh so that the doctor had to cut around or simply leave it. To make matters worse, Varma had a cold, and frequently paused in her work to cough or wipe her forehead.

"Cause of death is catastrophic injury to the heart caused by GSW," Varma said. "Which I'm sure you knew. He was killed, doused with accelerant and set on fire."

Meghan looked at the objects that had been removed from May's pockets. A key chain, some sort of Seahawks fob now blackened and bent. An old iPhone, screen burst, fused into its protective case. Coins, Zippo, an empty wallet collected from the beach. The nametag was already in evidence.

She looked at the bullet fragments that the doctor had removed from May's heart. Turned over the Zippo to see if it bore an inscription. Lifted the key chain—

Part of it snapped, two keys spilling into the metal tray with a cymbal crash. Meghan examined them. May had almost two dozen keys, on two concentric rings. Small snippets of masking tape had been applied over the shoulder and bow of various keys, each with a shorthand name written in smudged blue marker. *Apt. Fr Dr. M&D's Gar. Str Rm.*

Apartment, front door, Mom and Dad's garage and... store room? Of course, he'd have keys for the Price-Low. May would be used to early mornings, opening the store for deliveries, dealing with large amounts of cash.

Meghan looked at the two keys that had fallen off, and some crumbling substance between and around them. "What's this look like, doc?" she said.

Varma walked over and adjusted her glasses. Squinted and sniffled. Nudged the keys. Picked up a small amount of it and crumbled it between her hands.

"Rubber," she said. "It's an elastic."

"Makes a shitty keychain," Meghan said.

The separated keys hadn't been taped or markered. Meghan turned them over and saw on one, written in faint pencil, the numbers 3457. The other was smaller, for a cupboard or mailbox, with a black plastic grip that had melted slightly.

"Doc," she said, "say you live in an apartment and you ask me to grab something from there for you."

"Tell you what I could use," Varma said. "Nyquil dissolved in a shot of brandy."

"Gross."

"You laugh, but it's doing a bang-up job with this cold."

"Say I'm grabbing whatever from your place, but you don't want to give me your car keys. You'd slide the house key off the ring, right? But if it's two or three keys, like an apartment with a separate front door lock, you might elastic-band them so they stay together."

"Sure," the doctor said. "Makes it easy. Why?"

"3457 Sunset Lane is Alexa Reed's house. May told me he only talked to her once, but he has her keys."


The Reeds' house was still cordoned off. In the middle of the day, with rain falling heavily, it looked ominous. The houses on either side were lit up for Christmas.

Meghan ripped the barricade tape from the front door and tried the key. The bolt swung back and she entered. Denny Fong stamped his feet on the porch and followed.

Water streaked the walls, ballooning and creasing the paint, giving the place a moldy smell to accompany the faded smoke.

"A little spooky," Denny said.

"Stay here if you like."

"I was just saying, Sarge."

Meghan went upstairs to Alexa's bedroom and stood where she had on the morning after the fire. The area around the bed was still blackened, a silhouette of unburned floor where the body had been found. Water damage and stains around the bed. Not much furniture.

She began going through closets, shifting the bed and looking beneath. There was a dresser, burned so that opening the doors took effort and revealed only ruined clothing, a few necklaces and other keepsakes. Nothing of value, nothing requiring the second key.

She tapped the floor, examined the baseboards. Would it have been secreted somewhere? Burned up in a fire? Or was she looking for something that didn't exist?

If whatever it was belonged to Alexa's parents, it would be in their bedroom. Meghan opened doors until she found it—a room at the far right of the house. Hardly the size of a proper master bedroom, but with aging owners they probably wanted something on the ground floor.

A queen-sized bed with a canopy stood in the centre of the room, dust shimmering as Meghan trained her flashlight on the double closet doors. She opened the dresser inside and pulled out racks of clothing, blouses and skirts in dry cleaners' bags, the faded whiff of perfume mixing with old smoke. Shoes, maybe a dozen pairs. Before her stroke, Emily Reed had enjoyed accessorizing as much as anyone.

Beneath the shoe rack was a square of carpet that had been cut out and skillfully fitted back so that the outline was only just noticeable. Removing that revealed a hole carved in the floor, filled with a safe. The second key opened it.

Meghan told Denny to aim the flashlight up and to the right so as not to blind her. She knelt down and swung open the door of the safe. Found herself peering at neat stacks of hundred-dollar bills. She pulled out a stack and flipped through it.

So this was where the Reeds' savings had gone.

Wedged along the side of the safe, next to the stack of money was a manila folder. Meghan took it out and stood up. Denny adjusted the light so they both could read.

It was a legal document, signed and notarized, prepared on behalf of Richard Vernon Reed and Emily Alexandra Reed.

"A will?" Denny said.

Meghan read:

This document will set out in detail the activities I, Richard Reed, participated in, and in some cases instigated, on behalf of Roger Wilson Garrick. I write this freely, with a clear mind, in the hope of clearing my conscience. It is to be read only in the event of my sudden or unnatural demise.

Denny peered over her shoulder and scanned the first paragraph.

"Holy mackerel," he said.

# NINE

For a guy with his nickname, Tequila's chosen haunts were fairly dull. Top of the list was the Wendy's on Buena Vista. Cam ate something called a Baconator, paired with a peppermint Frosty, and watched cars slink along the drive-through. Sukhi had told him Tequila drove a champagne-coloured Navigator. Cam saw dozens of SUVs, a couple of Navs, but none driven by a thin South Asian with a goatee.

Next up was the Mumbai Sweets on 24th, a chain restaurant with a sports bar interior. Cam wasn't hungry, but he bought a samosa and a bottle of Kingfisher and nursed it for an hour. The clientele was mostly middle aged and white. The TVs around his booth showed football, soccer, pro wrestling.

Third stop: The Sandpiper Bowling Alley. Cam parked with a view of the door and waited, listening to the irritating banter of radio DJs to keep awake. Someone had shot a cop last night in Abbotsford, the shooter a disturbed man who'd tried to return a loaded pistol to an Outdoor Outfitters. The funeral was tomorrow and would be broadcast on local TV. Traffic jams on King George, construction along 152nd.

His list was ten stops long. After cycling through it twice, and still no champagne Nav, he phoned Sukhi to tell her he was giving up.

"Keep looking," she said, sounding more worried than the last time they'd talked.

"What's your brother done that he's run off for?" he asked.

"Not on the phone."

"You want him found, I need more to go on."

Sukhi told him she'd call back in ten minutes.

He waited, surveying the door of the Taco Del Mar from the strip of parking slots next to a second-run theatre. There was a Starbucks across the street. Other than locals driving by for coffee, this strip of 152nd didn't get much foot traffic.

Why these places? Cam thought. Chain restaurants with lots of parking. A dealer would want privacy, wouldn't he?

But Tequila wasn't a dial-a-doper, carrying merchandise or interacting with buyers. He was higher up and probably never handled anything himself. What he was afraid of was an ambush. Choosing public spaces with multiple escape routes showed Tequila was cagey, but didn't help Cam pin down the man's location.

His phone rang, the pre-set jingle it had come with. Sukhi said, "This *has* to stay between us. I'm serious, Cam. You can't breathe a fucking word."

"I swear," he said.

"'Member I said that Harv had plans to make a move on White Rock? Build the League up out here?"

"Uh-huh."

"Tequila was gonna handle that for us. Get things rolling."

"So why'd he disappear?"

"I don't know," Sukhi said. "Harv doesn't tell me the details, but I pick up on things. But this, no one's saying shit."

"Could the Vipers have taken him out?"

"Not without us knowing."

Cam wondered what that meant. "The other day I read about a fire," he said. "A girl who was murdered and torched. Could it be connected?"

Sukhi didn't answer.

"Just find him, okay?" she said. "Please."

One of the places near the bottom of the list was the South Surrey Athletic Park, known as Softball City. Four diamonds with bleachers and dugouts, a large all-purpose sports field, a skate park, hard courts and acres of parking. As a kid, Cam had seen punk shows in the rec centre, the audience lounging on couches and stools while the bands rocked out in front of the kitchen. The place didn't look much different from his childhood.

At night Softball City was closed up and dark. Not much need for softball in the heart of winter, the fields slushy, heaps of snow in the corners of the parking lots.

The roads looped around the diamonds and between the buildings. A dope dealer's paradise. Cam parked the Civic in the central lot, slumped down in his chair. Rain fell over the windows, and the daylight sunk behind the treeline of Sunnyside Acres.

Cam saw a patrol car creep through the parking lot next to his. No other cars between them. He got his driver's license out, prepared a story about working late and needing to sleep before driving home to Surrey. But the car prowled by.

Soon it was night and the stadium lights burst on, lighting up the parking lot and the softball diamonds.

Cam cracked a window and lit a cigarette. Another fucking waste. In the meantime he had to get working again. Maybe approach Doppler & Doppler, ask for a few containers. Not that he wanted honest work, but this—what the hell *was* this?

What had happened to him, these last months?

You're working for Zoe Prentice, he reminded himself. Getting in good with the League. *That* is your job. Your top concern. Finding Tequila is only a step toward that. Make Sukhi happy, maybe win some points with Harv.

You aren't one of them. You're only pretending to be because that's what Zoe wants.

A car drove through at the other end, high beams on. It passed by the entrance to the lot. Cam rolled the window farther down, watching. The car's driver did the same.

For a second they looked at each other. There were two bearded men in the front seat of a dark blue Honda Prelude. They glared at Cam, as if judging him.

Cam's cigarette had burned down to the filter. He pinched it between his thumb and forefinger, roach style, and made a show of bringing it to his lips. Inhaled deeply. Held it, coughed.

The men in the Prelude laughed at him, some working stiff just off shift, smoking half a joint. They rolled by. Cam noticed they pulled into the lot closest to the 24th Avenue exit.

The Prelude stopped but left its lights on. A few minutes later an SUV passing along the avenue spun into the lot, pulling up alongside them. A Navigator. Difficult to tell the colour in the dark, from far away, but possibly champagne. The SUV continued through the winding road of Softball City.

The Prelude spun around and followed. It parked next to the Nav, at the front of the rec centre. The men in the Prelude climbed out and stood under the building's overhang, one of them smoking a cigarette. After a minute the door to the Nav opened and a third man joined them. Even at that distance Cam caught the glimmer off the man's Thrive or Die jacket. Tequla Narwal. He was sure of it.

Tequila gave each of the men a chest-thumping hug and a right-angled handshake. They passed around a joint. More than a deal. These were friends.

Cam couldn't see them closely. He started the car, keeping the lights off, and crept closer. Parked again, facing the other way.

Both of the others wore black nylon jackets that added bulk to their small frames. One wore a black patka, the other a purple snapback. They'd looked older in the car. Their movements with Tequila were playful. Back slapping, fists tapped against their hearts as they nodded to what he was saying.

A minivan sped through the park from the north end. Cam squinted and saw a woman at the wheel, what looked like a kid in the backseat. Someone taking a shortcut home. The van crossed the parking lot, turned onto 20th.

When Cam turned back he saw the three men looking at his car.

Cam hadn't considered he might be spotted. Now Tequila was pointing at him. Despite the distance, he felt their eyes locked on him. Cam tried to reach for the ignition column, wondered why his hand wouldn't move.

The man with the purple ball cap unzipped his jacket.

Cam didn't hear the gun's report but heard clearly the *spang* as the bullet ricocheted off the light a few spaces to his left. He ducked down, started the engine. Heard the next shot and saw the right-side mirror spin off at a wild angle.

He backed up over the edge of the concrete and found the car sliding down a hill onto the field. Something pelted the windshield, spreading a crystal web across the glass. He stomped the accelerator. The car slogged across the field, broadsiding a mound of dirty snow.

Spinning the wheel, trying to see through the glass, the rain, hearing the shots now, some louder than others, Cam put the car in drive and floored it. The wheels spun—

The back window burst.

The car leapt forward and Cam banked right, seeing as he turned the men approaching, fire bursting from the gun in Tequila's hand. Shit. *Shitshitshitshitshit.*

The pop of a tire, the car rocking, going too slow.

He was going to die.

He processed this as he undid his seatbelt, popped open the door and rolled out onto the spongey grass. He was going to die here, in Softball fucking City of all places. He'd had time to consider death in prison, and while he'd faced a few close calls, it had been the slow, lingering death of incarceration that he'd feared. Not that he didn't fear this—he was terror-stricken—but it wasn't inside.

And at least he could make it hard for the fuckers.

Running bent over, hearing them slop and splash behind him, he bolted west toward the forest. There weren't other options, unless he wanted to run onto the road, hope that the cop car might go by again.

The last five metres to the forest was uphill. He pitched forward, scrambling as his feet sought purchase in the muck. Grabbed handholds, moving forward on his knees. Then he was up, crossing through the wall of ferns and brushes, thinking it had been a while since he'd heard a gunshot. Maybe they were out.

His shoulder caught fire. Cam pitched forward.

Inertia, that disconnected feeling of rising out of a dream, when you tell your body to move and watch it sit there, ignoring your commands.

His arm hurt and he felt his right hand slick with blood. He broke his command into smaller commands. Left arm forward. To his relief it began to nudge over the fern he'd trampled.

He'd fallen down a slope, into a grove between the winding bike trails of Sunnyside Acres. Downed trees and limbs obscured his view of the trail ahead. Unnatural light fell from behind and to the left, the direction from which he'd fallen. He nudged himself closer to the trees.

The last time he'd been in here—

Twelve or thirteen, sneaking out for a camping trip with a friend. Smoking a joint they'd rolled out of shake stolen from the Folgers tin where Uncle Pete kept his stash. Neither of them able to roll worth a shit. The thing had been conical, flat at one end, but they'd gotten two puffs each before it exploded onto Cam's chest. They'd spent the night drinking Old Grand-Dad mixed with Mountain Dew, reading *Hustler*s they'd found on previous trips through the forest, each pretending not to see the other jerking off. Lying down and staring up at this same canopy of trees. Watching it spin like a kaleidoscope as the pot and booze kicked in.

If you were going to die, it was a hell of a view.

Crawling forward, Cam dropped beneath a fallen Douglas fir, its root system upended, brown shelf fungus growing along the side.

The left shoulder screamed. A similar feeling to when Roger Garrick had slashed him. Cam's breathing was ragged and his feet frozen.

He dragged himself forward, up against the trunk of the tree. With his left hand, he crossed over and slipped his phone from his right pocket. The cheap clamshell seemed to be working. Who to dial, though?

He heard rustling and clutched the phone within the folds of his shirt, extinguishing the glow from its screen.

At least two sets of footsteps proceeded down the hill, stumbling, pausing to look around. One shone the light from his phone across the tree, above where Cam lay hidden. He closed his eyes.

"Never gonna find him," the one voice said.

"And who's fault is that, fucknut?"

"Don't yell at him, Tequila. You fired first, remember?"

"Like you were holding back, Gurv."

"Shut up."

The voices moved off, grew softer.

"Man, *fuck* this."

"He didn't vanish."

"Fuck you. Your fucking problem."

"Yeah?"

"Asked to fuckin meet like it's some big secret, then go all paranoid, some fool smoking a joint in his car."

"Think this is a fuckin joke?"

"See me laughing?"

"Both of you, just keep—"

"Aw, this little bitch is gone, man."

"I fucking clipped him."

"Clipped his fucking car and it took you all ten rounds."

"I saw the dude fall."

"Yeah, down the fucking hill. American Sniper over here."

"Stop fucking arguing," the third voice said. "The three of us gotta fix this together. We get a few of our people in here to look for him, smoke his ass out. That work for you, Tequila?"

"Whatever."

"Good." The third voice sounded relieved. "See, Gurv? We all on the same page."

"Either of you got any lighter fluid?" Tequila asked.

"Nah, man. Why?"

The gunshot caused Cam to jump, hitting his head against the bottom of the trunk. The first voice, Gurv's, saying "What the fuck—" before another shot quieted him.

No sound after that for what felt like a minute.

"Doesn't work for me," Tequila said, and giggled.


Cam heard rustling, Tequila searching the pockets of the men. A body flopped over, landing in mud. The suck of boots moving to dry ground. The log bounced, Tequila stepping over it, heading up the hill.

"Call Sukhi," Tequila commanded his phone, and muttered "Pick up, bitch," as he waited. Then his voice became sunnier, pleasant. "Hey sis... Just been busy, lots going down... I know he's looking for me, I'm'a talk to him when I'm ready. Explain everything... Yeah. I know. Don't tell Harv shit. He asks, tell him that Alexa bitch probably made it up... That's right... no, I don't got it."

He muttered "fucking bitch" again as Sukhi's voice continued on.

"Shut up for a second, okay? Tell Mom you need the car, then come pick me up... Yes right now. Would I ask it wasn't important?... The forest, right next to Softball City. You know the place... See police, you just drive past, loop back... No, I'm just saying *if* they're there... Just do it, will you?... All the shit I do for you?... Thanks."

Cam looked up and saw Tequila crest the top of the hill, disappearing into the white stadium lights.

He crawled free, saw the bodies of the two men. He bent at the waist, feeling his vision swim, but managed to retrieve their wallets. Between them they had six hundred dollars.

Cam took the larger one's coat, noting the man's arms were tattooed with serpents. Tequila had been meeting with two Vipers.

Both men had been shot in the head. Cam tried wiping the blood off the coat, finding his hands only added mud to the stains.

He hated to leave his car, but the police might be there already, and anyway, Cam was too weak to crawl up that hill.

Draping the coat around him, he limped farther into the forest, and when he found the trail marker, he followed it to the exit. From there he called a taxi.


The driver dropped him off two buildings over from his home. Cam tipped him an extra hundred. The driver nodded and cleared the meter.

Fatigue hit him as he mounted the steps to his apartment. Once inside, he stripped and stood in front of his bathroom mirror, craned his neck and examined the wound.

Once the blood was wiped off, it was a small black circle punched in the flesh of his tricep. It stung. There was no exit wound, which troubled him.

The sight of the blood and dirt pooling around the drain in his shower stall made his stomach roil. He threw up in the toilet, then turned the shower tap and drank and wiped his chin. He leaned back, worrying he might pass out again. Managed to hold up his phone and dial Ivan's number.

No, not Ivan. He cancelled the call before it had rung. Dialed Brad instead. Ivan hadn't taken part in the warehouse job, and Cam still couldn't figure out why. Brad felt he owed Cam—the five grand had meant a lot to him.

"What's up, bro?" It was two in the morning and Brad sounded more awake than Cam had ever seen him.

"Need a favour," Cam said. "How do I get in touch with that doc?"

The doctor wouldn't leave the house until six, and even then, only for one thousand dollars. "House calls are extra," he said.

He showed up, dressed in a sweatsuit and a foam-front Blue Jays cap. He used tweezers to prod the wound, pronounced the slug unremovable, and asked for his fee.

"I want it out," Cam said.

"Can't be done, buddy, not unless I take you to admittance."

"It went in straight. It's right in there."

"Yes, but it can't be done."

Cam stared at the doc till the older man looked away. "Cody said you'd get it out. Want me to tell him I asked and you said no? That the message you want me to take to Cody Hayes?"

The doctor put on a tough face. Cam didn't have to—the heavy-lidded sneer was created by pain and fatigue, and he wore it because there was nothing else.

"You should be anesthetized," the doc said. "All I have are tweezers and my prod. Nothing's even sterilized."

"So stick the fucking kettle on," Cam said.


He spent a day in bed, clutching the gun he'd taken from one of the dead men. The .22. A fifty percent chance it was the gun that had shot him.

Any time he heard noise on the landing outside his place, he grasped the gun and waited. The door would burst open, either Tequila or an army of the Vipers, or the League, his so-called friends, ready to finish him off.

He ran a fever. He sweated through his sheets. Then shivered with the wet fabric wrapped tightly around him. When he was lucid, he stared at the small piece of shrapnel the doc had removed from him. Thinking of what to do next.

Something had broken inside him. It was obvious his first trip outside, to buy scissors and peroxide and a case of soup from the cvs. He watched the other shoppers and couldn't care what they thought of him, standing there in his dirty jeans and the only clean T-shirt he had left, the one Tito had given him, with the League of Nations slogan across the front. He enjoyed the way the pharmacist rang up his purchases without making eye contact.

His strength came back to him. He checked his messages. His po had called, something about his car. Cam told him he'd been sick, but would come two days later, and if the po didn't like it he could come around to his place and check the puke bucket for himself. Okay, okay, the PO said. We'll reschedule for early next week.

Next was the car. Cam walked into the nearest police station and told them he'd been sick for the last week, and that when he'd opened his front door this morning his Civic wasn't there. No, he hadn't heard anything, but please, officer, it's got my stuff inside. I don't make much at my warehouse job, and I know it's a beater, but I need it to make my living.

Then there was the warehouse. He'd need to show income, and he couldn't spend his life climbing through cans. He phoned Scott Doppler and asked for a meeting. Scott told him of course, any time you want to come back, you're welcome. Cam said thanks, he'd be in next week to discuss terms.

That left only Tequila.


Sukhi Kaur opened her parents' door, moving aside as Cam entered.

"Just let yourself in," she said.

"Your parents home?"

"At work."

"Good."

He sat down at the kitchen table, ignoring her request to take off his shoes.

"Sorry I haven't called," he said. "I've been looking for your brother."

"That's all right." She was dressed in an oversized shirt, shorts, hair still wet from the shower. She offered him a beer and took one for herself.

"You still want him found?"

She shrugged. "Maybe it was dumb to ask you. Let's just drop it, 'kay?"

"It wasn't dumb."

"I'll pay you anyway. Half, okay? Just drop it."

He pulled off his T-shirt, exposing his bandaged shoulder.

"Your brother shot at me," he said. "One of his friends hit me. In the forest near Softball City. About an hour before you picked Tequila up."

"No." Her mouth hung slightly open. "Bullshit."

"You must know what happened to his buddies, right? You saw on the news."

She shrugged and tried to move away but Cam grabbed her arm and held her. Looked in her eyes. She spat at him. "Let me go, asshole."

"Your brother killed them, Sukhi."

"They were trying to kill him. It was an ambush."

"He shot them in cold blood. Asked them first for lighter fluid."

"What—"

"What the hell am I into?" he asked.

"Let me go."

He did. Sukhi rubbed her bruised arm.

"I didn't know till it was on the news," she said.

"You know now. Where is he?"

"Think he tells me? I just took him home. He was gone the next morning. Seriously, that's it." Her eyes moved over his shoulder. "Does it still hurt?"

"It's fine," he said, and kissed her.

A sound from her throat escaped the corners of her mouth and she pushed against his chest to free herself. Stared at him with shock. When he reached for her again, she came willingly, forcing his pants down, stepping out of her shorts. Letting out a trilling sound as he turned her and bent her over the table.

"My parents'll be home—"

She was wet and grabbed his neck as he pressed into her, grabbing his hair in her fist. A slapping sound as the table hit the wall. They fumbled and he sat her on the table top, kissed her, felt her fingernails tear at the bandage, a shock of pain as she touched the wound. Climaxing inside her, lowering her down, the both of them out of breath.

"My room," she said.

Racing through the halls, he scooped her up and threw her on the bed, Disney princesses on the sheets. Both of them making feral sounds as they tore into each other again. She liked to be on top. He liked the feel of her ass slamming down against the inside of his thighs. He held back until she came and then tore through his own orgasm, tossing her down next to him as he struggled for air.

"Holy fuck," Sukhi said.

Once his breath returned, Cam said, "Yeah. Now you're going to tell me everything."

# TEN

For the third time that week, Meghan closed the door of her office and examined the document from the Reeds' safe. It had been notarized by an attorney in Vancouver. Emily Reed served as her husband's witness, her initials on each page childlike and left-sloping, no doubt an effect of her stroke.

Richie Reed had dictated this confession a month before his accident. Why at that point had he decided to come clean with what he'd done almost ten years prior? And for what purpose—to avoid prosecution? Or to hold it over someone—and if so, who?

Meghan uncorked her bottle of Laphroaig and poured a dram into her travel mug. The last few nights she hadn't been sleeping well. The deaths of Alexa Reed and Michael May still demanded answers. Her chief suspect, Tequila Narwal, hadn't been seen in days.

And then came the double murder. Two bodies, found in the forest behind Softball City. Technically out of her jurisdiction: White Rock city limits ended at 16th Avenue, and the forest was above 20th. Surrey PD had promised her a report once their initial investigation was complete. They'd gladly taken copies of her files.

Four bodies, all around the same age, all killed within two months. Hell of a way to end the year. If there was a connection between this double homicide and the deaths of Reed and May, Meghan didn't see it.

She stared at the document. Exactly how it tied to the murders was difficult to say. Meghan took a generous sip of Scotch, then poured more into the mug. She began to read through it again.


On or around June 7th, Roger Garrick came to see me at work, at the gas station I then owned and operated with my wife. This would be close to three years before he died.

Despite being related by marriage, we'd never been close with the Garricks. Frankly, Emily told me they were snobs, and up till then, I'd never had dealings with Roger or Liz that proved otherwise. At our wedding they'd given us an espresso machine, including the receipt "in case we'd prefer drip grind and the money." I heard later, second-hand, that Liz had made some comments about Emily marrying a "gas jockey," and how she'd end up living in a double-wide in Parksville if the business didn't pick up.

That day, Roger walked in and greeted me like an old friend. I don't think I'd ever been embraced by him before.

Noticing my shock, he said, "We're brothers-in-law, or the next thing to it." He asked me to follow him outside.

He'd parked his M1 in the stall next to the building. Roger asked me to humour him and sit behind the wheel. The car was beautiful, a few years old but in excellent condition. It was his firm's work sedan. The way he told it, the lease was up, and Roger had been given the option to buy it.

"Liz wants something sportier," he told me. "If it was up to me I'd keep it. What do you think?"

I told him it was a fine car—it was—and that he could do a lot worse.

"I mean what do *you* think," he said. "For yourself and Em."

"We don't have that kind of money kicking around," I told him. "If you want to put up a for sale notice on our bulletin board, that'd be okay."

Roger laughed and shook his head. "No strings," he said. "It's yours if you want it. Liz feels bad about her and Em not being that close, and we thought we'd try to make amends. I want you to have it, Richie."

It was a dream car, the M1. I'd never owned anything under a decade old. Certainly nothing that nice. I was grateful, but said I'd have to talk it over with Emily.

The gas station was turning a profit, but housing prices had inflated, and in truth, we were struggling. Alexa had almost finished high school, and we were scraping up tuition for her first year of college. Even the applications amounted to a few thousand dollars that we plainly didn't have.

That didn't mean we weren't somewhat suspicious of the Garricks' motives. But we weren't the kind of people to hold a grudge, and their offer was generous. I called Roger to accept. He seemed as happy as we were.

Over the next few months we were invited to parties at the Garrick home. Liz and Roger were warm and genial and made a point of introducing us to the "better people" in the community, such as Mr. Marquez at the bank, Staff Sergeant Sutter and others. When the parties ended, we'd sometimes stay late to play bridge or lounge by their pool, occasionally spending the night.

Roger was charming and well-respected, Liz even more so. The two of them together were brilliant, so much better as a couple than separate. Quickly we came to see them as our best and closest friends—though I'm sure many others felt that way.

Those were enjoyable times for us. Em and I worked brutal hours, both at the store and with bookkeeping and inventory. We rarely spent a free night together. At Liz's insistence, we began coming over once a week.

Business began to pick up. We were able to pay for renovations, and when Karl Garvey's widow decided to close their station on Crescent Road, we bought her out. Mr. Marquez began helping us set money aside, enough for Alexa's first year at SUNY. Our retirement portfolio began to take shape.

Roger did have a temper, but it only came out on long nights of drinking and using cocaine. He'd occasionally insult one of the party guests, mock them. Roger could be cruel. Once in a while Em or I would come in for our share. But he would always apologize, tell us it was the day he'd been having, or the fact that Liz had been bothering him again to have children.


Meghan stopped to pour another dram in her mug. She tried to remember those parties. Hadn't she and Rhonda been at one of them? Long before Meghan became detachment commander, they'd been invited to the Garricks' Christmas open house. Vaguely she remembered paying her respects to Liz, who'd been seated on a dais surrounded by friends. The invitation had been written in Liz's handwriting, and Meghan had taken it as a sign that Mrs. Garrick wished them to be close.

"Hey Lizzie," Meghan had said, possibly tipped into familiarity by the abundance of free wine. "Just wanted to say thanks for the invite. The house lights are beautiful."

The look on Liz's face had been confusion, quickly displaced by a mask of public courtesy. "Oh, of course, it's our pleasure," she said.

Once Meghan had thanked her again, and started back into the crowd to find Rhonda, a nasty jolt of laughter carried to her from the dais. A joke at Meghan's expense.

All in the past, of course. Liz had been nothing but friendly since then.

Meghan could picture the Reeds, on the dais to the left of Liz. Emily with her squarish, slightly muscular body concealed in a flowing chiffon gown, and fleshy Richie in a tux, sweating from the heaters near the dais, mopping his red forehead with handfuls of black cocktail napkins.

Meghan remembered them because, walking away, she'd thought: *fuck you all.* Liz's condescension she understood— she'd been raised a spoiled bitch from early adolescence, had been born perfect, found the perfect husband. But the Reeds, in their hilariously over-the-top clothes? Those dressed-up gas station clerks?

*Fuck. Them.*

She'd told that to her wife later that night. Rhonda had enjoyed the party a lot more than Meghan. "Do I detect a little blue collar resentment, Meg? Or maybe just too much vino? They all seemed perfectly nice to me."

Of course they had.

Meghan read on.

One weekend in late November, Roger called me to his office on Oxford Street. When I showed up he asked if I'd mind taking a brief walk with him. "A constitutional," he called it. He had a business proposition to discuss.

We walked around the small collection of professional buildings, past the bank and the learning annex. Roger smoked. He asked if I wanted to make some real money. He needed someone he could trust, and wasn't sure anyone but a close friend, a relative, would be up to it.

I said of course, but then asked if what he was talking about was legal.

"It's a hundred percent above board," he told me. "That doesn't mean I want the world to know."

He made it sound as if his life and fortune were in danger. Maybe they were. In any case I agreed—to help him out, of course, but also for the money he'd hinted at.

It was a simple operation. I'd hold something for him at the gas station. A man would come in and pick it up. I'd be paid five hundred dollars for nothing more than providing a space for the transaction.

He didn't tell me what it was, nor did he give me anything in person.

The next morning Liz dropped off a thick grey envelope. It weighed maybe two pounds and felt full of paper. If I had to guess I'd say it was full of money, but I didn't open it. Liz told me she didn't know its contents, either.

"Richie said you'd know what to do with this."

I'd nodded and put it in the receipts drawer and didn't think much more about it. That may sound incredible, but it's true. I didn't want to know anything that would make me think worse of my friend, and the five hundred dollars had come at a welcome time, paying Alexa's airfare home for Christmas.

A week later, the 30th, I believe, a man entered. He was wearing a purple bandana around his head, black jeans and a green jacket. Around twenty years old, maybe younger. Brown skin, black mustache, maybe five nine. He said I had something for him. For a second I didn't know what he was talking about, and that seemed to make him angry. But I remembered the envelope and handed it to him.

As he reached for it, I noticed his right hand bore a tattoo of some kind of snake. He shook the envelope as if to judge its heft, then walked out.

At the end of the night, before I'd closed up, Roger phoned me and asked had I mailed those Christmas cards we discussed. It seemed unnecessary to use such vague language, but I've always loved spy films, so I said yes, the courier picked it up today. Roger said he'd reimburse the postage next time we spoke.

And he did, taking us out for a meal at the Mumbai Sweets, handing me the money while Em and Liz were in the washroom.

"No problems?" he'd asked. When I said no: "Think you'd be up for making this a regular thing?"

I joked that I'd always wanted to be a postman. Roger smiled, but it was clear he brought no humour to the operation.

We agreed that I'd be paid a monthly fee of two thousand dollars. The drop would alternate between our stations at Five Corners and at Crescent Road. I would have to be working on pickup day— he didn't want Emily to know.

Eventually, after a few months, I told her. More precisely, she found one of the envelopes and threatened to open it if I didn't tell her the truth. I've never been comfortable lying to my darling; I told Em the entirety of the operation.

I can't say we were desperate for money—certainly not the way we'd been when Roger had given us the car. We *wanted* the money. We wanted nice things. To be able to put Alexa through school, to renovate our home, to pay for our share of the lavish parties and dinners we'd been invited to.

I worked all my life for nothing. This was a shot to make up for that.

That New Year's we threw the first party at our house, spending five thousand dollars to beautify the backyard and provide our guests with first-rate food and drink. If that sounds shallow and materialistic, I can only say that after a lifetime of strict budgeting and doing without, it felt wonderful to splurge, to be able just once to do things right, create the kind of memories that Liz and Roger seemed to fashion so effortlessly.

Around that time, Em had an odd conversation with Liz. We'd spent the night at their place, getting absolutely sloshed. In the morning, Roger and I had gone out fishing. Liz and Emily had stayed home to clean up after the party and drink some more.

My wife would have been thirty-seven at the time. Liz asked her, out of the blue, if she was still getting her period.

She and Roger couldn't have children, Liz explained. They'd been looking at options, and one would be artificial insemination. Would Emily and I consider helping them conceive?

Em remembers it as being very awkward. Liz cried, and said the child would be raised as if it were her own, and that we would be well taken care of for any inconvenience. My darling said she'd talk it over with me.

Roger and I returned from fishing and the topic was dropped.

Later, before we left, Liz cornered Em and told her not to say anything, not to think about it any further. It had been one option, there were others, and the last thing she wanted was to jeopardize their friendship. Don't think about it any further, please, and please don't tell anyone.

Emily promised. It was only much later, when everything went wrong, that she told me.

It was hard for Meghan to believe that Richie Reed had compromised himself so willingly. But then who hadn't? She thought of Bob Sutter, streaking out of Liz's pool. Not so different from the Reeds.

Had Richie really been so naive—or was this all a construction, put together later, to show how the dead man had led the Reeds down the primrose path. Seduced them.

What was Emily's role in all this?

What was Liz's?

Sometimes there would be weekly pick-ups from the station. Other times a month would pass with only the one envelope. After the first, Liz never brought them to us—it was either Roger himself, or one of the messengers at his firm.

The young man who picked up the parcels was always the same. Sometimes he was accompanied by a woman or another man. Once, his travelling partner called him a nickname. Tequila, I think it was.

The next summer was one of the best times in our life. Em and I had achieved a comfortable retirement parachute, and were thinking of investing in a third gas station. I barely considered what I was doing and certainly didn't think it was wrong, or that it would somehow come to an end.

In July, Alexa flew home to spend the summer. We were so happy to see that she was thriving out east, near the top of her class in one of the best undergraduate programs in the country.

What more could we hope for, other than more peace, more prosperity?

Occasionally I took days off, or ran between the stations depending on the schedules. I think I believed, as long as I was working, I wasn't to blame for anything between Roger and his associate in the purple bandanna. I was a working man and a family man. That's how I justified this.

Alexa often hung around the stations. We gave her an allowance but if asked, she would gladly pick up a shift here or there. My daughter is an innocent in all of this. A victim.

She was working at Five Corners while I was at Crescent Road. The young man called Tequila entered and demanded the package. Alexa had no clue what he was talking about and asked him to leave.

The man was insistent. He even pointed at the drawer below the till and told her the envelope would be in there. Alexa made a scene, said even if it was, who are you to think you deserve it? She called me, told me, there's a strange man here, angry, who says she has to hand something over. Do you know anything about that, Daddy?

Imagine how I felt, telling my daughter it was all right. He was a friend, go ahead and give him the envelope.

That dinner she asked me what was in the package, and when I told her I didn't know, Alexa stopped speaking to me.

A few days went by, tense days where Emily tried to keep us together. Her efforts seemed to be working. Alexa warmed, and eventually things seemed to be normal.

In early August, I believe the 11th, Tequila approached me at the store. We'd had, I think, one previous meeting after the events with Alexa, and nothing had been said, other than an apology from me that it wouldn't happen again. I'd received an envelope from

Roger's courier the night before. When I opened the drawer to fetch it, it wasn't there.

I've never had a gun pointed at me, and the last fistfight I was in occurred in high school. I didn't even know what was happening at first, only that I found myself on the floor, tasted blood, and saw the man pointing a chrome plated pistol at my head.

Tequila asked again for the envelope, and I said I didn't know, but that I'd find it, by tomorrow, please just give me time. I was struck repeatedly with the handle of the gun.

I cried.

I pissed myself.

I believe I passed out.

The next few hours are hazy. I remember someone standing over me, a customer, I think, asking if I was all right. I convinced her it looked worse than it was, and that I'd already phoned an ambulance. She offered to stay till it arrived, but I said my wife was coming by in a minute, and got the lady out of there.

I phoned Roger and told him what happened. I'd never heard him so angry, and I broke down at the words he called me. "You fat fucking moron, if someone took it you better find out before I have to."

Em arrived, and I confessed. My darling knew before I did what had happened. She insisted on taking me to emergency, where I was treated for a concussion, a broken nose and given a total of fifty-eight stitches.

Alexa met us at the hospital. My daughter bawled at the sight of me. "It's my fault, Daddy." She'd opened the envelope, seen that it was full of money, and thought it wouldn't be missed. It wasn't theft; as far as she knew it was mine and Emily's. We were doing so well that it seemed plausible to her that we wouldn't miss a few thousand.

The story I'd told at the admittance desk was that I hadn't gotten a look at the person who beat me. A random malicious act. If only it were.

Bob Sutter himself questioned me later that night. He asked if I thought it had been a robbery. I said I didn't know.

He said he was glad, in any case, that I was okay. "Family and health are most important," he said. "After that, it's good everyone holds onto what's rightfully theirs."

The remark sounded suspicious, but I didn't think much of it. As I said, it was a hellacious day, and I think a lot of what followed happened on account of those events.

When I got home I had Alexa bring me the envelope. I made up what she'd spent from our savings. We taped it shut, with all the money inside. The next day I went back to work.

That afternoon, I saw Tequila for the last time. He laughed at my face and said I looked like I'd slipped in the driveway. He feinted a punch and laughed again when I backed up into the battery display behind me.

After that there were no more envelopes.

At the Garricks' Halloween party, Roger told me our business was finished. *Our* business, he'd said, as if it would continue with someone else. He cooled toward me after that, though socially we remained friendly, and Emily and Liz continued on as they had.

That is the sum total of what I did on Roger Garrick's behalf. A few months later the Shaw boy killed him, in front of poor Liz, who had finally managed to get pregnant. I'll admit that I cried when I heard about Roger's death. But part of me was also relieved. My tie to that world was severed, as far as I knew.

So why record this testimony, if the principle player is dead? Partly as confession. Partly as insurance, should anyone seek to

harm me or my family. If that seems farfetched, I don't disagree—
just as I didn't when Roger first approached me with that car.

Christ, did Meghan need a cigarette.

She ran off a photocopy of the document, then returned
the original to its evidence bag, along with the recovered
money. All told there had been one hundred and forty-eight
thousand dollars in the safe. The money was more baffling
than the note, and the note was plenty baffling.

How much of it did Meghan believe? Most, she decided. A
working-class guy like Richie Reed wouldn't invent scenarios
of pissing his pants or breaking down in tears.

Her doubts lay with the women, specifically Richie's
repeated exhortations of their innocence. Calling his wife
"my darling."

Emily didn't know—except she went along with it.

Alexa didn't know—Richie described her theft like she'd
borrowed bus fare from the drawer, not several thousand
from an unmarked envelope.

And Liz—certainly not a wide-eyed innocent who stood
meekly by the side of her husband. Why throw in mention of
her struggles with pregnancy?

Liz had told Meghan she'd been paying for Alexa's college.
That didn't square with Richie Reed's account. Was this whole
thing concocted to blackmail Roger's widow? If so, why did
the Reeds withdraw their own life savings? Who the hell pays
the person they're extorting?

If the money came from the Garricks, then what happened to the cash siphoned from the Reeds' account?

The mention of Tequila was the most troubling. Ten years ago he'd been a member of the Vipers, before his defection to the League of Nations. The document didn't specify what business he'd done with Roger Garrick. Only that he'd acted as bagman, with Richie Reed's station as the drop. That connected Richie to the chief suspect in his daughter's murder, for all the good it did.

Mysteries on top of mysteries. Meghan dialed Liz Garrick's number.

"This is becoming a weekly session," Liz said.

"We've got a lot to talk about."

"We do. Tomorrow at the same time, my place again?"

"How about mine?" Meghan said.

"If you insist." Liz gave a self-deprecating laugh. "I'm not sure I have your address, Meg. Could you give it to me?"

"No problem at all, Lizzie. It's 15299 Pacific Avenue. From the beach you head up Johnston, turn right at Five Corners."

"Perfect, thanks. Wait. That's—"

"The station," Meghan said. "My office. See you around eight."

Hanging up shouldn't have provided so much satisfaction.

Before she left for home, Meghan checked her emails. Surrey PD wanted the slugs and casing from Michael May's murder, for comparison with their double homicide. Both involved a .45 ACP.

Denny Fong was on night duty. He smiled at her as she came out of her office. Denny's confidence was up since the forensic conference. She told him to transport the slugs from the evidence locker to the lab in Surrey and to make sure he got the proper signatures.

"Chain of custody," he said. "I'm on it, boss."

She remained a step away from him, to keep him from smelling the whisky. No need to get rumours started. Her shift had ended, she was on her own time and Meghan Quick could handle her liquor.

"Going home," she said. "Have a safe night, Denny."

"Night, boss. Sleep well."

She treated herself to a cab ride home, thinking she'd ask Amanpreet or Katy to swing by in the morning and pick her up.

"You're the police?" the taxi driver said, as they rolled through quiet intersections. The trees around the Semiahmoo Mall were garlanded with white Christmas lights, a SEASONS GREETINGS banner across the entrance. Meghan remembered taking Trevor there, eons ago, for his first visit with Santa.

"Yeah," Meghan said, "I am the police."


At the curb in front of her house she paid the driver too much. He returned the fifty to her wallet and helped her select a twenty instead. He thanked her for the tip and they wished each other a merry December.

The season of stress was upon them. The season of breaking up pointless fights, struggling to find shelter for the homeless when the snows hit. The season of endless booze- and drug- and stress-related issues, any of which could spark off into horror. The season of depression and loneliness, of pills taken and razors dragged across wrists. Suicide by Christmas, she thought.

But it would also mean time to spend with her son. Maybe Rhonda would fly back. They'd left things at a reasonably good point their last conversation. Not that it would ever be entirely repaired, but they could be civil, could give Trevor the best Christmas he could expect.

And in truth, she missed Rhonda. And always would. And accepted that.

Give her a call right now, she thought. See if Ronnie can spare the time. Or maybe wait till you've sobered up a little.

Meghan had the phone in her hand, was dialing, when she noticed a sound like drowning coming from upstairs.

In an instant she was sober, mounting the steps with her gun drawn. "Who's there—Trevor?" Thinking of the man she'd fought the other day, Tequila, who'd left the bruises on her cheek and shoulder.

Would he lay in wait for her—here?

*I'm in fucking charge of the police force here*, Meghan thought.

As if that meant anything.

The hallway split in two at the top of the stairs. Meghan saw a light on from the left, and peered around the corner. Then heard the sound behind her, turned, nearly fired.

Her son was on his side, unconscious. Arms and legs secured behind him with plastic zip ties. Trevor had been doused with something. Meghan recognized the smell.

Kerosene.

# ELEVEN

**S**ports memorabilia decorated the walls and shelves of Scott Doppler's private office. Framed and signed jerseys, balls and pucks in shadow boxes. Photos, Scott with his arms around retired defencemen and designated hitters taken at auto mall meet-and-greets. He'd been trying to get his father to sponsor a Doppler & Doppler hockey team for years; as Scott told Cam, the old man was coming around.

Cam was seated on a commemorative chair, green laminated wood, taken from some long-gone stadium. He leaned forward, sending a creak through the chair, which caused Scott Doppler to grit his teeth.

"About the job," Cam said.

"Like I told you in the hospital, we're happy to have you back when you're feeling up to it." He pointed at the faded scar on Cam's cheek. "Looks like you healed up nicely."

"Nights might be a problem for me."

Scott rubbed his hands together. "Yeah, that's a toughie. A lot of container work has to be done by morning. We could put you on swing shift, how'd that be? Four to midnight? What about three to eleven?"

"Days might be a problem, too."

Cam stretched his legs out leisurely, keeping eye contact with the vice president. Part of him was enjoying this. Watching Scott's brow furrow, the man sputter and act confused.

"Let me remind you what we do here, Cam—"

"You get a piece of the containers Tyson and Sheedy empty," Cam said. "That will continue."

Scott's eyes bugged out, his jaw motored soundlessly. "I'm not exactly clear—"

"My schedule changes up," Cam said. "Sometimes at the last minute. What I'll do is, end of the week, I'll call and tell you which shifts I worked. You make sure I get paid for them. You personally."

"I'm not—"

"Then if anyone asks, you can show them your records."

"Hold on a sec, buddy, let's you and me—"

"Also," Cam said, "I want my forklift ticket. I'll arrange for it and get them to invoice you."

"We don't, our policy is not to—"

"Then I'll be getting the ticketed rate, same as my friends."

"Cam—"

"Like I said, what you've worked out with Sheedy and Tyson for the cans, that'll continue."

Scott sighed. Clasped and unclasped his hands. Stared at Cam as if the younger man had pointed a gun at him.

"What happened to you?" Scott said. "You started here, you had a great attitude, great work ethic."

"I still do," Cam said. "My price went up is all."

The Surrey police told him his car had been found. Would he mind stopping by and talking to them about the circumstances of its disappearance?

Cam was relieved that he wouldn't be dealing with the White Rock cop, Meghan Quick. She'd sense something off about his story. Since Softball City was technically over the dividing line in Surrey, he was dealing with a larger but less personal force. Cam was greeted at the station by two officers in suits who were probably from IHIT, the Integrated Homicide task force, and sure as shit weren't talking to him about a car theft.

His story was brainless and simple. He'd been sick for a week, barely able to leave the house. The only place he'd gone was the local pharmacy. He'd even rescheduled meeting his PO—call him if you don't believe me.

The car could have been stolen at any time that week. Sorry I can't be more specific.

He knew with his record they'd look hard at him. But there was nothing to see. When they brought up the two dead men in Sunnyside Acres, he pleaded ignorance. Had never seen their faces, which was the truth. Had no idea about the Vipers. He'd been away a long time, and his work schedule at the warehouse was gruelling.

Even knowing that his movements from then on would be scrutinized, that he was possibly a suspect, didn't alarm him. For one thing he hadn't shot them—Tequila did. Except for the small puncture wound in his forearm and a slight numbness when he rotated his wrist, there was no evidence he'd been involved at all.

More than that, though. Cam had been through the machinery of the justice system before. He knew the hoops that would have to be jumped through to get a warrant for his place, let alone an indictment. An arrest on suspicion alone was out of the question.

The fact was, even if it went to trial, there was no way twelve jurors would convict someone based on their car sharing a parking lot with that of two dead men. A crown prosecutor would know that. If not, a lawyer like Zoe Prentice would make them see it.

He was off the hook. Legally, at least.


Cam took precautions when he next met with Sukhi, changing taxis at the bus loop at Newton Exchange. He arrived fifteen minutes late, and when she opened the door of her parents' place, he moved in for a kiss and a grope. Sukhi pulled away.

"Harv's here," she whispered.

He was inside at the kitchen table, nursing a beer. Dressed in a polo shirt and slacks, a black workout headband. He nodded at Cam and told him to have a seat.

"You haven't been around," Harv said, his tone friendly, conversational.

"Sick. And then had to catch up on work."

"Glad you got that sorted. Sukhi said you figured out what we're doing and want on board."

Cam nodded, deliberately not looking across at her, but wondering what her game was.

"Shit's delicate," Harv said. "You heard about the two dead Vipes in the forest?"

Cam shrugged.

"I knew those guys. An act of aggression like that, their people're gonna want who did it. Makes keeping the peace a fucking challenge."

Harv pointed at Sukhi, who was studying her phone.

"Her brother's off the fucking grid right now, and the Vipes want his head. Know anything about that?"

Not sure what the play was, Cam said nothing. He could only guess that Tequila had been the one Harv sent to work out a peace, and that Tequila's actions had royally fucked things up.

Harv stared at him, emptied his beer. Pressed a fist to his mouth to stifle a belch.

"I've got a lot riding on this," he said. "You're smart, you get shit done, and you don't got the baggage a lot of us do. Only thing is, can I trust you?"

"Course," Cam said.

"Makes it hard when I find your car's left at the fucking scene. Got an explanation for that?"

Sukhi's eyes told him to say nothing. He repeated his story about being sick, about the stolen car. Harv nodded thoughtfully.

"You think it's possible that Tequila jacked your ride?" he said.

Too emphatic an agreement would be a bad sign. "Possible," Cam said. "I don't know him."

"But if your car was there and you weren't, that's what must've happened. Like logically. He finds out where you live, heads there and boosts your ride."

"I guess."

"Lying *fuck*." Cam turned, hearing the voice from the hallway.

He saw the gun first, that same chrome automatic from the parking lot. Tequila Narwal entered the room and placed the barrel against Cam's temple. Hard enough to push him a step back, cornering him against the wall.

"You lying fuck. You were there. You shot them. You fucked up me and Harv's work."

"No."

"Face the fucking wall."

Harv began patting down his legs, then bound his arms behind him. Zip ties, he thought.

"Fucked my sister, too, didn't you?" Tequila prodded him in the spine with the barrel suggestively. "She gets around. Fucking initiation rite. Didn't I tell you, Harv?"

"You told me." Harv ratcheted the ties tighter till Cam's wrists were bleeding and his arm sockets ached.

Sukhi had backed toward the kitchen, tears on her cheeks. She wasn't meeting Cam's gaze.

A kick to the back of his knee knocked him to the tile floor. Cam sprawled, felt himself pulled upright, felt the pistol grip connect with his ear. The pain broke loose a shiver of fear, and he realized what was in store.

Harv paced in front of him, talking low. "Tito? Yeah. We got him. Where's Cody want to meet?"

Tequila crouched in front of him, smirking. He pressed the barrel into the centre of his forehead.

"You on your way to court, son."

A grey membrane had fallen over him, like being submerged in freezing water, till even the sensation of cold began to fade. He imagined Death sitting next to him in the back of Tequila's

Navigator. A pale-skinned, clerical-looking woman, not unlike Zoe Prentice. Maybe he could get a message to Zoe. She could extract him—

There wouldn't be a chance. No phone call, no due process, no presumption of innocence. They'd want him to beg, and use his begging as proof of guilt.

And Tequila would be standing there gloating the entire time.

That enraged him, pushing the fear out. That he'd been manipulated by the three of them, and that he'd end up taking the fall that was rightfully theirs. Who knew how many others had done this before him, taken the same ride, spent their last moments trying to work out a way to save themselves.

*Fuck you*, he thought, staring at the back of Tequila's head. Hip hop blared from the stereo. Pusha T. In the passenger's seat, Harv was lit by the glow from his cell.

*I'm going to kill both of you.*

*If my hands weren't tied—*

They drove east out of White Rock, Cam noticing signs for the border crossing. At Zero Avenue they left the road, bumping down a hill, and he recognized the farm they were taking him to. In the daytime the farmhouse looked even more ruinous, a corner of the roof caved in as if by cannon fire. The barn loomed, its grey doors flung open, swallowing up the Nav in blackness as Tequila drove inside.

Court.

Ivan and Brad and Tito and six others he didn't recognize stood around the horse stalls, smoking pot and vaping and scowling at him. Cam saw the aluminum and wood bats at their sides.

He was shoved out of the back seat, onto the hard-packed dirt floor. Harv stood him up. Someone laughed, and he heard the *chuff-chuff-chuff* of the bats striking the ground, the sound meant to frighten him.

Seated on the broken staircase leading up to the hayloft was Cody Hayes, holding a pink-handled machete. He was older than he'd seemed the first time Cam saw him. Maybe late thirties. Steroid-swole, face flushed pink from the cold. Simian features curled in a smile.

"Shouldn't take fuckin' long," Cody said. "There's a way my brother likes shit done, so let's get through it. Anything to say?" He was looking at Cam with the same contempt he'd held for the couple that night.

"Yeah," Cam said. "The person you want is over there." He nodded in Tequila's direction.

Tequila laughed, and a few of the others joined in. More striking of the bats. Cody shut them up.

"You're gonna accuse someone else to save yourself?" Cody said. "That what kind of man you are?" He pointed the machete, sabre-like at Cam's temple. "You tell the truth and we're done quickly. Maybe even let you go."

"He's playing you," Cam said to Cody.

"Fuck you. Fucking traitor."

"Shut up," said Cody. He looked at Tequila with the same dull hatred. "What do you got to say?"

"Me?" Tequila's head spun between Cody and Harv. "I've been making money for you. That's what I do, isn't it? Since day one. Who earns better than me?"

Cody looked to Cam as if it was a salient point.

"He was selling you out," Cam said. "Making a deal with the Vipers. Then he shot them when he thought it'd get back to you."

"And you know this how?"

"Check his gun," Cam said. "It's the same one he used on them. Idiot doesn't know enough to toss his shit after a job."

Cody stood and walked forward and held the machete against Cam's throat, so that drawing breath hurt. "And. You. Know. This. How."

"I saw him," said Cam.

"Bull*shit*." Tequila spat on him, Cam feeling flecks land on his cheek, eye. "Pieceashit'll say anything."

"I was following him," Cam said, not caring if Cody believed his innocence or not. If this was it, he'd have company. "Wanted to talk business. Then I saw he was meeting with the Vipes."

"Prove it, lying asshole."

"The gun's the same. He was gonna burn them, too, but he didn't bring any gas." Cam smiled. "That's his thing, isn't it? How'd I know 'less I heard?"

Tequila struck him, a weak punch that Cam backpedaled from. His next one made up for it, knocking Cam into a support post. He slumped to the floor, felt Tequila's boot impact his ribs.

"Off him," Cody said, pointing the machete at Tequila, who stopped everything and retreated, still staring at Cam.

"I should say something," Harv said. "Cam *was* following Tequila."

"Yeah?" Cody said.

"I asked him to."

Tequila's response was a wordless, open-mouthed stare at his friend.

Cam wanted to crane his head around at Harv, gauge his expression. Instead he nodded, looking at Cody.

Harv said, "Sukhi told me her brother was acting weird. I was worried he might try to make a deal for himself with the Vipes. I asked Cam to follow him."

"Lying pieceashit," Tequila said. "You know—"

"Shut up." Cody turned to Cam. "And you saw him shoot them?"

"They chased after me," Cam said. "Shot me in the arm. When they thought they'd lost me, Tequila finished off the others."

"It's a fucking lie," Tequila whined. "They're lying, Cody."

"You had your say," Cody told him.

"But I'm serious—"

Cody stuck him with the machete, a short jab to the stomach that caused Tequila to scream.

"I fucking *told* you, shut up," Cody said. "I can't fucking *think*."

He drove the blade into the ground and pulled out his phone. Tequila sank down to the dirt next to Cam, clutching his chest with both hands, sobbing.

Harv quietly picked up Tequila's gun.

"Bro," Cody said into the phone. "Nah, it's a whole fucking—I can't tell... Harv said he asked him to, yeah... That right?... Cool... See you soon."

Hanging up, he turned back to the two men on the barn floor. "Dalton's on his way."


Before Dalton Hayes arrived, his brother told the others to wait outside. Except for Harv, Cam and Tequila.

Twenty minutes passed before Cam heard the snarl of an engine. Doors slammed. Two men walked in, almost the size of Cody, one white and one South Asian. They looked at Cam and Tequila with blank expressions. Despite their hoodies and black jeans, they looked like Secret Service.

The third man who entered was slim, narrow-shouldered and dressed in a white long-sleeved T-shirt with a League of Nations vest over it. His hair was the same light brown as Cody's, though his features were smaller, less ape-like. Definitely the same genes—Cody was the outsized funhouse-mirror version. Dalton was the original.

Dalton Hayes looked at Cam, then at Tequila. Then sighed. His face showed compassion for them, but also aggravation. Like an employer asked to fill in last minute for a sick subordinate.

He sat on the barn's staircase and asked Harv what was going on.

"That situation with the Vipes, he kind of caused it." Cam couldn't tell if Harv was indicating Tequila or himself. "Shit got out of hand. My fault for not thinking he might try something."

"Mmm-kay. You can't use Mountain Grove anymore. The cops're looking at their electrical bills. Shady Acres or Greene & Son."

"Got it," Harv said. "How d'you want it handled?"

"You decide. Wait till I'm gone."

Dalton bumped fists with Harv and Cody, and motioned for his bodyguards to lead the way. Passing next to Cam, he leaned down.

"That thing at the port," he said. "Nice piece of business. Inspired, brother."

"Thank you," Cam said.

Tequila began to cry.

Cam was helped to his feet, his hands cut free. Harv asked him how he wanted to handle things.

"Think you can do it yourself?" He held out a bat in his left hand, Tequila's gun still in his right.

A thrill went through Cam, a stray impulse—grab for the gun, take it and shoot them all. Shoot and run far away from all of this.

He took the bat.

Cody Hayes smiled. "Get at 'er," he said, stalking out. Harv put a cigarette in his mouth and followed, sliding the barn door closed behind them.

Tequila looked up from the dirt floor, strands of ancient grass stuck to his face, saliva and snot leaving a trail down his neck.

"Not fair," he blubbered.

Cam placed the bat on the ground between them. He took one, two steps back. "How's that?"

Tequila feinted and scrambled for the bat—was the first to wrap his fingers around the taped handle.

Cam kicked him in the face.

Tequila screamed and reached up to cover his broken nose. Cam fell onto him, knees striking the killer's ribs, beating his head into the dirt. Tequila crawled across the ground, seizing the bat and swinging it wildly to ward Cam off.

Like timing a windmill shot in mini-golf. When the bat hit the ground, Cam stomped down on Tequila's hand. Heard the bone break. Booted him again.

"Please," Tequila said.

"You'd've killed me and not thought fuckin' twice." Cam strolled around the prone killer, tapping the bat like the others had done, enjoying the reverberations that sped through his arms. Building himself up to what he had to do.

"Nuh-uh," Tequila said. "I'd've—I'd've—I'd—"

He rolled and tried to reach the barn door, and Cam struck him with the bat. Tequila flopped onto his back, arms up defensively.

The door opened a sliver.

Harv stepped in, looked at Cam and made a hold-off gesture.

Tequila started laughing maniacally, relieved. "Gonna get it now," he said. "Had me going for a second, bro."

Harv pointed Tequila's gun at him and shot him in the head.

Tequila stared up at them, gawped, then stared at nothing. The dirt beneath him grew slick with blood. Smoke curled out of his forehead, mouth.

"Not a fucking word to Sukhi," Harv said to Cam. "Far as she knows we got him out of town."

He handed the gun to Cam and nodded toward the corpse.

"Now on, we're in this together."


The use of the bats became obvious. Brad carried in two blue body bags, and he and Cam slipped Tequila into one. After it was zipped, Harv opened the barn doors, and Ivan, Tito and a few of the others entered and went to work.

"Bones got to be crushed," Harv said, handing Cam a bat. "'Specially the skull. They can reconstruct that shit. Can't be anything left."

Soon the canvas bag was soaked and its contents pulverized. The bats made a snapping sound against the fabric, sloshing the contents around. Harv called them off. He unzipped the bag and took a photo, the flash blinding in the dim light.

Cam and Brad placed the bag inside the second one, noticing the black trails of blood on the earth.

Harv and Cam drove to Shady Acres Funeral Home, backing the Navigator up to the rear entrance. They carried the bag inside and placed it in a long rectangular cardboard box.

The room was high-ceilinged, concrete walled and cold. A tall blonde woman in a black polo shirt and grey slacks shook Harv's hand.

"It's always sad to see a pet go," she said. "Of course you can use the machine. Is this a pet with a lot of bones or metal?"

"No."

"No pacemaker? I ask because they tend to explode."

"No pacemaker," Harv said.

"Good. No need for the cremulator, then. Come back in about six hours."

They drove Tequila's SUV to a chop shop in North Surrey. Harv handed the keys to the head mechanic, who nodded and drove the Navigator around the back.

Ivan was waiting in a blue Dodge Charger. He handed the keys to Harv wordlessly, ignoring Cam, taking the fifty dollars Harv offered.

On the ride back to White Rock, Harv drove recklessly, pushing the Dodge's engine up to a hundred, one fifty. The highway flew by.

"Why you and not him?" he said to Cam, as if anticipating Cam's question to himself. They hadn't spoken since leaving Zero Avenue.

"I've been wondering."

"'Side from the fact that Tequila wasn't reliable, if he was meeting the Vipes, someone on their end will know. They'll want him taken out, if things are gonna stay cool between them and us."

"Is that what you want?" Cam asked.

Harv looked over at him. His face showed mild annoyance. "I'm not afraid of the Vipers," he said.

"All right."

"They think it's a competition, Coke and Pepsi, but really it's Coke and Coke Zero. So why not recognize that? What we're doing in White Rock is the future. A casino goes in, we're all rich. Generational wealth with no risk, brother."

"How's that work?" Cam asked.

"You control the casino, you control the money that goes through there. No better way to wash cash. We'd be in business with the right people—and every dollar that goes through there, we get a taste."

"So why deal in the Vipers?"

Harv slowed and took the off-ramp, down the industrial road leading to the crematorium. "Blood always costs more than you think," he said at last. "If we have to take them out, so be it, but there's enough for everyone."

"You really believe that?"

"Yeah, I do. I've been in this since I was a kid, Cam. Since a buddy at elementary school told me to keep something in my locker for him. That was Tequila Narwal. He thought to make money you got to take it from others. He never saw that the really rich people, the ones with fuck-you money, sit back and get it given to them. Just takes owning something everybody needs. Setting terms so they got to deal with you."

"Like PayPal," Cam said.

Harv smiled. "Knew you'd get it. That's why I cut you in."


The white-grey ashes of Tequila were handed over to them in a plastic sack. Harv drove by the beach, along Marine Drive. He pulled over near the pier, waited as Cam walked out onto the promenade.

Cam stood at the edge, with the breakwater of piled white stones the only object separating him from the ocean. Other than an elderly Vietnamese woman checking her crab traps, the promenade was empty. Cam crouched and loosened the knot in the bag, and shook the ashes out over the water. They were sucked below the pier, the fine dust coating the barnacles growing on the near-black wood.

Cam crumpled the bag and watched it float down to the water.


"I don't know what happened to him," Sukhi said on the phone nights later. "Harv won't tell me anything. Just that you straightened things out. Do you think the Vipers got him?"

"No clue," Cam said. "Maybe he's out of the country."

"No, he'd at least tell mom. Promise you'll tell me if you hear anything?"

"Course," he said. "When can I see you again?"

It was Harv's decision for who would replace Tequila. White Rock–South Surrey was lucrative, relatively safe. He offered the territory to Cam.

Cam tried to talk him out of it.

"I can't be doing that while I'm on parole," he said. "Plus there's guys been waiting for their shot, they'll resent me."

"It's serious money," Harv said.

Cam nodded, thinking, *and serious trouble.* Tequila was the perfect dealer. Flashy but not too flashy, smart but not too smart. Canny enough to only meet people he knew, in public areas with multiple routes of escape. Cam might make a go of it for a while. But eventually he'd trip up. The law of averages. Those cop cars that had driven through Softball City—one night they'd be ten, fifteen minutes closer, and that would be that.

All of which was a concern. But Cam also didn't want to spend his time looking out for the Vipers.

"Ivan's the one," he said.

"And why's that?" Harv asked. Cam sensed it was a test.

"Tito's got mood swings. Too erratic. Brad is good all-around, but not self-motivated. Ivan wants it. He's smart."

"He's the one that didn't go for your warehouse heist," Harv said. "Told us it wouldn't work. And not to trust you."

"Smart, but not *that* smart," Cam said.

Harv smiled.


He booked a hotel in Harrison Hot Springs and took Sukhi there for a weekend. They spent their Christmas in bed.

Boxing Day Cam was sitting in the hot tub near the hotel's indoor pool, watching Sukhi do long laps, pop up near the shallow edge and smile at him. Then push off, splashing into the water, only to emerge on the other side.

The next time she got close to his end, he was there to lift her out, laughing, kicking at him lightly, and carry her to the hot tub. Her hands reached down through the turbulent water and worked him out of the swimming trunks she'd bought him for their trip.

After, lying on the hotel bed eating room-service hamburgers at thirty bucks apiece, Cam checked his messages, saw one from Harv.

*Call now.*

Not on his cell, of course. He dressed, slapping away Sukhi's hands as she tried to strip him, her toes as they brushed his ear and neck. He kissed her and headed to the lobby.

On the concierge's phone, he dialed Harv's number.

"Get back here soon's you can," Harv said, once he was sure the line was secure. "Dalton says we gotta tool up."

# TWELVE

Once, when Trevor was an infant, Meghan had left her service weapon out. Her son had spotted it on the end table by the door, slipped out of her arms and began to waddle toward it. Meghan had been half-asleep, lulled by the cartoon they'd been watching. *Great Mouse Detective.*

She'd felt the situation before understanding it. His familiar weight next to her was absent. Was he by her feet, on the edge of the couch? Motoring her arms and legs confirmed that he wasn't. Opening her eyes, she spotted Trevor, now on all fours, rocking the legs of the little table.

Meghan had fallen off the couch and out-crawled her son, scooping him up before the gun toppled.

It would never happen again—to this day she locked her SIG up every night when she came home. She'd only brought up the incident to Rhonda as an example of a crisis averted, to make a joke about her own reflexes. Rhonda hadn't found it funny.

That was their first major argument, and had set the tone for the rest of their relationship.

Carelessness, danger, long hours, stress. The job was killing their marriage. Meghan couldn't see how it was affecting Rhonda and Trevor. That was Ronnie's point, anyway. Meghan admitted the job had its drawbacks. She agreed with her wife—hadn't she said she'd lock up the gun from now on, and done so?—but the argument continued.

They'd both had a few drinks by that time.

Rhonda had said, and taken it back immediately, but meant it: "I carried him, Meg. That's always going to count for something."

"Meaning I'm less his mom because he came out of you."

"Let's just drop it. I'm sorry I brought it up."

Meghan, on occasions, would throw those words back at Rhonda. "You should decide, since you carried him," or "I guess that's another thing you carrying him counts for." Sometimes playfully, though it always had an edge. She'd come to regret it, much more than Rhonda regretted saying it in the first place.


The kerosene had soaked into his clothes. Meghan cut her son loose and slung his arms over her shoulders, dragging Trevor down the stairs. When the ambulance arrived, she rode with him to Peace Arch Hospital. Panic churned the alcohol fog in her head.

At the hospital, he came around and smiled at her. The doctors sedated him, and Trevor fell asleep with Meghan holding his hand.

Cuts on his wrist and ankle, a concussion—but safe. Fine. Not to Rhonda.

"He should come and live here," Rhonda said on the phone.

"I'm sure Chicago is *much* safer than White Rock."

"Meg, you said the attack was a message, right? *To you.* How fair is that, for Trev to be hurt, on account of your—"

"Don't, Ronnie," Meghan said. "I neither wanted nor caused this. I'm tired. I'm with him now. I'm not gonna fight."

She braced for the hysterics, instead hearing a loud sigh. She imagined Rhonda leaning back in her office chair, a backdrop of the city skyline outside her window.

"You're right. You're not at fault, Meg."

"Thank you."

"But it happened regardless. He'll be safer with me."

"In Chicago."

"In Oak Park. With my family close by."

"I guess Trevor should be the one to decide that." Meghan was glad she'd beat Rhonda to making the point of Trevor having the final say.

"I just—I worry about our son, Meg. His safety means everything. Yours too."

It was difficult to hear Rhonda break down the way she, Meghan, wanted to. Wanted to and couldn't, because she was detachment commander, and her co-workers were watching, and because years of old-boy's-club bullshit had taught her to conceal her emotions. And because Rhonda would eventually cast blame on her, for not protecting Trevor, even though Rhonda was a thousand miles away.

Meghan wished their roles were reversed and Rhonda was comforting her.

"Will you let me know when he's better?"

"Of course," Meghan said. Then, before she could stop herself, "Why don't you fly home?"

"Meg, I can't."

"For the holidays? Trevor would love that."

"I'll try."

"I would, too. Like it, I mean." Grimacing but hopeful.

"I promise I'll try," Rhonda said. "Take care of him, Meg. And yourself. Promise."

She promised.

She stayed at the hospital, pulling rank to overrule visiting hours. Her phone's battery ran out. She bought a coffee from the cafeteria and immediately came back and harangued the night nurse to make sure Trevor was comfortable.

Denny Fong stopped by the hospital to take their statements. He'd gone through the house, found no forced entry, nothing amiss. Meghan reminded him to have the techs fingerprint the zip ties.

Denny looked at Trevor, asleep. "Does he remember anything?"

"Just unlocking the door. He never saw his attacker."

"What was he doing there? I thought he'd moved out."

"Surprising me," Meghan said. "His student loans had come in, he wanted to take me to dinner."

Denny patted Trevor's foot. "I'm glad he's okay. You need anything, boss, just holler."

"Make sure they print those zip ties."

At eleven the next morning the door to Trevor's room opened and Liz Garrick stepped through, carrying a coffee tray. She looked down at Trev and her mouth pursed in a look of sympathy. To Meghan it appeared rehearsed, artificial.

Liz presented her with the tray.

"You missed our meeting," Liz said, "and your phone is off. When I heard what happened I came here. I hope that's not indelicate."

"Of course." Meghan took a cup off the tray, smelled cinnamon and vanilla. "Thank you."

"Who would do such a thing," Liz wondered, after Meghan had explained roughly what happened.

"I'll figure it out," she said.

"I hope so." Liz indicated the seat next to her and Meghan nodded. "I know we left things a little rough," Liz said, "but if you need anything, I'm glad to be of help."

"Thank you."

"Was the business you mentioned yesterday terribly important?"

Meghan had almost forgotten about the money and Richie Reed's letter.

"Liz, do you know a lot about your husband's business dealings?"

"Everything." She smiled. "It's my business now, after all."

"Was there a side of it that was less than legal?"

"Of course not."

"I don't want to dig up ancient history," Meghan said. "But if Roger was involved in something illicit with the Reeds, it might bear on Alexa's murder."

"Nothing."

"Nothing about envelopes, members of the Vipers making pickups from the Reeds' service stations?"

"Meghan, that's asinine." Liz looked over and patted her hand. "You're stressed out, aren't you?"

"Badly," Meghan admitted.

"And maybe you're predisposed to believe cynical rumours over friends. Bob told me that's an occupational hazard."

"Have a lot of talks with Bob, don't you?"

"Meg—"

"Liz, I don't give a shit what corners Roger was cutting. He's gone and there's no sense covering it up—unless it's still going on."

"Think what you want," Liz said, placing her coffee down on the bed stand, beginning to gather her purse and coat.

Meghan watched as the woman slung the coat over her shoulder and walked out, leaving a residue of lavender in the air. Ever fashionable. Meghan followed her out to the elevator bank.

"You have a chance to get in front of this," Meghan said. "Explain it now. All of it. That way when it comes to light—and it will, Liz, every damn thing—there'll be no surprises."

"There are always surprises," Liz said. "I'd've thought a cop would know that."

The elevator doors opened and Liz joined the people and the food trolley inside. Turning to look at Meghan, she said, "Do what you feel is best for you and yours."

She spent Christmas Eve at Trevor's bedside. They talked and ate a turkey dinner just short of abysmal, watched the stop-motion *Rudolph* on the small, cube-shaped portable television.

No internal bleeding, no signs of brain damage. Another night and he could go home.

Rhonda didn't fly back. Work issues. Their Christmas was a quiet one.


Back at work on Boxing Day, fielding her co-workers' notes of concern, catching up on what she'd missed.

The two murder victims found in Sunnyside Acres had been ID'd as Gurvinder Atwal and Joe Bains, both members of the Vipers, both with records for minor thefts, impaired driving and drug possession. The .45 ACP slugs matched those from Michael May.

The stadium's easternmost parking lot had held a Dodge Charger registered to Atwal. The only other car in the lot was an empty, bullet-ridden Civic registered to Cameron Shaw.

*Well fuck me*, Meghan thought.

She phoned Surrey PD and asked for details on Cam's involvement. Learned he'd declared the car stolen two days after the shooting.

"Bullshit," she'd told the detective from Major Crimes.

"Probably is," the detective said.

"You know he's got a record? Has killed before?"

"Yes we do, matter of fact. Anything else you think we're overlooking?"

"Sorry," Meghan said, wanting the conversation to continue. "Have you found Tequila Narwal? He's our main suspect in the May killing."

"I understand you had a run-in with him."

"At the victim's home, yes."

"We'll let you know if he turns up," the detective said. "Happy Holidays."

"You too," Meghan said. And thanks for nothing.

Sukhi Kaur pulled the same tantrum when Meghan showed up at her parents' door and asked about her brother. She didn't know anything. Tequila barely spoke to the rest of the family. She never saw him do drugs, let alone sell them. Why you got to harass me all the time?

Meghan was having none of it.

"Let's see how you like a night in the cells," Meghan said.

"Okay, okay. I don't know where he is."

"Fine. Want to leave your parents a note?"

"C'mon."

"You'll get a phone call once you're processed."

"For what? What'd I do?"

"Impeding an investigation to start with," Meghan said.

She nearly dragged Sukhi to the car before telling her she could come and talk nicely or in cuffs.

Meghan put her in a hard interview room, white-painted brick walls, a wobbly chair in the far corner. She watched the young woman on the monitor from her office. Sukhi picked at her shoelace.

Meghan entered the room, shoving a Dr. Pepper across the table.

"I'm going to ask you what your brother was up to, and if you lie to me or give me any more shit, I'm arresting you. I am fucking through playing around, Sukhi. Your brother attacked my son."

"He wouldn't do anything like that—"

"You have the right to remain silent—"

"*Okay*," Sukhi said. "I don't know what he did but he hasn't been around. I been kinda worried about him."

"When's the last time you saw him?"

"I don't know, a few nights ago?"

"Which night?"

"How do I know—"

"Anything you say will be—"

"Okay, okay," Sukhi said. "Like a week before Christmas. He asked me to pick him up. I forget from where." Seeing Meghan's expression: "Okay, from 20th and maybe 148th, near the forest."

"Near Softball City."

"I guess."

"How'd he get there?"

"Just said to pick him up."

"And you didn't ask?"

"No," Sukhi said. "I don't ask him shit because he won't say shit. And that's the truth, okay?"

"This was the night of the shootings."

"I don't know about that."

"Get up," Meghan said. "You're going to the cells."

"Yeah, okay, it was the same fuckin' night. But he didn't say anything about it."

"You abetted him."

"No way."

"What do you do, Sukhi?" Meghan asked. "You have a job? You in college?"

"I help my parents. Look after their place."

"I think you're as dialed into the League of Nations as your brother," Meghan said. "And this act? The dumb spoiled bitch who doesn't know anything? It's about played out."

"Whatever." Sukhi slumped in her chair, arms crossed.

Meghan rolled her chair closer, cutting off the room.

"Young lady," she whispered, "if you don't tell me something, you're going to prison. Your brother made choices. Those don't have to affect you."

"I don't know where he is, okay?"

"But if you hear from him, Sukhi, if I find out you've seen him and didn't tell me? Jail."

The girl wiped her nose and nodded.

"Last thing," Meghan said, "then we'll get you out of here. You know a guy named Cameron Shaw?"

She'd thrown the name out, thinking the girl would deny it. And she did—but not before her face bugged out. As if Meghan had thrown a live grenade in her lap.


According to his PO, Cam was a model parolee. Pissed clean and reported regularly, other than once when he was down with the flu. Cam's employer vouched for his work ethic, said he'd been on nights for weeks now, driving a forklift and emptying shipping containers.

The picture of Cameron Shaw they were selling was too glossy and airbrushed to fool her. But Meghan was in a bind. The double homicide wasn't her case, and if she questioned Shaw again without informing IHIT, she'd risk an interagency feud. Right now she needed all the cooperation she could get.


Meghan slept on the couch, letting Trevor take her bed. She woke to find a plate of cinnamon toast in front of her. Her son entered, carrying a Bodum press full of coffee.

"You shouldn't keep your butter in the fridge," he said. "It clumps when you spread it."

Meghan ate some of the toast and told him it was perfect. "Feeling better?" she asked.

"My wrist itches a little. And my head has like this ringing, like a dial tone."

"The days before the break-in," Meghan said, "did you notice anything weird? Maybe someone at school gave you a funny look?"

"No, nothing."

"You sure?"

Trevor groaned. "Do you really have to go full Cop Mom on me right now?"

"You're right, honey, I'm sorry."

They talked about school, about plans for New Year's. Christmas had been a wash, but maybe a small party here? A bottle of Laphroiag 15, beer for Trevor, some sausage and Ritz crackers and that cheese spread that comes in the red tub?

"Ronnie's coming for New Year's," Trevor said. "We should get her something."

It was news to Meghan. They'd talked yesterday, Trevor and Rhonda. She'd booked her flight home for the 30th.

"If it doesn't work out," Meghan said.

"Yeah, I know, I won't get my hopes up too high."

"A little high is fine." Meghan smiled. "It would be nice to have her home."

"I don't get why you didn't stay together," Trevor said. "And believe me, I know that's what every child of divorce says, but—oh shit."

Meghan looked at him, thinking it was something internal, reaching for her phone to dial emergency.

"I just realized," Trevor said, "like you were asking. There *was* something at school."

He'd been at Newton Exchange, waiting for the express that took him across 72nd to the college. There'd been another passenger who was kicked off by the driver. Some kind of altercation. Trevor saw the guy flip off the driver and stomp away. But not before he'd looked through the back windows and made eye contact with Trevor.

"He just looked pissed," her son said. "Someone on the bus said he was a gangster and the driver hadn't wanted to drive him."

"What did he look like?"

"Just a guy. Kinda short. Purple bandanna on his head."

"And you thought the look he gave you was important. Was meant for you specifically."

"Looking back, maybe, but not at the time. I had my headphones on and wasn't really paying attention. But that night on the ride home I saw somebody I thought was him, but it turned out not to be."

"You're sure they weren't the same," Meghan said.

"Positive. The second guy was taller and had a Khalsa tattoo on his neck. I was staring at the back of his head for most of the ride home. Different guys, just dressed the same. Guess there's no law against wearing purple, is there?"


The safest place for Trevor was at work with her. Meghan drove to the office and parked him at her desk with a laptop. She told him not to leave and informed the staff to keep an eye on him.

She dug up the Gang Task Force number and asked to be put through to Inspector Nora Epstein. Explained about the attack and the men tailing Trevor.

"That does sound like the Vipers," Epstein said. "They've been known to operate in Surrey, but rarely in colours. Riding public transit is unusual for them."

"Who's the head of the Vipers?" Meghan asked.

"Million-dollar question. Marco DaSilva is de facto head, but he's currently in Kent, not up for parole till next year."

"The last name sounds familiar," Meghan said.

"DaSilva's nephew Tito is a member of the League of Nations. Tito was part of the defection a few years ago, along with Harvinder Singh and Tequila Narwal. My source tells me Tito is a heavy meth user, and there's not much love between him and his uncle."

"I want to talk with Marco."

"I'd really rather you didn't, Staff Sergeant Quick. After the shootings of Bains and Atwal, the rank and file are riled up. The situation is volatile."

"So am I," Meghan said. "My kid was attacked. I want to talk to Marco."

"Suit yourself," Epstein said. "Only don't be surprised when he claims not to know anything about the attack. He might even be telling the truth."


Marco DaSilva's counsel wasn't responsive. They said Marco was dealing with severe depression, was thought to be a suicide risk. If Meghan wrote down her questions, Marco's attorneys would give them to him when they thought fit. In any case, Marco DaSilva didn't sound like someone actively running a gang.

A message had come in from Bob Sutter. *Horrible what happened. Let me know how I can help.* Meghan tore the slip in two and let it waft into the garbage.

Bob. Her friend and mentor who was what now, exactly? Still a friend, but lowered in her estimation. If you were going to have an affair, Liz Garrick was a good choice, beautiful and rich and probably discreet. But Meghan couldn't help thinking Bob had been led by his dick into supporting Liz Garrick's casino bid.

That was the worst part. Not that Bob would cheat, but that he'd be taken in by such an obvious ploy.

Speculation, Meghan reminded herself. As far as she knew Bob and Liz were just two adults who both liked swimming. It could be totally mercenary or the truest of true love, and only they would know.

The case kept coming back to Elizabeth Garrick, didn't it? Alexa was her cousin, once removed. Michael May had keys to the Reeds' house, which Liz had put up for sale. Cameron Shaw, her husband's killer, had left his car near the bodies of two gang members, the same gang which Roger Garrick had done business with.

And the attack on Trevor in Meghan's home? That part she couldn't tie in. At least not yet.

"Can I go home?" Trevor asked. He'd been left alone to wander the station for most of the afternoon.

"Soon, honey." Surrey PD had posted a car outside Trevor's apartment. Meghan had done the same for her house. No activity at either so far.

"Can we at least order pizza?"

She gave him her credit card. "Get whatever you want, but something everyone would like. None of that white gunk on mine."

"Béchamel. It's good."

"It's heresy. Red sauce, cheese, mushroom and green pepper."

"Got it. One Boredom Deluxe on its way."

Meghan opened the office door to see if Amanpreet or Katy wanted a slice. She found Amanpreet standing at the front desk, listening intently to the scanner. Denny Fong's voice filled the room.

"Ten Thirty Three, the emotionally disturbed person I mentioned, he—oh Jesus. Shots fired. Shots fucking fired. I'm sorry. I'm gonna be sick."


Totem Park was a small outcropping between Marine Drive and the beach, watched over by a row of boxy postmodern residences. A walkway, a small plaza with two red cedar house poles, benches and floral displays. Denny's Interceptor was parked next to the curb, behind a sporty looking orange Dodge. A figure lay slumped against the rear wheel.

Meghan arrived along with the other units. She caught sight of Denny, sitting on a bench near the poles, crying.

"I told him to put it down," he said, looking up at Meghan as if imploring her to explain it to him. "I told him to."

White male, early twenties, dressed in track pants and a Raptors jersey. A black automatic lay in his lap. The bullet had entered under his eye. Blood and brain matter gleamed on the pavement. It was starting to snow.

Meghan checked his pockets, found a baggie of small

white capsules and a wallet. Ivan Stepcic of 214 Southmere. Beneath the jersey, she could see the glittery letters on his shirt.

Thrive or Die. Some choice.

"Why didn't he listen?" Denny said.

Meghan didn't answer. Across the street, holiday lights twinkled, out of synch with the lights from the Interceptor. She put an arm around Denny and let him sob into the folds of her coat.

# THIRTEEN

**W**ord of mouth.

Among the boys, *Ivan flipped out, drew a gun on a cop* quickly became

> *Ivan got set up*

which became

> *The Vipers set up Ivan*

and finally,

> *The Vipers took out Ivan as retaliation.*

The story kept changing, till Cam had no idea what to think. The only thing that remained a constant was that the Vipers deserved to be put in their place. The Hayes brothers were making plans for that.

For Cam, that meant waiting around his apartment, staring at his collection of cellphones. He had three: a legitimate one for his PO, one for the League, and one that Harv had given him for private communications only. A hardworking parolee, a loyal League member, a conspirator in secret talks with the brains of the organization. He was a different person on each line.

Beyond all three was the pact he'd made with Zoe Prentice. She hadn't contacted him in a long time. If she was working for a government agency, they were thinking long-term.

Or maybe they'd left him out to dry.

Sukhi texted every few hours. Cam often woke up to a library of unread messages. At first they were about her brother, if there was any news. But after a few days, anxiety and self-interest trumped family. She wanted to see him. He was leery, not knowing how things stood between her and Harv.

But Harv didn't seem to care.

"Ever hear of the Marshmallow Test? An experiment where kids were given a marshmallow, told if they didn't eat it, they'd be given two later on. Most couldn't wait. Know why?"

"Hungry, I guess. I dunno."

"A lack of vision." Harv had used the vape pen they'd been sharing to point at Cam's chest. "That's Sukhi in a nutshell. She's a great fuck, but she's dangerous, brother."

And Harv had laughed.

"Anyway, she's your problem now."


He'd stopped sleeping through the night, instead crashing at odd intervals. He was staring at the stationary blades on the ceiling fan when Tito phoned.

"We're on for tonight."

"Yeah?" Rubbing fatigue out of his eye sockets.

"You, me, Brad and the new kid. You got something?"

The .22 was drywalled into a hole Cam had cut behind the medicine cabinet in his bathroom. He said he'd be ready when they swung by.

A few minutes later Harv called.

"That dumb sonofabitch Cody," he said. "Walking us straight into war. I tried talking to Dalton, but he just shrugs and says sometimes you have to send a message. Our plans are fucked if this goes wrong. Could set our shit back years."

"How?" Cam asked.

"Scare off the people we need to make friends with. Make them think we can't play nice. This is thug shit. One marshmallow shit. Not businesslike."

Cam said he'd do his part.

"Stay safe, brother. Shit's out of my hands for now."


An hour later Cam was dressed in a black hoodie, his pistol resting in the centre pouch. No League clothing. No ID.

You get stopped, forget it. Go straight to jail and serve out your two years and change, on top of the gun charge and the consorting with criminals charge and whatever else they come up with. Tonight you're a walking parole violation.

He thought about what he'd do if the cops pulled them over. If Meghan Quick was approaching him, asking him to step outside the vehicle. Go quietly? Run? Which Cameron Shaw would emerge?

It was cold outside. The weight of the gun was some comfort.

A white work van that he'd never seen before pulled into the parking lot of his building. Cam didn't recognize the driver. The side door opened and he was helped inside by Tito. Sitting in the middle bench next to Brad and an Asian kid with blond hair who was introduced as Chalk.

There was no heat in the car. "Where we going?" Cam asked, his breath steaming.

No answer. On the floor of the van, near his feet, what looked like an assault rifle.

"3-D printed this morning," Chalk said, grinning.

A pump shotgun next to it. On the middle seat two pistols and a box of ammunition.

As much as they all run their mouths, he thought, this is the first violence for some of them. Chalk looked maybe twenty, the kid adding piece after piece to the wad of gum he was chewing. Even Tito looked downcast and pensive. Not like beating a traitor to death. Their faces looked like those of soldiers you'd see in war movies, the transport hold full of fresh-faced kids taken out of boot camp and dropped into the shit.

Cam found himself the calmest person in the car. He bummed a smoke off Tito and said, "Let's fucking *do* this." And told the driver, "Tunes, man. Let's get in the fucking mood."

A thick, syrupy bass line poured out of the tinny speakers. The *ch-tink* and swoop of an 808 hi-hat. The others began to nod their heads. Cam didn't know the words but he nodded harder than the rest.

They drove along Zero Avenue, in the same direction as the barn. But when they neared the turnoff the driver continued on. Down a branching side road, asphalt turning to gravel.

The van jostled and lurched over an uneven path, through a wooded area with a LOT FOR SALE sign across the entrance. The van pulled over at the gate. Cam and the others dropped down into a ditch half-full with melted snow.

Splashing across, pulling themselves up the bank, they stopped in a copse of tall maples. A three-quarter moon shone through the branches above. Cam couldn't see any stars.

"What do we do?" Brad asked. He and Chalk seemed to look at Cam and Tito for answers.

Tito looked at Cam, shrugged. "Cody just said we wait and hit them when they show," he said.

"Then that's what we do," Cam said.

He smoked a cigarette. The others passed around a bag of crank. On the second pass, Cam gave in—and, holy shit, he was out of practice with anything hard. He found himself trembling, bouncing in place, and stopped when he realized the noise he was making. He hunched down and nodded as if the music was still playing.

They heard the gargle of a motor and crushed out their smokes. Brad lay down sniper-style in the foliage, the rifle pointed at the highway. Tito had taken the shotgun.

The motor sound was coming from the south, from the border, and above.

He saw the plane, a small two-seater, skimming dangerously close to the tops of the trees. Heard a rustle and felt the ground thud. A bomb? He saw Brad swing his gun up from the forest floor and aim skyward, tracking the plane in its site. Cam brought his hand to the barrel, down, stopping him.

The hell—

He saw something fall through the trees, tearing branches, sending a thousand invisible critters scurrying through the undergrowth. A black plastic bundle of something. Then the scream of the plane banking, gaining altitude.

The others ran toward the package. Cam saw pinpoints, headlights along the road.

"Down!" he called.

Tito didn't listen. Running knee-deep through leaves and sucking mud, he examined the fallen cargo. Started toward the other package beyond that. He was carrying the shotgun over his head, drifting farther from them.

Cam thought of going after him, or calling out to him, but the lights were growing closer. He tucked his mouth inside the collar of his shirt so his breath wouldn't give him away, and sunk down behind the trunk of an ancient evergreen.

Insanity. What the fuck was he doing? If Tito was in charge, where was he running? Were they even in position?

"Hold on," he called to Brad as the car slowed. Brad whipped around, aimed the gun at Cam's face. Then, realizing what he'd done, said "Sorry, bro," and redirected it at the headlights.

A procession. An suv in the lead, behind it a panel van not unlike the one they'd arrived in. The convoy turned onto the road—

—and Brad fired, and suddenly there was light and gunfire and nothing made sense.

The suv swerved and skidded off the road. The van carried on, stopping when it rear-ended the suv. Brad was firing wildly. In a second the rifle had run through its magazine and Brad was scrambling to reload it among the leaves.

Doors opened. Shots lit up the road, chunked into trees nearby. Cam kept down. He saw Chalk open fire to his left, knocking holes in the van, pitting the windows. To his right he saw Brad look up at him, panic on the kid's face. The plastic magazine wouldn't slide home.

Gunfire cut into the brush between them. Cam crawled backwards. "This way," he called.

A shadow moved across the van's headlights. Cam aimed and shot at the figure, missing, focusing on the centre and imagining it was a paper target, holding his breath, firing, the second shot catching the man in the belly. He heard a scream, voices of confusion. Cam's heart was pummelling his chest from the inside.

Chalk had fired his pistol empty and was reloading when the bullet hit him. He collapsed down, thankfully falling behind the edge of the root system of Cam's tree. Cam looked over at Brad and saw the kid finally ram the magazine home, pull the trigger and, panicking, pull it again, and again, with nothing happening.

"Your pistol," he called out, as another volley hit them. When next he looked over, Brad was on his back, hands over his bloody face.

*Fuck.*

He saw movement, a shadow, heard footfalls across gravel and saw someone coming toward them. Tall, gangly, cradling an automatic rifle.

Cam shot him twice. Waited, and shot at the man who went out to retrieve the other.

Screaming from somewhere. Cam slunk back, keeping the tree between him and the vehicles. Once he was back far enough he saw the lights from the vehicles had died.

He didn't think he'd killed any of the people he'd shot. Brad and Chalk were injured. He couldn't guess how serious. And Tito—where the fuck had Tito gone?

Cam peered from behind his tree and saw a shadow standing close to where Brad had been. Another behind it. Both walking toward him.

Movement to his left. Cam turned and saw Tito crash land behind a tree a few yards from him. Bullets slapped at the area around him. Tito was coughing, out of breath. Hands free of the shotgun.

The shadows moved in the direction of Tito's hiding place. A roar, a muzzle flash, and then Cam felt himself pelted by slivers of the tree. He could hear the sound of their feet crackling the dry and frozen leaves. Saw Tito stand, his head swing around. Then run—run toward Cam, nearly tripping over him.

Tito spun around and saw Cam and his brow furrowed in curiosity as he fell. Guns went off, close by. Tito scrambled over him, rushed toward a thicket of blackberry bushes. The pair of shadows passed by Cam, laughing.

Facing away from Cam, a tall thick-bodied man, the shorter one carrying the shotgun. The ends of their bandannas trailed down their spines. They stopped and took aim at the bushes where Tito had gone.

"Marco's nephew. The fucking traitor."

"Come out, Tito. Come out, come out."

Cam leapt up and shot the short one in the back of the head. The other man spun. Confusion at his fallen partner, no time for fear before the second bullet snapped his head back. He shot them both again.

More fire from the road, distant and inaccurate. Cam kept in a crouch, reaching for the shotgun, finding shells in the dead man's coat pocket. The smell of blood and blackberries.

He saw the white van pull in behind the convoy and heard shots, screams. Creeping forward he saw Cody Hayes walk into the headlight glow and take aim, shoot at a prone figure on the road. Two volleys with an AR-15, walking up and putting another in the dead man's skull.

"It's me," yelled Cam, holding up the shotgun from behind a tree.

"Where're the others?" Cody asked.

"Tito," Cam called. Hearing no response, he told Cody, "Brad and Chalk got hit. It was a fucking mess—"

A groan from nearby startled him. Chalk wearily raised a hand. Cody picked him up and dragged him to the van, slung him one-handed into the back seat.

"Fucking assholes." Cody walked to the dead man in the road and fired again between the man's legs, into his mouth. Unzipping his camouflage trousers, Cody spattered the mutilated corpse with a stream of piss.

Cam busied himself locating Brad, dragging the body toward the road. As he did, Tito appeared from the bushes. "So glad you showed up," he said to Cody. "Goddamn. There were so many of them, we got surrounded. They were waiting by the package—"

"Told you to fuckin' wait till they loaded up," Cody said.

"Should I get it now?" Tito said.

"You gonna carry it that far?"

"No. Sorry."

"Fucking right. Turns out only one of you is worth a shit."

Tito climbed in beside Chalk and Cam. He looked at them tentatively. Cam felt numb but managed a nod. Tito returned it. That was all the thanks he'd get.

Cody Hayes directed the driver to head to the barn. He hauled Chalk out and told the driver to call for the doc. Brad's disposal was left to Tito and Cam.

"Brad didn't deserve this," Tito said. "He should be buried right."

Cam said nothing. He wrangled the corpse into the body bag himself and found a sledgehammer among the rusty tools in the barn.

It took twenty minutes and wasn't nearly as thorough as the others had been with Tequila, but it was all he could manage. Tito drove the van to the crematorium and waited while Cam made arrangements with the director.

He'd shot people, surprised them, the same way Tequila had done. Now he was helping with disposal the way Harv had showed him. What would Zoe think if she saw this? Or was this what she wanted?

Everything was fucked.

"Not right to do Brad like this," Tito repeated as they left.

"No."

"He was solid, man. He really was. Nobody could make me laugh like Brad."

"Shut up," Cam said.

In the course of the night they'd swapped places. Cam knew he was calling the shots now. Tito seemed to know, too, and be grateful. He smoked a joint and emptied a bottle of Coors while they waited for their friend's cremation to be over.

Cam let Tito drop Brad's ashes off the pier.

He was home by seven and slept till noon, staggered to the washroom, threw up and went back to bed. At three thirty he was roused by polite knocking on the door.

Panic surged through him. Had he kept the guns? No, he'd forced Tito to drop them off the pier along with Brad's cremains. Cam's shirt and hoodie, bloody from the night's work, had been incinerated.

Shit. His shoes—still mucky from that night—lay by the door.

You could never think of everything.

He kicked them aside and looked through the peephole, ready to confront Meghan Quick. Instead he saw the face of Zoe Prentice.

"Tumult," Zoe said, snapping open her filing case, "is a very useful thing. People that thrive on the status quo don't tend to last long in our world. You're a good example of that, kiddo. From what we hear you're making yourself indispensable."

"When can I get out?" he asked.

Seated on the couch next to her, clutching a beer in two hands, he tried to look calm. Like someone doing well.

In truth, seeing Zoe brought back the reality of the deal he'd made. He wasn't a member of the League of Nations; he was Zoe's employee. Her *client*'s employee, more precisely.

"Soon," Zoe said. "If that's what you want."

"And my money."

She smiled. From her case she produced a piece of paper with a sequence of numbers. "This is you," she said. "A bank based in the West Indies, though the money can be transferred electronically."

Cam examined the sheet. "There's only nine grand," he said.

"To start with. The rest will be deposited when you finish."

"And when will that be?"

"The longer you stay, the more valuable you are," Zoe said.

He let the paper fall to the cushion between them.

"Fuck that. I already had more close calls than I want, and that White Rock cop is looking to send me back. I've done things—"

"I don't need to hear that part, kiddo."

"Maybe you do," Cam said. "I shot my way out of a forest last night. These people don't know what they're doing. If they're not looking at me as a traitor, they're putting me in situations to get taken out."

"But you're still here," Zoe said. "You have our full support."

"Who the fuck are you, anyway?" Cam stood, willing himself to keep from shouting. "And don't tell me you can't say, because I've nearly had my lights put out twice now for you."

"We know, and we appreciate that."

"'We,' huh?" He couldn't tell if Zoe meant an agency or a person. "What do you all want, anyway? If it's intel on the League, fucking ask me, I know as much as anybody."

His mind went to the darkest place, and he found himself comfortable with the thoughts he found there.

"If your client wants someone removed—if that's what this is leading to—tell me."

Zoe sighed, put the bank statement back in her case. She looked at Cam with sympathy of the it-sucks-but-what-can-you-do? variety.

"We want you to keep on keeping on," Zoe said. "For a little while longer, at least. You'll be rewarded for it, and protected as much as we can."

"Thanks for that. Tells me nothing."

"Being vague isn't something I relish. I have orders, too. If and when there's a specific task, I'll be only too happy to relay instructions. For now, at least, they want you to stay the course."

"How'd I get here?" Cam said.

Zoe stood and brushed couch lint off her skirt.

"Maybe you think you were manipulated," she said. "A better way of looking at it, a more useful, practical way, might be that you're here because you *want* to be here. And maybe, kiddo, it's not as dire as you think."

Tito DaSilva looked older and frailer in the daylight, two days after the ambush. His face had the same effect on Cam that seeing Uncle Pete after seven years had: someone still familiar yet unmistakably diminished. Tito smoked and sat quietly on his couch next to Chalk and Tyson Lee.

Cam felt a slight shame at seeing Tyson, a family man, decked out in League colours, knowing he was here to insulate Cam from the law. It was Cam's suggestion to bring in Tyson and Sheedy, further in than simply emptying containers at the warehouse. Ironic, since Tyson and Sheedy had put Cam in contact with Tito in the first place. That felt like ages ago.

But there was no one else he trusted, and he wasn't going to take Ivan's place, run around White Rock carrying drugs. Chalk and Tyson would each handle calls from reputable clients only. They'd recruit who they wanted from outside the League to carry and collect. In return they'd kick up to Tito, who would act as enforcer; any problems, come to him. Cam didn't know if that would work, but it was what he'd want to hear in their place.

Cam told them all carefully—if the cops pull you over, don't say shit but don't resist. We'll send someone to bail you out, and you'll be taken care of in prison.

After the others had left, Tito asked Cam to hang back a bit.

"You really want me as muscle, after what happened?"

"That wasn't on you," Cam said. "That was about organization. Won't be happening again."

Tito hugged him, slapped his back. "Thanks, bro. Sometimes I think I'm not—that I should get out. Go and, I dunno, fix cars or something. Learn how to code."

Cam felt like a shitheel for what he said next. Tito was trusting him with doubts and worries that Cam shared. There was something horrible about not being able to commiserate with the only other person going through what you were.

But part of him also thought: if I can't get out, why the hell should you?

He gripped Tito's arm and grinned until the man was looking into his eyes.

"And miss all the fun we're gonna have?"


He spoke with Harv every week. They talked about organizational structure, planning, ways to limit exposure. Cam tried to sound him out on his plans for White Rock, and the status of things with the Vipers.

"They know it was us," Harv said. "You can bet they're planning something. And then we'll clap back at them, and them at us, and it'll keep going till the Exiles force a sit-down. I try to tell Dalton and Cody that, but they don't listen to anyone. Now it's about pride."

"So how do we move forward?" Cam asked. "You and me."

"Survive. Wait things out. Try to make it clear to the Vipers that it's the Hayes brothers' kick, not us. Hope they're smart enough to see that."

Sometimes Sukhi would sound him out about business, usually while in bed. She seemed able to guess more than Cam told her. He hated being that predictable. She no longer asked about her brother.

Difficult not to think of Tequila's broken and bloody face every time he looked at hers. Extricating himself from her would be just as dangerous. So he stayed, meeting when she said to, fucking at her whim, taking care to be discreet.

Rising, by some accounts, falling by others, feeling himself locked in place.


He showed up at the warehouse to collect his pay stubs and make sure the container business was running unimpeded. Sheedy had brought on a pair of Filipino brothers to help him. Cam felt a surge of power, the way Scott Doppler handed over his paperwork and nodded and looked away.

On his way home that night, he noticed a silver sedan behind him, making no effort to hide its intentions. Cam gunned it, turning onto the highway. The sedan followed.

No gun, he thought, turning his rent-a-wreck into the left lane. The sedan pulled alongside. Behind the wheel was a silver-haired white man wearing aviator shades. He signalled to Cam, pull over.

Cam hesitated, wondering if it was a trick. The man had the look of a cop—but what if the Vipers counted on that?

Down the highway they continued, the sedan switching lanes to tailgate him. The driver signalling, sometimes gesturing toward the shoulder. He took both hands off the wheel for a moment, showing Cam the unarmed-I-come-in-peace gesture.

Cam slowed and stopped the car on the shoulder. He climbed out, feeling the breeze slap against him as traffic hurtled past. He walked back to where the sedan waited.

The driver rolled down his window and removed his glasses. Cam recognized him. It was the cop who'd slapped cuffs on him, who'd testified at his trial. Former commander of the White Rock detachment, Bob Sutter.

"You remember me?" Sutter asked as Cam approached the driver's side of the sedan.

"Who could forget?"

The cop smiled. He'd never seemed to bear Cam malice, although part of his testimony was about what an upstanding citizen Roger Garrick had been. Retirement agreed with him: the sedan was new, the watch on his wrist was platinum, and even his teeth seemed whiter.

"I'm a councilman now," Sutter said. "And you, you look like you're staying out of trouble."

Cam's junk car and worn threads could hardly make that impression. He nodded, figuring the cop would get around to his point eventually.

"I see your uncle around town, here and there."

Cam shivered as another car passed them.

"I hear you're reformed now. That right, Mr. Shaw? You fully rehabilitated?"

Another wide, shit-eating grin.

"Just work at a warehouse," Cam said. "You can check, you want."

"I'm sure you've got that covered," the cop said. "Sewn up a nice little alibi for whatever shit you're up to. Isn't that right?"

Cam drummed his fingers on the roof of the sedan.

"We both know what you are," the cop said. "If you hurt her, or even look at her sideways, they'll be finding pieces of you in ditches from here to Acapulco. *Comprende*?"

"Hurt who?" Cam said.

"Mrs. Garrick. The woman whose husband you killed. She asked me to get in touch. She wants to see you."

# FOURTEEN

City hall had flooded. The commander's address to city council was moved to the boardroom on the top floor of the White Rock Library. Catering ran to bottled water and a carafe of lukewarm coffee. The boardroom table was crammed, the few open seats going to a reporter from the *Peace Arch News*, the head librarian and two council hopefuls who were looking for ammunition.

No Liz Garrick, Meghan noticed.

She ran through her statistics, her goals, touted the department's decrease in auto thefts thanks to the bait car program. Property crimes were down. Overdoses remained alarmingly high, prevalent in the summer along the beach-front bars and restaurants. Homicides were up exponentially. Investigations were ongoing, but Meghan was hopeful they would solve both murders soon.

She fielded questions. Said she stood behind Denny Fong as an officer and a friend, but that an impartial investigation needed to be conducted. Councilman Bob Sutter asked if she felt her department was up to handling the killings.

"I believe we are. Not only that, but we're working with Surrey PD on a double homicide, which we believe to be related—I'm not at liberty to say how just yet, but it's being handled to the letter."

Meghan cleared her throat and turned over the page of notes she'd brought with her. She paused to take a drink of cold coffee, mostly as an excuse to survey her audience and gird herself for what she'd say next.

"I've been asked by Elizabeth Garrick to speak about the implications of a possible casino. She wants me to assure you that your police force will be prepared to handle the increase in crime that often accompanies gambling. I'm sure you've studied the numbers yourselves, so all I will offer is my professional opinion: I'm against it."

A rattle of papers, the reporter tapping furiously on her laptop.

"I have three reasons: One is the increase in crime, not just from desperation but the money being laundered through casinos. Two, this will hurt our current tourist economy—the beachfront shops and family restaurants will lose their clientele. Three—and this might sound peculiar, but I don't think we know our city. The events of the last few months make it clear there's an undercurrent of resentment and growing frustration—of rage—among young people here. Until we understand that, we shouldn't add further stress. Thank you."

Applause, interrupted by a question from Bob Sutter. "Are you saying you don't feel your department could handle a minor uptick in crime?"

"That we shouldn't welcome it, that it won't be minor and that there are other problems to address."

Bob was responding even before she'd finished. "Meg—Meg, if I may? You're saying you don't feel confident in a few extra B and E's, but you're fine handling two homicides? You don't see that as a teensy contradiction?"

After the meeting, Bob timed it so they'd exit together. The brick walls of the stairwell had construction-paper snowflakes taped to them. Rubbing against one, Meghan saw blue glitter stick to the shoulder of her dress uniform.

"I wasn't trying to be malicious, Meg," Bob said. "I'm genuinely concerned about you."

"Bullshit, Bob."

"I mean it. Hopefully we can sit down soon, you, me and Liz, and stay friends."

"You, me and Liz," Meghan repeated.

She thought she saw Bob blush.

Outside, they paused at midpoint between their cars.

"Things haven't been great at home for a while," Bob said. "I have so much love to give the right person."

Meghan couldn't help but laugh.

"Go ahead and think it's funny, Meg. But I mean it. I'm not happy sitting on my ass. I want to be a part of this world. Liz makes me feel connected. Vital."

"She's using you to help get the casino."

He shrugged. "A casino is inevitable. You can't fight change, Meg. You just try and steer it as best you can."

"Or let it steer you," she said, opening her car door.

Bob tapped her window. "Happy New Year, by the way, Meg."

"Happy New Year, Councilor."

The Independent Investigations Office was handling Denny Fong's shooting. Until it was over, Denny was deskbound, which meant the department had to draw from the ranks of its auxiliaries. It took Meghan time to get the schedule squared away. One of the auxiliaries, a computer programmer in his regular job, had asked how many of his personal firearms he should bring to work.

The joys of command.

Meghan doublechecked every lead on the Reed and May killings. She reread the statements from relatives and friends. Michael May's parents phoned often. She told them she was hoping for a break in the case soon, sickened by how false the words sounded.

The fact was, some crimes didn't solve. Or solved for bullshit reasons. You could get lucky, or the perp could get unlucky, and then it all came together.

Rhonda didn't show for New Year's, but promised she'd really try for Easter.

Trevor went back to school, seemingly over his trauma, and resistant to Meghan's pleas to see a counsellor.

The money and Richie Reed's confession sat in evidence.

Things were fine. Murderously, bafflingly, fine.

Her cell exploded in "Jolene" by Dolly Parton while she was struggling into a pair of jeans that had somehow shrunk over the holiday season. Meghan answered it on speaker phone, leaving her hands free to wrangle the material up to her waist. Stretch denim next time. Stretch denim every goddamn time.

"Yeah?" she said, suppressing a "fuck" as the material tore.

"Meg?"

Liz Garrick's voice.

"Meg, I'm in trouble, and we need to talk immediately. Could you come to the house, please?"

"Yeah, Liz, I can come." Thinking it would be a waste of time, another pointless battle of minor barbs between people who knew each other too well. High school played out all over again. The hall monitor versus the homecoming queen.

"Would right away be okay?" Meghan heard urgency in Liz's voice.

"Sure. I'll be there in ten, Liz, okay?"

"That would be great. I'd really—"

The phone cut off. Meghan dialed back, dialed as she hurried into her clothes, dialed as she drove across town.


The lights were off inside the Garrick house. As Meghan tried the front door she realized the incidental lights were off, too. No Christmas lights, no computer flicker from upstairs or pale fluorescent porch lamp. Not even the muted orange of the door buzzer. Someone had cut the power. Meghan unsnapped her holster as she walked around the side of the house.

The glass of the pool room had been turned opaque with smoke. Peering inside she could see only vague shapes—the diving board, an overturned white plastic chair. A form on the ground.

"Possible fire at the Garrick home," she radioed in. "Persons injured."

The door was locked but Meghan knocked out the pane with the butt of her pistol, turning her head as smoke billowed out. Working the lock and handle from the outside, she pulled in a deep breath and entered, approached the direction of the form, nearly tripping over the body.

She felt legs and took hold of ankles and dragged, her breath easing out, the strain causing her to suck smoke into her nostrils. Coughing. Her carry form was wrong, she wasn't protecting the victim's head at all, but her eyes were watering and she pulled both legs, lost her grip and held tight to one wet calf, dragging, clearing the building and collapsing onto the lawn.

Air. Her eyes cleared.

The figure was Bob Sutter. The towel that had been wrapped around his body had come loose and was now grass-stained and bunched beneath his head. Meghan checked his pulse and examined his airway, directed a breath down his throat. Pumped at his chest, one, two.

Nothing.

Meghan wiped her mouth and leaned back, away from the corpse.

A headache was cleaving her skull. Meghan stood up and looked into the pool room. The smoke seemed to hang over the water like a fog. But it wasn't spreading.

She radioed again, emergency, and tried the handle of the house's side door. It wasn't hot and it wasn't locked. She drew her gun and entered.

No smell of smoke in here. She headed down the hall into the high-ceilinged foyer. Heard footsteps from upstairs.

The main entrance led to a living room on the right, a curved staircase on the left. Meghan scanned the stairs and the landing above before slowly ascending, her footsteps nearly silent on the carpet.

Glass smashed from the end of the upstairs hallway. Meghan took the rest of the flight and moved forward, checking the bathroom, the guest room.

A pale form in green lay on the floor of the master bedroom, face shrouded in silver-black hair. Meghan rolled her over and felt for a pulse. Liz Garrick was breathing.

The door to the balcony was ajar. Banging it open with the toe of her boot, Meghan looked out. A figure had slipped down the roof and was slithering toward the overhang. Male, dressed in dark clothes.

Meghan shouted at him to halt. Then dashed down the stairs, toward the back.

Bursting out of the solarium door, she saw the figure hit the ground five metres in front of her. She yelled, "Hands up, police!" and drew a bead as he began to run.

Her first shot went wild as the figure sprinted down the back alley that led to the beach. She fired again as the gate swung and heard someone scream and a light go on in the house across the alley. She could hear a convergence of sirens now, fire and police.

"Pursuing on foot toward North Crescent," she radioed, following through the gate into the alley. Across the road, over the tracks. The figure had stumbled on the beach and was pulling himself up, darting west toward a parking lot.

Meghan jogged down the shoulder of the tracks, saw the figure running and fired, smashing the headlight of a Jeep at the edge of the lot. The figure turned. Meghan made eye contact.

Then Cameron Shaw bolted through the treeline, and was gone.

When Katy Qiu and Auxiliary Officer Ted Sommers arrived, Meghan was sitting near Bob Sutter's body. The white cups from the AED machine still clung to Bob's chest, staring at Meghan like pupil-less eyes. Emergency had taken Liz Garrick away.

"Do you smoke?" she asked Ted.

"Well, sometimes..." The auxiliary stumbled.

Meghan held out her hand. "Let's have them."

She lit up one, a Camel Light, and watched as the beach breeze carried the smoke toward the water.

The fire team swept through the building and said there were no other people inside.

Meghan knew, if Bob had been over, then Max Garrick was probably staying at a friend's house, or with a sitter. But she let out a sigh once the house was cleared.

Dale and Emmet walked out of the house, Emmet waving to her. He removed his fire helmet, noticed she was smoking and shook his head. "Old habits die hard, huh?"

"Where'd the fire start?" Meghan asked.

"Sauna," Dale said. "That's a new one, isn't it?"

Meghan shrugged, not up for black humour with Bob Sutter lying dead and naked on the grass.

Emmet explained that the fire had started close to the sauna. Bob, trapped inside, had inhaled the fumes, struggled, had freed himself only to collapse. A heart attack brought on by arson. Greg Grewal would have his hands full.

Once the arson investigator arrived, Meghan said, "Careful with this one, we've got a suspect."

"I'm always careful," Greg replied. "Should tell the thousand other people trampling through." He looked down at the former detachment commander. "Poor old Bob."

"Cold out here," Dale added, pointed at the dead man's shrunken pubic mound.

"He had to pick January, huh?" Emmet said.

Meghan walked away, telling Katy and Ted to follow her.

Sukhi answered her door in drawstring pants and a blue silk kimono. Her hair was up. "What do you *want*," she said.

"We're gonna talk," said Meghan.

"I *told* you I don't *know* anyth—"

"In my car or on your lawn. You choose the venue."

Once Sukhi was in the back seat of the Interceptor, Meghan turned in her seat, staring at the young woman through the safety guard.

"Any bullshit, Sukhi, and I'm holding you as an accessory. Where can I find Cameron Shaw?"

"I don't know—" She caught the look Meghan was giving her. "He has a place in Surrey."

"Is he there now?"

"How should I—I mean, I don't know."

"Phone him," Meghan said.

Sukhi dialed and waited through six rings before saying, "He's not answering."

"Where'd he go if he's not at home?"

"I dunno, maybe Tito's?"

"Tito DaSilva?"

"Yeah."

"Address?"

Sukhi told her.

"Where else?"

"I don't *know* anything else."

Meghan pointed at Sukhi's phone. "That stays off tonight."

Tito DaSilva was rousted out of bed, tossed down on the carpet of his living room. Meghan quickly searched upstairs and waited as Tito tried to talk her out of checking the basement.

"Don't you need a warrant or something to do that," he said weakly.

"Reason to believe you're harbouring a dangerous fugitive," Meghan answered. She signalled the other officers to follow her down.

Bats, pistols, League of Nations flags and shirts. Hash pipes and a baggie of what looked like crystal meth. No one was hiding in the basement.

Back upstairs, she handcuffed Tito and pulled him up so he was sitting on his heels. "Lots of bad shit in plain sight," she said.

"Plain sight my ass, basement door was closed."

"Difference of opinion. Where's Cameron Shaw?"

"No idea."

"Tito," Meghan said, making a *tsk-tsk* noise as she pushed the man back to the floor. "Know what happens if you don't tell me where he is? I'm going to walk out of here."

She waited for Tito to puzzle through this, and ask her, "And what?"

"And nothing. Certainly not arrest you. Fact, I'll tell people to make sure to steer clear of our buddy Tito, that his residence is off limits." She smiled and patted his shoulder, enjoying the way his head swung back and forth. "We'll look out for you, buddy, I promise."

"I'm not a rat," Tito said.

"Of course not. I will personally tell everyone that. Loudly."

"You're fucking killing me," Tito said. Then figuring out what she wanted. "Cam might swing by. He sometimes does."

"And what'll you do?"

"Tell you."

"What else?"

"Keep him here?"

Meghan patted his head. "Attaboy, Tito. Now tell us five other places we can look."


Surrey PD had an alert out for Cam. He wasn't at his apartment or at work. They'd alert his parole officer and check the regular League haunts.

Only one place left to look. Meghan drove along Crescent Road to where it met the Nicomekl River. She pulled into a small house with a sagging porch and weathered stairs.

A rental car sat at the edge of the drive. The driver's side window was cracked.

Meghan clambered onto the porch and knocked on the door. She heard the house awaken, footsteps and muttering, the lock being snaked back. Pete Shaw greeted her with a bleary-eyed nod.

"You just missed him," he said.

The old man sat on a milk crate on his porch and lit two cigarettes, handing one to Meghan.

"'Scuse my lips. Cam took my work truck. Wouldn't say where he was heading." Adding, "We're not on speaking terms these days."

"But he came here. You lent him your truck."

"Couldn't stop him taking it."

"Couldn't or didn't, Pete?"

He shrugged. "He was my apprentice."

Meghan heard a metallic clang from inside the house and shoved Pete aside, quick-drawing her weapon. The old man put his hand up, tried to say *relax*, but Meghan was moving past him.

"Don't," Pete said. "The gun. Please. You'll frighten him."

The interior was small and the lights were off. Meghan moved toward the kitchen, clearing the living room, seeing a light on and hearing the burble of a toilet tank replenishing itself.

The door opened and a child walked out, dressed in blue pajamas with glow in the dark sharks, their mouths open in gleaming smiles. The kid had a blue gob of toothpaste stuck to his left cheek, an aluminum toilet paper roller in his hand. He stared at her before smiling.

"Hi Mrs. Police," Max Garrick said. "We're out of tee-pee, Uncle Pete."

Meghan holstered her gun, feeling Pete's hand stroke her shoulder.

"Guess there's a few things I should tell you," he said.

# FIFTEEN

It had all gone to shit in two hours' time.

Cam had followed Bob Sutter's sedan into the rich area near the east end of the beach. He remembered the house, thinking of the additions he and Uncle Pete had made. They'd framed and wired the pool room, tiled the kitchen, re-grouted the bathrooms after the Jacuzzi tubs had been installed. The most beautiful house in the city, owned by the most beautiful couple. Something surreal about it, even now.

Bob had let him in the front door with a key.

Elizabeth Garrick's voice carried down from somewhere above the double staircase. "Come on up," she said. "Bob, would you give us a few minutes?"

The old cop had nodded and muttered something about a schvitz, glaring back at Cam. "Don't make trouble for the lady," he said.

Mrs. Garrick appeared, leaning one hand on the banister at the top of the stairs. She was dressed in a black robe of some soft material, her feet embedded in thick pink slippers. She smiled at him. Cam suddenly felt younger and smaller, and deeply uncomfortable.

"Your face," she said, making a sympathetic frown.

He touched the scar on his brow. It had been a while since he'd thought of it. "Work accident," he said.

"Let's talk upstairs."

Cam hurried up the stairs and followed her into the bedroom. It was nothing like he remembered from his time working on the house. She'd removed the wallpaper and the crown moldings, expanded the balcony so that the room looked out on the lawn. You could see all the way down through the skylight to the aquamarine of the pool.

"It's somewhat ironic it would be you," Mrs. Garrick said. She was kneeling at the entrance to her closet. "Frankly I'd rather deal with the person my husband did—I believe his name was Tequila?—but Bob tells me things are up in the air with that organization. Yours is more stable."

Cam nodded, not sure what she was getting at.

"Change is overwhelmingly positive when it comes to business. We have to be willing to grow." She turned back and smiled at him, a tight, mean-spirited smile. "Thrive or die, I believe is your motto."

Cam tried to speak but found he was tongue-tied. "I always wanted to apologize," he said.

"Of course. You didn't mean to kill him any more than I wanted him to die."

She lifted something out of the closet and stood up.

"I imagine we've both spent a great deal of time living with our regrets. But Roger is dead despite them, and I've decided to forgive myself. This, Cam, is what I want for his legacy."

She held up a glossy brochure and unfolded it. A nighttime landscape of White Rock beach, aglow with smiling faces strolling the promenade, walking into and out of a large neonlit sphere. The Paragon Casino and Resort would be *right on the water, serving a cross-border, international clientele, offering fun games of chance, gourmet restaurants, and the very best entertainment from around the globe.*

Cam pointed at the brochure. On the beach a nuclear family stood smiling, watching something leap out of the water. "Is that an orca?" he asked.

Mrs. Garrick smiled. "Artistic licence. The zoning will go through, and financing is secure. All we need is for the violence to stop."

She held out something plastic-wrapped and vacuum-sealed. Money, four stacks of fifties.

"Twenty thousand dollars, to be used to calm the waters," she said. "If more is needed we can come up with more—within reason, of course."

Cam took the money and tore a corner of the plastic away. The currency looked real. He said, "What exactly are you buying?"

"Peace," Mrs. Garrick said. "Violence over the next two years could put the project in jeopardy. I don't care how, but something must be worked out."

"Can't promise anything," Cam said.

"Just tell your people. This would be a start. A down payment of sorts."

"All right."

"But the violence stops. That's non-negotiable. And whoever murdered Alexa and this other young man, they're to be handed over to authorities."

Cam thought about Tequila, saw him in the second before Harv fired. Remembered the weight of his ashes.

"Might be difficult," he said.

"If it's possible the person isn't in a position to be handed over, I'd understand." Mrs. Garrick's eyes lingered on Cam's, making sure the point was driven home.

"I'll tell them."

"Excellent." She ruffled his hair, running fingers over his scar. "I always knew how you felt," she said. "How you used to watch me."

"Everyone watches you."

She didn't deny it. Her index finger brushed his mouth, chin. "Roger thought you were a threat to me. He didn't want you in the home when he wasn't there. He was silly-sweet with his jealousies."

The lights in the room wavered and Mrs. Garrick's smile turned to a look of concern. Then they were in darkness.

"Bob," she called out to no answer. Again, louder.

"Someone else here?" Cam asked.

"There shouldn't be." Her phone lit up the room, her face determined, half in shadows. Walking toward the bedroom. "Please check, would you?"

Cam moved to the staircase, looked down and saw a man press his face into the bevelled glass of the front door, then come around to the window and look through. Not seeing Cam, he continued along the perimeter of the house. His forehead was covered in fabric—too dark to make out the colour, but Cam guessed purple. What were the Vipers doing here?

What was *he* doing here?

He crept down the stairs, searching for something he could use as a weapon. Where was the kitchen? The place had been renovated and his orientation was off. Cam held to the banister and slipped along the hallway.

Steam was coming from the back of the house. No—smoke.

Cam stepped into the parlour and peered out. A man in a purple snapback stood in the entrance to the kitchen. He coughed and spat. Smoke teased out from below the door to the pool room. Another man joined him from the opposite hall, dragging a pry bar along the floor.

For a second they stood there looking at Cam, and Cam at them. They started toward him and Cam bolted to the stairs, rushing upward, hearing them behind.

Ducking into the guest bedroom, he heard the men pass by him. Knocking, then banging on the master bedroom. Maybe he could sneak past, down the stairs. A kick, a splinter of wood. They were after her—

In a panic he looked around the room for something solid. He heard Liz Garrick scream and abandoned the search, grabbing the second man just as the first breached the entrance.

Cam snared the man's neck and dragged him back. Choking, elbows flailing at Cam's ribs, the man went down. Cam felt something sink into his arm, saw the man's fingers claw at his bicep. Cam thumbed his eye. When the man released his grip, Cam struck him in the throat. He struggled free, kicked the man in the head, lumbered toward Mrs. Garrick's room.

He saw the other man strike the widow across the face. She gasped and thudded to the carpet. The man bent for the package of money and Cam tackled him, the two crashing through the balcony glass.

In the melee, Cam's head struck the railing and he felt the money slip through his hands. He was kicked in the chest and stomped and saw the man's boot come down. His hand went up to shield himself—too late—

—he woke to a woman's voice echoing through the house.

Stirring, he saw that the men were gone. So was the money. Mrs. Garrick was on her side, wrist bent at a wrong angle. But breathing.

Pulling himself up and picking out glass, he staggered down the hall, stopping when he heard the voice of Meghan Quick.

*I know how it looks, officer...*

She'd never believe him.

He lowered himself from the balcony to the roof of the pool room, heard the cop shouting, ignored it, worked on controlling his drop as best he could. Up. Then sprinting across the lawn as she called again, hands up, police, and fired.

The train tracks. The beach. Falling, scrambling up, that nightmare feeling of moving over sand. Onto the grass and the parking lot. Seeing the headlight explode to his right, an additional surge of adrenaline sending him through the lot and back out to the street where he'd parked.

He drove off, turning away from the beach as the bubblegum lights of a police cruiser lit up the opposite end of the street.

Christ, what a mess.

Where to go?

"You're not coming in," his uncle said.

Cam could hear a voice inside—a child's? He tried to peer over the old man's shoulder, but Uncle Pete shut the door behind himself, leaving the two on the porch.

"The truck, then," Cam said.

"Wait here. I'll grab keys for you."

Cam inspected the marks on his arm. His attacker's fingers had left deep bruises, a fingernail embedded in the skin. A small splotch of blood pasted the fabric to his forearm.

Uncle Pete returned, tossing him the keys.

"Not that you asked," he said, "but you ought to hand yourself over. I could call Meg Quick, have her come out herself. That way nobody gets hurt."

Cam had already backed off the porch, toward the blue pickup.

"I'll take my chances," he said.

The old man nodded and didn't seem surprised.


In a drug store, he bought a burner phone and dialed Zoe Prentice's number. She didn't pick up and there was no messaging service. Cam dialed Harv's private number. Waited, then texted, *It's cs, new phone, what's going on?*

A moment later Harv phoned him back.

"The cops just got through with Sukhi," Harv said. "Something happen?"

"I don't know, man. I was picking up something from Mrs. Garrick and the Vipers attacked. They took the package and torched her place." Cam drove the pickup over a bridge, slowing as he approached the turnoff for the freeway. "The cops saw me there."

"They'll be at your place soon, if they're not already," Harv said. "You're gonna need to stay out of sight. You got money on you?"

"Next to nothing," Cam said.

"There's a stash at Tito's, inside one of those green ammo crates. Couple credit cards, too. Enough to get started."

Cam pulled the truck onto the shoulder of the off-ramp, reversed down to the turnoff that led back to White Rock. The oncoming cars moved too fast to notice a truck cross the rumble strips and make a U-turn.

"Where'm I going?" Cam asked.

"Figure that out once you get the money," Harv said.

There was an unmarked car parked up the street from Tito's house. No hubcaps. Tinted windows. The car screamed police.

He drove on, slouched in his seat. Uncle Pete had left one of his old baseball caps in the truck, and Cam wore it with the brim pulled low. He could feel the fabric against his forehead, greased smooth from years of his uncle's sweat.

How had his life ended up so damn different from his uncle's? Did he simply not measure up? Was there a point in the mess of decisions where he'd swerved left, while Uncle Pete would have taken the straight road? Or had the old man simply been blessed never to have to make those types of choices?

Cam thought about Zoe and his money. He'd phone her and tell her to have it ready. Role-playing time was over now. He wasn't a member of the League of Nations. He was a guy who'd bought himself a second chance and was now entitled to it.

*Bullshit*, he thought, parking the truck behind the Bay Ridge Elementary soccer field. You're entitled to nothing. You want that chance? Then it starts with you getting into that basement.

Crossing the field, he wound his way through a figure-eight-shaped pair of cul-de-sacs, down a small chain-link walkway to the alley behind Tito's home. The yard was as neglected as the rest of the house. A standalone garage was piled with furniture, the lawn both spotty and overgrown. His footfalls crunched against the frozen lawn.

Up the back porch and a little pressure to the door. Why he hadn't called Tito first he wasn't sure. Maybe so that if asked, Tito wouldn't have to lie.

In the kitchen Cam texted him. *This is cs. You home?*

He heard the *shump-shump* of stocking feet running downstairs. Saw a shadow pass across the hall, heard Tito's voice say, "Aw, fuck me."

A moment later a text came through: *Yeah u ok?*

*Check yr back door,* Cam typed. Then crouched and waited as Tito walked past him through the kitchen, tapping him on the shoulder and whispering, "Surprise, motherfucker."

Tito screamed and dropped something that smacked off the tile. A pistol. He turned and embraced Cam. "Scared me, asshole."

"*Shhh.* Harv told me to grab something from the War Room. You alone?"

Shaking his head as if waking himself up. "Yeah, dude, everything's fine."

Something in Tito's eyes—shame, the same look he'd had coming out of the forest after abandoning Cam and the others—told him things were not fine. That Meghan Quick or someone else had talked to him. Tito had weighed things up and made a choice.

Cam looked down at the gun, a long-barrelled target pistol, probably a .22.

Tito's hands swept down for the gun but Cam kicked it, spinning it into the bottom of the cupboard. Their bodies collided and Tito grabbed his forearm, close to the bruises, and sensing the pain it caused, embedded his fingers in the flesh. Cam howled and batted at Tito's face, and as they fell, reached for the gun.

Tito's arms were longer. His middle finger rested on the handle, snaked it closer to his palm. Cam clamped down his hand on Tito's arm, freed his left and elbowed Tito in the eye socket. Cam grasped the trigger guard, felt a kick land in his stomach. The gun slid underneath the lip of the oven.

Tito panicked and Cam struck him in the face. Pulled out the oven drawer and launched it at Tito, crumbs and aluminum cake pans scattering across the floor. He bent and retrieved the pistol.

"Who," he asked, his breathing starting to return to normal.

"No one," Tito said. "Let me go. Please, brother."

"Did Harv tell you I was coming?"

"Nuh-uh."

"Was it the cops?"

"No. Swear."

Cam gestured with the gun and Tito stood up. Walked to the basement door and started downstairs. At the bottom, Tito turned, watching Cam's hands, licking at the blood that trickled from his mouth.

"Face down on the concrete," Cam said.

Tito complied, shivering when his cheek brushed the floor.

Cam found the crate and loosened the top. Dug out the money and cards wrapped up with what looked like a gram of cocaine. Leaving the coke, he told Tito to sit up.

"Why the fuck did you do this?"

"I didn't," Tito whined. "I just got scared, the cops were here, I don't—"

"You told them I might be coming back?"

Tito shook his head but didn't meet Cam's stare.

If he were a true outlaw, he would've shot Tito there. Part of him wanted to. Could imagine the cowardly shit's look of surprise and pain.

"Stay," he told Tito. "If I hear you breathe, the next five minutes, I don't care what happens to me. Down."

Tito embraced the cold concrete.

Cam ran up the steps, heard front-door knocking, dashed through the kitchen. Saw the back door burst inward. Turned, saw the play of a flashlight over the front entrance. Cam went left, into the living room, smashing at the window with the butt of the pistol. Knocking out the glass shards and stepping onto the ledge, dropping down, landing with a *woof* on his knees in a gravel bed.

His hands pawed the concrete walkway as he pushed to his feet. Confusion from inside, the bubble lights out front. Diving over a neighbour's fence, dragging down some sort of vine that snared his right leg. Patting his pockets to make sure he still had the phone.

He could get back to the truck.

Running crouched across the property, motion lights flicking on. Into the alley, the walkway, scraping the chain-link, rattling the bushes. He darted down the centre of a cul-de-sac toward the school.

Leaning against a beige power box in a darkened corner of the street, he dialed Harv.

"You get it?" Harv asked him.

"Tito sold me out."

"We'll deal with him later," Harv said. "You still got wheels?"

"Maybe."

"There's a big house on Blackburn, backs onto the Ravine. A little shack behind there. Entry code is triple eight, triple six. Do *not* come if anyone's following you."

"Understood," Cam said.

"And no more calls on this line."

Cam tossed the phone and bolted across the field.

He ditched the truck in an alley behind the row of beachfront houses, working his way on foot up the ravine to the address Harv had given him.

The house was a three-storey postmodern castle, staggered to create multiple verandas and bent at a right angle to wrap itself around the curve of the hill. Cam struggled over the gate and followed a rambling brick path to a two-floor cottage that looked built from a kit.

The code worked. The interior was wallpapered and floored with vinyl. A steep staircase rose from the middle of the kitchen. Battered appliances sat on the Formica counter. Garbage overflowed from a green bag on the floor.

Cam went up the stairs without turning on the lights. The small room at the top held a pull-out bed and a bookshelf. A bottle of Johnny Walker Black sat on the ledge of the window that looked out over the ravine.

Not a bad place to lie low. Cam helped himself to a drink from the bottle. He cleared junk from the bed, sat on the mattress, not meaning to sleep, but finding his head reclining.

He awoke to prisms of light. There was no clock upstairs. His arm was aching and hunger rumbled his stomach. He went back downstairs and found a box of old granola bars, chewed one with a cup of water from the small bathroom. Then he cleaned the blood off his forearm. Showered, had another granola bar, thinking he'd be here for a while.

It was a lot of trust to place in Harv, but he didn't have a choice.

He was about to deposit the granola wrappers in the garbage when he noticed something sticking out of the bag. An aluminum canister, PREMIUM STOVE AND LANTERN FUEL. Red oxidation speckled the lid. Liquid still sloshed inside the can. It smelled pungent, like kerosene.

He didn't have time to consider what it meant.

When the door was kicked in, his hands flew up. He felt the cold kiss of a shotgun barrel against his neck. Cam didn't resist as he was thrown on the ground.

# SIXTEEN

**P**ete Shaw chain-smoked American Spirits and drank two cans of Pabst as he told Meghan how he'd come to be the biological father of Elizabeth Garrick's son, and what lengths he'd gone to keep that a secret.

"Liz and Roger tried for a long time. You know how proud he was—the thought of her going to one of those sperm banks, of people in town knowing the kid wasn't his—that would've ate at him. Her, too. They had this image back then of being perfect."

"I remember," Meghan said.

"She's pretty, of course, Liz. But I always thought there was something sad about her. 'Magine having all that, and still not being happy? It's a cruel world that way."

He cracked a fresh can and offered Meghan another cigarette, which she accepted. From inside, Max opened the door of the pantry and began pulling out bread and peanut butter. Pete watched for a second, smiling in that misty way that parents do.

"Anyway," he said, "Liz was on the phone with her doctor, one day, talking about it while I was doing some work. And she remembered I was there and asked me not to say anything. I told her, of course, her business is her business. You overhear a lot of strangeness working in peoples' homes. I'd lose customers out the ass if they thought I was spreading their secrets around."

Meghan watched Max for a second. The child had some of the porcelain beauty of his mother. His hair was darker, though. Like Pete's, she thought. Or Cam's.

"'Bout a week later, Liz lays it out for me. How she's reaching the age where soon it'll be impossible, and Roger doesn't need to know. And if I wanted her, we could do it like that."

He grinned, seeing the look on Meghan's face. "'Magine a homely bastard like me turning down a woman like that. I told her I wouldn't feel good forcing her, but if she wanted a donation, I was willing. So we set it up with her lawyer. Drew up a contract and everything. Here."

Her smoke had gone out. Pete took it and chained it off his own, then lit a fresh one for himself. His attitude to the events was more bemused than anything else.

"Soon after that, Roger got killed. I didn't see much of Liz after that. Me being Cam's uncle maybe put her off seeing me."

"So how'd this happen?" Meghan asked, gesturing toward Max's sandwich-making in the kitchen behind them.

"Small town, and we just kept running into each other. One day we were both in line at the post office. We say hello and get to talking. I asked how Max was doing. She said why don't I come over and see? The kid and I took to each other. Now, time to time, Liz asks me to look after him. My age, there's not much else I have going on, and the kid's pretty happy here."

"He looks it," Meghan said. "I'm glad there's people in his life like that. And yours."

"We're lucky," Pete said. "You lose people but you still have others. That's got to be good enough, else you go crazy. I don't think Cam ever reckoned with that."

"You worried for your nephew?"

Pete smoked, looking thoughtful. "My brother bought it when Cam was young. His momma left him with me. Lord knows where she ended up."

"Doesn't answer the question," Meghan said.

"I'm all he's got. But he's not all I got. He wants my help to make a change, I'm here for him."

Her phone shook. Amanpreet Brar texted that a tip had come in. Cam was on en route to Tito DaSilva's.

"I've got to go," Meghan said, deciding not to share the news.

Pete nodded. "Stays between us, right? What we talked about?"

Meghan made the zipper motion across her lips.

Arriving at Tito's house, she found Amanpreet standing on the lawn. Ted Sommers waited with Tito on the front step, taking the gangster's statement. Meghan noticed the broken window along the side.

"DaSilva says Shaw pulled a gun," Amanpreet said. "Would've shot him if we hadn't arrived."

"Any idea where Cam is headed?"

"None. And he won't speak about his other associates."

Meghan nodded. "A man of principle."

"Had to be one somewhere, I guess."

She went home to check on Trevor. Her son was sprawled on the couch, asleep in front of the TV. Meghan took the easy chair, muted the volume, and allowed herself to nod off.

She awoke to Trevor standing over her, holding out her phone.

"You had it on vibrate," he said.

"Thanks, sweetie." The number on the screen was private. "Who's this?"

"A friendly citizen." The voice was male. "The dead girl and boy you've been looking into? The killer's name is Cam Shaw. He killed a man last night, too. He's just out of prison for killing someone else."

"You don't say. Where can I find him?"

The voice gave her an address, a laneway cottage on the side of Duprez Ravine.

"Make sure you get a warrant. You'll probably find evidence there, too."

"Anything else?" Meghan said.

"Have a Happy New Year."

Meghan led Ted and Katy Qiu down the back alley. Her vest made her sweat despite the cold. The shotgun was heavy, built for the dimensions of the average male, like everything else in this fucking job.

The door of the shack had a code lock instead of a key. They battered it open. Inside, Cam was shirtless, standing in the centre of the tacky little room.

"Hands, Cam. Easy."

He didn't put up a fight.

Meghan had him booked and placed in a cell, then escorted into a hard interview room. She contacted his parole officer, ate a Wendy's plain double cheese, then headed into the room with a can of 7up. She sat down and regarded Cam for a minute before handing over the beverage.

"Parole is over," she said. "You go before a judge on Monday morning. The only question, really, is what else we charge you with. Which depends on what you tell me now."

Cam said nothing. She could tell the gears were grinding inside. He was putting together just how badly he'd fucked up.

"Bob Sutter died yesterday," she said. "Murdered, while you were in the house. Mrs. Garrick was beaten—how's the court going to look at her husband's killer coming back for more?"

"I didn't hurt either of them," he said.

"I'm absolutely willing to hear your side of things."

No comment from Cam.

"If I don't," Meghan said, "I'll be forced to think the worst of you—which we both know isn't far from the truth."

Beneath the stoic prison stare, she thought she saw shame flicker over his face. He knows what he's done, she thought. Knows how bad this will get.

"You look worried," she said. "Do you think your friends in the League of Nations will stick with you when you're back in Kent? Or did they maybe help put you there?"

She opened the soda and drank it herself.

"Probably not hard for them to get at someone who's locked up with a half dozen of their pals."

"You think you know," Cam said.

The words stopped Meghan. Alexa Reed had written something similar. And while cop cynicism and age made

Meghan want to dismiss the words as generational griping, something nagged at her about them. It wasn't unfairness they were complaining about, it was indifference. Blindness.

"What don't I know?" she said.

Closing his eyes, Cam said, "This wasn't supposed to go like this. I was only supposed to pretend."

"And it got out of hand?" she suggested. "Is that what happened with Alexa? You were just going to talk and things got out of hand?"

"I didn't have shit to do with that."

"Right. You say I'm missing something, but won't elaborate. You know what, Cam? You *wanted* this. And you knew this would be the result."

Meghan stood, stifling a burp with her fist.

"I'll get someone to take you back to your cell. We've got all weekend together, Cam. We'll talk more in a few hours."

The killer didn't look up at her.


A full night's sleep had never felt so well deserved.

The next morning, she visited Liz Garrick at her home. The widow was in her solarium, wearing ski boots and sweats, wrist wrapped in a cast, hair loose to cover the bandage on her forehead. Liz was directing two men in overalls to be careful with the replacement glass.

"Meg," she said, neither friendly or perturbed, but as if she were another entry on her list of chores.

Meghan sat down unasked in the chair next to the pool. The water had been drained. A smear of blood could be seen on the tile near the edge.

"Poor Bob," Meghan said, surprised by how little grief she felt.

"He was a good man. I hope whoever did this pays dearly."

Once the window was in place, Liz took the chair next to Meghan. The workers left, returning with caulking guns and paint.

"Cameron Shaw was here when you were attacked," Meghan said.

"Was he?"

Meghan gave her a don't-bullshit-me grin. "I chased him away from you. I didn't see anyone else."

"You arrived a bit after the fact," Liz said.

"What the hell are you mixed up in?" Meghan lowered her voice. "I talked with Pete Shaw. Remember when I told you there'd be a time when your secrets would come out?"

Abruptly, Liz pushed out of her chair and started toward the kitchen.

"If that's true, Meg, then I think we require a drink."

Perched on the edge of the loveseat, with a tumbler of gin in hand, Liz Garrick told Meghan about Roger's business.

"He had vision, even back when this was nothing more than a pissant border town," she said. "The casino was his dream. He laid the groundwork years ago. Or tried to."

"What groundwork?" Meghan asked.

Liz gestured through the window of the living room, out toward the beach and the water.

"We are so incredibly sheltered, you and I," she said. "The power of those waves are nothing by the time they reach the sand. The bay protects us. Insulates us. Roger sought to do that economically for the town."

Meghan didn't touch her drink. She let the widow continue.

"You see White Rock as a sleepy hamlet that would do fine on its own, and me as this monstrous witch who wants to turn it into a playground for the wealthy. What Roger saw was a town with a steadily creeping median age, a population getting older, wealth concentrated in the hands of fewer and fewer, and no means for younger people to obtain the lifestyle their parents enjoyed."

"And a casino would solve that?" Meghan asked.

"Not by itself, but it would employ thousands—who else works in hotels and bars, as dealers, as valets?"

"Immigrants," Meghan said. "Don't pretend they're all union jobs, Liz."

"They're decent jobs people could use to pull themselves up."

"And you and the Garrick Foundation would do this out of charity."

"For a healthy profit," Liz admitted, "which we pay taxes on, and which feeds back into the community."

"We're never going to see eye to eye on this," Meghan said.

"Probably not. But you asked for the truth. Roger had his faults, but he saw this town as stagnant and wanted more than anything to revitalize it."

"Then explain how the Vipers and the League of Nations fit into that?"

"Bribes," she said simply. "And protection, and the thousand and one things that come up when you work as a developer. Do you think Roger was alone in dealing with them? Or that he enjoyed it? He was extorted by every criminal group under the sun. But he was a practical man. He did his best."

"And you knew about this."

"Roger and I knew everything about each other."

"Even about Pete Shaw and Max?"

Liz smiled dreamily at the mention of her son. Looked at Meghan but said nothing.

Meghan thought it through and then blanched as something fell into place.

"He found out, didn't he?" she said. "Roger found out Max wasn't his, and confronted Cam, thinking it was him. That you were pregnant with his child."

"Really, Meg," Liz said.

"Cam didn't know, did he? And Roger attacked him for it. And you watched the whole fucking thing."

"Worse," Liz said, refilling her glass. No longer meeting Meghan's gaze. "The trim guard Roger was brandishing. I helped take it away from him."

She drank and *ahhh*'ed like someone in a commercial. Looked at Meghan evenly.

"I was hysterical for months," she said. "I heard them arguing, walked in and saw Roger slash at Cam. I grabbed my husband's arm, trying to convince Roger it wasn't what he thought. While I was holding him, the kid knocked the tool from Roger's hand, picked up a hammer and struck my husband."

"And you hid your role in this," Meghan said. "You cost that kid years of his life."

"I was traumatized, Meg. I hope you never have to face something like that."

Before Liz could drink, Meghan covered the glass with her palm, demanding the widow's attention.

"Do you know who killed Alexa? Or Michael May? Are you hiding anything else from me?"

"I wouldn't be party to murder," Liz said. "If I knew, Meg, I'd tell you. Or do something about it myself."

Meghan left, wondering what she meant by that.

A thick-bodied woman in an expensive suit was waiting by the station's front desk. She stood up when Meghan arrived.

"Zoe Prentice," the woman said. "I'm Cameron Shaw's counsel. I'll see my client now."

"Like hell," Meghan said. But she led Prentice through the station toward the holding cells. "How'd he afford a hired gun like you?"

"As that's immaterial, I won't dignify it with an answer."

"How very proper," Meghan said.

Cam was poised on the edge of the stainless steel bunk, elbows on his knees like the statue of the pugilist at rest. He looked up at Zoe Prentice with gratitude, fear.

"Hey kiddo," Prentice said. "How are you being treated?"

Cam shrugged.

The lawyer said to Meghan, "Some time alone, please. Here is fine. Then you and I should talk."

"Can't hardly wait," Meghan said.

In her office she blew on a scalding cup of coffee, the station fridge having run out of milk, and phoned her son. Trevor was between classes, on his way to crim, with only a second to talk. He was doing fine. No nightmares. No more sightings of gangsters.

"You're not in any danger, are you, Mom?"

"I'm fine as long as you are," Meghan said. "Be careful, okay? Situational awareness at all times."

"You be careful, too."

A quick online search revealed that Zoe Prentice practised criminal law in Surrey. Mostly pro bono defence cases. An abused wife charged with spousal homicide. A homeless woman who'd smothered her roommate during a psychotic episode. And now Cameron Shaw.

Meghan finished her coffee. Richie Reed's confession still sat on top of her in-box. She looked at the canister of kerosene found in the cottage. It would need to be chemically matched to the residue from the homicides, and on her son.

The can was half-empty. Three attacks on half a can? Not likely.

Alexa Reed, dead from a broken neck, her body burned. Found in her old bedroom, in a house once owned by Richie and Emily Reed, both now deceased. The house placed on the market by Elizabeth Garrick, Emily's cousin. The Reed family had seemingly gone broke, in fact hoarding their money in cash.

Strangled. Burned. Bankrupt.

A thought hit Meghan.

She pushed away from her desk and stood up, only to see Zoe Prentice waiting in the doorway.

"Mr. Shaw needs to be r.o.r.'d," the lawyer said.

"Like hell. He's a suspect in multiple homicides, not to mention a violent offender whom I saw at the scene of a crime. Try again, Ms. Prentice."

"Have new charges been laid?"

"That depends entirely on his cooperation," Meghan said.

"There are certainly multiple violations I can charge him with. Trespassing, breaking and entering—"

"Are you sure Mrs. Garrick would support that?"

Meghan picked up the phone receiver. "Should we check?"

Prentice smiled. "Please."

Her bluff called, Meghan had no choice but to see it through. Liz admitted to inviting Cam into her house—or rather, that Bob Sutter had. She wouldn't give a reason, but insisted Cam was there as a guest, and hadn't been involved in her attack.

"Mr. Shaw will happily answer any charges placed on him," Zoe said. "He will appear in court on Monday with regards to his parole. In the meantime, though, he deserves to be released on recognizance."

"And I have your word he'll be there Monday morning?" Meghan said.

"My word?" Prentice smiled at the quaintness of the term. "Don't you trust your own system?"

"I'll take that as a no," Meghan said.


If you took all the lies people had told her in the course of her career, quilted them together, you could fashion a garment large enough for the city to wear.

A significant part of that garment—a sleeve, say, or a collar—could be sewn out of only the lies told by Sukhi Kaur.

Since the beginning she claimed innocence, and only admitted knowing Alexa, knowing Cam, when confronted with evidence. Even then, she hadn't told Meghan the truth.

Well, if she had to go back to the girl yet again and force the whole story out of her, so be it.

When Meghan arrived at the house, there were no cars in the driveway. She knocked and waited. Eventually Sukhi appeared, wrapped in a robe, her hair and makeup a mess. Instead of defiance, though, the young woman was oddly muted.

"What now?" she said.

"I'd like to look around your garage."

"My parents's garage," Sukhi said.

"You gonna let me in?"

The garage held a 1970s Jaguar under a dust cover, its tires flat. Boxes of old tax returns. Little else. Sukhi looked bored.

"You done?" she asked.

"Now the shed." As they walked through the house, Meghan asked, "When did you last see Cameron Shaw?"

"Dunno. Days ago. Why, he do something?"

"I know you're not dumb, Sukhi."

The shed was piled with vintage camping gear. Coleman lantern, portable stove, the green metal heavily oxidized. A prominent spot in the corner held nothing. Meghan shone her light on it. Noted the circular stains of rust.

"You burn a lot of kerosene?" she asked.

Silence.

Meghan followed as Sukhi trudged into the house, letting herself fall onto a living room couch, arms folded in a profound sulk.

"I think you know who set that fire," Meghan said. "Who killed Alexa Reed."

"Don't know nothing," Sukhi said.

She made to stand up and Meghan said, "You know who did it, because Alexa came to you. You were introduced through Michael May, who's also dead. If I had to guess, I'd say your brother killed them. Tequila or Cam. Or you did."

Sukhi glared at her from the couch. She unfolded her arms and let them fall with a deep sigh. One trailed the floor. The other sunk between the cushions of the couch.

"Sukhi, you are going to tell me the truth. You met with Alexa, didn't you?"

"No clue what you're saying."

"She told you about the money, didn't she? The hundred and fifty grand her parents had taken out."

"No."

"Did you send your brother to her place to take it? Or were you with him?"

"Don't know anything," Sukhi said. "Why're you always—"

"Because a young woman is dead and you know what happened. I'm giving you an option to come clean and not spend the rest of your twenties and thirties in prison. I walk out of here, that's what happens. How about that?"

Sukhi said nothing. Meghan watched her, waiting for the woman to recognize that her options had officially run out. Meghan opened the front door, thinking a few hours in an interview room would probably nudge her into a confession. She heard Sukhi spring off the couch.

Turning, Meghan saw the eye of a nickel-plated .45 leering at her, wavering slightly between the woman's hands.

"How 'bout this instead, bitch?" Sukhi said.

# SEVENTEEN

"**L**et's get an ice cream," Zoe said.

There was a Baskin Robbins near the beach, along with a gelato parlour and a small kiosk run by an eighty-year-old woman who still hand-churned her own three flavours. From her, Zoe bought a double-scoop strawberry and a single chocolate for Cam, despite his protestations.

They walked out onto the promenade. Holiday lights were still strung in parabolas above the boardwalk. A grey mist covered the breakwater and the bay. To the east, Cam could see the roof of the Garrick home.

"I'm fucked, aren't I?" he said.

"If you mean are you going back to prison," Zoe said, "almost certainly, yes. The system makes it very hard for parolees to receive the presumption of innocence. One of its many flaws."

Cam couldn't tell if she was fucking with him. He licked at the grey-brown runoff that threatened to cover the knuckle of his index finger.

"My parents used to bring me here in July to watch the fireworks," Zoe said. "We'd buy ice cream and get to the beach early, park a blanket on the sand. I used to love inspecting the tidal pools, or walking across the train tracks."

A dozen sarcastic replies came to Cam's mind. He had spent his summers working, maybe slamming an extra couple beers at shift's end. No days off, boy, Uncle Pete liked to say.

"I wonder about children today, if they'll have that same urge to explore the world." Zoe lapped at her cone. "But then the world's a more frightening place now, isn't it?"

"It's not the world that frightens me," Cam said.

Zoe looked at him with what he took for sympathy

"No way I'll last inside, not with the Vipers and the League."

"I can't guarantee it, kiddo."

Cam lobbed his cone into the water, brushed his hands on the weather-greyed railing. He felt cold.

"My decisions," he said.

"Sorry?"

"I did this to myself. And I don't see a way to un-fuck things. Not unless you can offer me a get out of jail free card."

A trio of elderly women speed-walked by, laughing. When they were out of earshot Zoe said, "Your friend Harvinder Singh is an interesting man."

"He handed me to the cops," Cam said.

"Anyone would under those circumstances. Harv, though, seems to have maintained close ties to his former group."

Zoe's expression admitted nothing.

"Harv, Tequila and Tito," she said. "They were the most likely, since all three defected from the Vipers. Tito has no ambition, and with Tequila gone, it's obvious who's been brokering this unwanted merger."

"Unwanted by who? Your clients?"

Zoe sunk her teeth into the crisp wafer of her cone.

"I take out Harv, they'll protect me inside? And the money's waiting for me when I get out?"

"That would complete our deal."

Cam took in a deep breath of icy, ocean-scented air, looked back toward the beach. A family was walking along the sand, all three of them in padded coats and boots. The little girl was being dragged along by the red leash connected to her mittens.

"You'll have to get me a gun," he said.

Before she left, Zoe gave him two hundred dollars cash and a disposable credit card. He waited on the bench, looking at the green water smothered by fog, the ash-coloured sand. Smoking cigarettes, warming his hands.

After maybe an hour, he heard a honk from the parking lot behind him. A silver Honda waited in the midway between lanes of parking. A middle-aged South Asian man in a suit behind the wheel.

Cam approached, saw the man unlock the passenger door. He climbed in.

They drove away from the beach to a street in front of a low-rise apartment building draped in a white fumigation tent. Here the man got out of the car and gestured for Cam to follow. They both went around to the trunk.

Inside was a grey hoodie, a black Mariners cap, two burner cellphones and a Smith & Wesson .357 with a box each of .38 Special and Magnum rounds.

The man tossed the keys into Cam's cupped palm and walked to a dark Lexus parked down the block. His farewell was a salute of the index finger to his brow.

Cam ripped the price tag off the hoodie and struggled into it. He pulled the cap low over his head. He tucked the gun in the compartment between the seats, then stared at the instrument panel. He hadn't driven a new car in—well, ever. Certainly not since going inside. A button started the engine instead of a key. The panel and interface took a minute to figure out, the gauges and odometer only light green spectra on a screen.

Where would Harv be right now? Not at the house on the beach, since the cops had been there. Not at Sukhi's. Face facts: Harv was smarter. More resourceful, better connected, more plugged into the city. He would soon know Cam was out. He'd be preparing for him.

The problem with smart people? They were always a little arrogant, gave you less credit that you deserved.

He dialed Harv's number, waited three rings, five. A connection. For a long moment, neither of them said anything.

Then Harv asked, "Who is this?"

"Who do you think, asshole?" Play angry, make him think you're in a rage.

"You're out." Harv's voice was calm.

"No thanks to you. All that 'we're in this together' bullshit."

"Things happen," Harv said.

"Yeah, they do, but I notice not to you." Softening his voice. "Look, man, I got nowhere else to turn. You gotta get me some cash and a way out—and I'm not talking about Tito's weed money. Ten grand and a plane ticket."

"All right," Harv said, agreeing too quickly, the way Cam thought he would.

"Maybe a boat would be better. Get me down to Mexico."

"Sure."

"And what about ID? You must know a guy, right?"

"I'll take care of it," Harv said. "Are you in town?"

"Close," Cam said. "How soon can you get the cash and ID?"

"Almost noon now. Let's say two o'clock at the port."

"All right," Cam said. Then adding a calculated note of suspicion, "The ID, you'll need a photo."

"We'll bring the equipment, take it right there."

"Bullshit, this is a fucking set-up." Suspicion mixed with despair, imploring Harv to say it wasn't so. "You're fucking with me."

"Wouldn't do that, brother," Harv said. "A laptop and the right printer is all it takes." Chuckling, "Not like you got a choice, Cam."

"No," Cam said, realizing the truth of that statement for the version of himself he was presenting to Harv, and the even more terrified version gazing at himself in the rearview.

"Two o'clock, the parking lot near the port," Harv said. "The spot of your great heist."


There was a small off-leash dog park too close to the port to be used by anyone but the locals. The red loading cranes towered over it. The sloping grass led to a rocky beach which wound along the coast, culminating in a pile of rubble, from the top of which Cam had a view of the parking lot he'd broken into months ago.

Maybe that had been the turning point. The moment he lost the plot. If he hadn't been so desperate to prove he was smarter than everyone, so enthusiastic...

In truth, the heist had been the first moment he'd felt good since the days before the killing, when he'd worked for Uncle Pete and felt useful and content.

He watched the entrance to the port and waited for the soldiers of the man he had to kill.

No way Harv would come himself. He'd send his people, the members of the Vipers or the League who were loyal to him.

So they get to the parking lot and don't see Cam. They wait around. And then?

Then they notice the note.

Cam had raced to the parking lot as soon as the meet had been set, knowing there was a small chance Harv would have people waiting. Along the way he'd stopped at an ATM and grabbed a bank envelope. With a pen and a page torn from the Honda's mileage log, he'd written Harv a note.

*Had to run*
*Will call tomorrow*
*Don't trust our friends*
*Instead get in touch with CPG*
*thanks brother*

He'd noticed a decrepit Sedona that had been in the same spot at the edge of the lot the last time he'd been there. He'd addressed the envelope TO H.S. ONLY and placed the corner under the wiper blade.

Cam congratulated himself. CPG was gibberish, a red herring, something Harv would puzzle over in private. The soldiers would take the note to Harv, leading Cam right to his target.

His stomach rumbled but he couldn't think of food now. The gun was tucked beneath the hoodie, the metal warm against his skin. The rough texture of the handle's side plate had begun to itch.

At one fifteen a white sedan drove by the lot, paused for a second, then continued along. Cam clocked it, watched the car disappear down a side street. Ten minutes later it circled back. This time a man stepped out and walked through the gate of the lot.

This would be the hitter. Cam tried to make out the man among the parked cars. He'd been near death for so long that what chilled him wasn't the fact the man wished to kill him, but the casual nature of it. Click/bang/over.

Maybe it was over already.

He waited.

Two o'clock, two fifteen, three.

At three thirty a blue van pulled into the lot. Two men exited, both in purple ball caps. Cam watched as they moved down the rows, checking each of the cars that had been parked or abandoned there. They met the hitter, conferred.

At ten to four they returned to the van. All three of them. One clutching the envelope. They drove off, leaving the sedan behind.

Cam scrambled down the rock pile, raced to the Honda and gunned it. He turned onto the same street the van had gone down, spotting them in a lane feeding onto the highway.

They'd call Harv, tell him Cam didn't show, but they'd found some kind of letter. Harv being cagey, he might ask them to open it and read it to him. Unable to make meaning out of CPG, thinking there must be more to it, he'd tell them to bring it to him to study for himself.

The van pulled off the highway at the exit before White Rock. Cam almost lost them coming out of the merge lane. Weekend traffic to and from the border was heavy.

The gun sat next to him on the seat, shuddering slightly along with the car.

They passed onto Crescent Road, following the Nicomekl beyond a driving range, a Christian camp. This had all been trees eight years ago. Cam could see where the land had been flattened, divided into lots. Billboards proclaimed FUTURE SITE OF and some bullshit development's name. OCEAN DRIVE VILLAS.

The van pulled into a tract that rose to the left of Crescent Road, the entrance so hidden that Cam missed the turn and, realizing a uey would be conspicuous, drove around till he could double back.

It was a subdivision, or would be in a year. Several cream-coloured duplexes were already up, beyond them the wooden skeletons of their future cousins. Cam saw the van pull into the driveway of Unit 7, disappearing into the mouth of a garage.

It was nearly five o'clock, the sky almost dark. Lights on in the house. No blinds. Cam saw movement, the figures trudging single file through what looked like a kitchen. Stopping as someone met them in the dining area.

The action moved between the windows till Cam couldn't see anything.

A soft light went on inside the car, and he heard the 8-bit tinkle of a generic ringtone. He stared at the unfamiliar number on his phone. After a minute the words *new message* filled the screen, along with the graphic of a sealed envelope. He hit playback.

"It's me, it's Harv. Guess you couldn't make it. No worries, brother, it's better to be safe. Got your message. Who's this CPG? Hit me back on this number."

Cam put the phone down. He saw Harv saunter past the window of the duplex, holding something to his ear. Cam's phone rang again. He turned it off.

Four people in the duplex, at least.

He could lay in wait till nightfall, till they were all sleeping, then break in. Find Harv, kill him, escape. He could lure Harv out, try to shoot him and make a run for the car. He could shoot him *from* the car—if his aim was better, if luck was on his side, if a million things went just the right way.

He could shoot his way in now.

The more he thought about his options, the more he realized he had none. Any plan was likely to fail. Even if he managed to reach the target, work up his nerve, he'd still have to escape—and a gun was loud enough to make more problems than it solved.

So how, then?

He watched the duplex for an hour as darkness settled and the streetlights in the cul-de-sac lit up. An ambulance passed, no siren or lights. He imagined Harv inside the house, studying the note. His soldiers waiting around him. Who did Harv trust? Who was on board with his plan?

Cam started the Honda and drove back up Crescent Road.

At the turnoff for the highway was a gas station and convenience store that had once been owned by the Reed family. Their second location; Cam remembered seeing flyers for the grand re-opening. It was an Esso now, one frightened uniformed man in the Plexiglas cage.

Cam bought a jerry can and filled it at the pump, paid the man and asked him for matches. Then bought a lighter and a pack of cigarettes so the purchase wouldn't look suspicious.

"Friend of mine's car ran out of gas," he said. "Actually I'm going to light some shit on fire."

The man in the cage nodded indifferently and rang him up.

The garage door of the duplex opened. Two men emerged on foot. They saw the blaze and started down the driveway, through the gate, to see what exactly was burning in the middle of Crescent Road.

Cam was already halfway up the block, cutting across the narrow muddy yards, careful with his footsteps. Flags and stakes where cement would be poured. The laneways of the development felt empty and unreal, an amusement park after closing time.

He walked right through the garage door, hit the button to close, then ripped the system from the wall, twisting the wires so that the light on the box went dark.

A minute later the basement door opened and a lanky shirtless white guy in a purple snapback stepped over the threshold. He looked at the panel and paused, eyes popping when he saw the pistol.

Cam put a finger to his mouth, *shhh.*

He slipped the man's gun from his belt and had him kneel down. Cam had wondered what to do in this situation— tie him up? Gag him? Kill him quietly?

He struck the man on the back of the neck with the butt of the gun. The man let out a squawk of pain, and Cam hit him again, and a third time, the last catching him on the temple as he turned over. The man lay on the concrete, silent, hopefully unconscious.

Cam flicked on the light. Saw the van, empty. Tools, a car seat, flats of crushed beer cans. He turned the light off and shut the door behind himself.

A car fire only held so much interest. He'd have to hurry.

Up the carpeted steps, quickly, not worrying about sound. He heard Harv's voice. "The fuck was it, a crash?" The

260

staircase turned and Cam rose out of it, quickly brought the gun's barrel above the white railing and held it pointed centre mass at Harv.

Genuine shock on the man's face, which gave Cam a sinister pleasure.

A living room with dining nook, behind him one narrow hallway with a door. Everything beige and new. Cam moved into the room, closed the distance. Harv was in jeans and socks, a white undershirt.

"Wait," Harv said. "Listen, brother—we can talk. Who's this CPG?"

His eyes flicked from Cam's face to something over his shoulder. Someone approaching, or trying to make him think so.

Cam shot him.

Harv spun back, driven down between two lounge chairs. In the room the Magnum's sound was a terrific roar.

Cam stepped toward the downed man, heard footsteps besides his own. Turned.

Standing naked in the hallway, his enormous pale pink stomach slightly greasy with sweat, was Cody Hayes. Something silver in his hand, arcing down.

Cam didn't see what struck him, but felt himself falling.

# EIGHTEEN

Everyone was stupid, according to Sukhi. Her parents. Harv. Her brother. Cam. They all saw her as shallow and weak. None of them realized her value. When you're that good at disguising yourself, it works against you.

"It was *my* goddamn plan," Sukhi said. "And he just took it, like it was his."

"Cam did?" Meghan asked, staring into the gun.

"Harv," Sukhi said. "I just played Cam, in case the others tried to fuck me over."

"Men, huh?" Meghan said.

As Sukhi paced and monologued, Meghan calculated distances and movements. She watched the gold-tipped fingernail resting inside the trigger guard. The gun bobbed. Sukhi transferred it her left, took a precautionary half step back. Meghan's hands were still up at shoulder level.

"Harv's obsessed by this 'generational wealth' shit. Meanwhile all his cash is tied up. I bring him this score, he gets cold feet, sends my brother instead. What's he expect? Stupid."

"Your brother killed Alexa?" Meghan asked.

"Not saying shit about that." Sukhi's eyes focused on Meghan's holster. "Drop that gun."

"Why don't I hand it you? Might go off if it falls."

"Give," Sukhi said.

Meghan turned slightly so her hip was closer to Sukhi. Her right hand touched the firing pin, slid off the side of the holster. She fumbled with the snap on the trigger guard.

"Nervous," she said.

"Here. Hands up." Sukhi approached, reaching for the holster with her free hand.

Meghan spun, hip-checking her, at the same time locking her arms around Sukhi's elbow. The .45 went off, ear-splitting, punching into the floor. She bent the elbow and the woman screamed and the pistol clattered to the ground. Meghan drew her own, pointing it at Sukhi's throat.

"Hands on the top of your head," she said. "Face down."

When Sukhi was proned out, searched and cuffed, Meghan allowed herself to crow. "*That*'s how it's done."


The hard interview room. Sukhi in the corner on a stationary chair, leaning against the white brick. Meghan stood over the table and threw down pictures of Alexa Reed. A candid shot printed from social media. A grinning family photo. The dead girl, burned, her blackened chest sewn up with a post-autopsy Y-scar.

"Who?" Meghan said.

And waited.

Sukhi started from the beginning, with Harv's defection from the Vipers. His realization that if the League of

Nations ever wanted to be more than a feeder gang for the bikers, they needed territory of their own. Income of their own. Her brother had told her of the deals he'd worked for Roger Garrick back in the day.

"Tequila was just a pickup man," Sukhi said. "He remembered this rich guy was trying to get a casino going before he got killed. So a couple years ago, Tequila finds out this dude's widow is thinking of doing the same thing. He told me and I told Harv. They approached her to buy in."

"They dealt directly with her?" Meghan knew Liz Garrick had spearheaded the project, but found it difficult to put the woman directly in business with gangsters. If nothing else, Liz was smarter than that.

"Her people," Sukhi clarified. "The guy my brother used to pick up from."

"Richie Reed."

"Mr. Reed, yeah, Alexa's dad. Harv got in touch with him. The deal was five million to buy in, but then Mr. Reed started making noise about not wanting to be involved."

"So what did Harv do?" Meghan asked.

"*Ka-boom*," Sukhi said, grinning. "Hit him while he was crossing the road. Harv said just to warn him, but Tequila had that big Nav, knocked him flying. Dude went straight up in the air, *pew*, like a fat little football."

Hysterical laughter ended in a coughing fit. Meghan folded her arms and waited.

"Anyway. Tequila was pissed about the damage to his car."

"And Alexa?" Meghan asked.

"That was a lot later," Sukhi said. "She came to me. Said she knew about all the shit my brother did. The whole casino deal."

"She was going to the police?"

"Fuck no. She wanted in."

"Alexa didn't know you killed her father, did she?"

Sukhi paused for a sip from the bottle of Perrier Meghan had given her.

"She said she had some money, and could get more with our help. Her parents' house was for sale, but that money would go to Mrs. Garrick to dish out. Alexa wanted us to threaten her. Obviously we weren't gonna fuck up our deal for one little white girl."

Meghan tried to comprehend a bereaved child finding a hundred and fifty thousand dollars, and whose only thought was how to get more.

Sukhi coughed and sipped bottled water. "So Tequila and I, we go talk to her at her parents' place. Do a line or two. Alexa starts beaking off, how she needs the money, she's already got a hundred and something thousand. Tequila asks where it is, let's see. She goes quiet, says she can't trust us. Shit get real tense. Alexa pushed me. I don't let anyone do that, so I push back. Only she slips and bangs her stupid head. Totally an accident, but who's gonna believe me?"

Meghan was having a hard time believing it, though she could imagine how it really happened.

"So my brother gets an old fuel can from our parents' shed, was in there when they bought the place. He set the fire and we were good to go. Took her keys, so it'd look like she did it to herself."

"And Michael May?"

Sukhi nodded. "Tequila just wanted him to keep quiet, since he made the introduction 'tween us and Alexa."

"May wasn't involved in the deal with the money?"

"Lady, there *was* no money. We searched that house top to bottom. Bitch was obviously lying." Sukhi coughed and looked at Meghan. "She was, right?" Seeing Meghan's look. "Fuck."

Meghan made it clear to Sukhi that in court, it would come down to whose version of events a judge and jury put more faith in—Meghan, the fucking detachment commander, or a dropout who'd been stringing along two gang members, one a convicted killer. Credibility advantage to Quick.

But there are ways to tell a court what happened. Was Sukhi a cold-blooded psychotic who pointed a gun at a police officer? Or a confused kid who got carried away and, who knows, maybe even relinquished the firearm non-violently?

"What do I got to do?" Sukhi asked. As she stood up she bunched the fabric of her jeans at the waist and held them in her fist. No belt or shoes in the cells.

Meghan thought for a long minute about saying, "Nothing." Telling this girl, who'd giggled at the death of a man, who'd been partly responsible for how many deaths on her own, to go rot. Sukhi might have shot her had Meghan not been lucky.

Bob Sutter would have cut her zero slack, Meghan thought. Negative slack.

But the girl's help could be valuable.

"You pointed a weapon at a cop," Meghan said. "That's not going away, Sukhi. But there are others we want more than you. Cameron Shaw and Harvinder Singh, for starters. Help us get them and you'll improve your position."

"By how much?" Sukhi said, before reverting to her innocent-ditz persona. "Seriously, I dunno where they are."

"Can you find out?"

"Like how?"

Meghan shrugged.

"That's not fair," Sukhi said. "I'll help you, it's just I don't know."

"Then it's your neck," Meghan said.

She walked to the door and knocked on it to be let out. Stared at the camera for a second as Sukhi worked out her strategy, then called Meghan back to her seat.

"All right, so I maybe know about one other thing," she said.

Meghan showed the girl her hands, let's have it.

"Harv's planning something—I'm not sure exactly, but he's been trying to get Cody to make some introduction."

"Cody Hayes?"

Sukhi nodded.

"What kind of introduction?"

"I don't know. Really."

"That's too bad," Meghan said.

"I really *don't*," Sukhi said. "Dalton Hayes is the only one that deals with this person. Harv's been trying to get Cody to set something up for ages now."

"To go around his brother."

"Cody's pretty dumb. Harv's been working him for months."

Meghan studied her face. No question that Sukhi knew the value of what she was saying. That if Meghan made the right overtures, she would magically remember more details.

"Tell me what you know about this higher authority," Meghan said.

Sukhi smiled. "What are you gonna do for me?"


Alexa Reed inherited a fortune and found it wasn't enough. She'd turned to the wrong people to put pressure on Liz Garrick. The decision had cost Alexa her life.

But whose decision had it been? Her father had done business with the same people when Alexa was in her teens. The Reeds had liquidated their savings, maybe planning to give the money back if it meant avoiding prison. Or maybe they wanted to buy into the casino themselves, the same illegal investment Harvinder Singh was after. Generational wealth.

This spoke to something more than greed—a sense that money couldn't buy safety, only a *chance* at safety. A longshot, and as it turned out, the wrong play.

Sunday morning, with the warrant for Harvinder Singh in place, Meghan and Katy Qiu started toward the housing development on Crescent Road. Surrey PD had allowed them to handle the search since Meghan's interview with Sukhi had led them to the spot. Meghan parked her Interceptor behind the burnt husk of a silver Honda.

Sukhi had told her that Harv owned two properties in the unnamed development. Units 7 and 8. Maybe others as well. He'd only brought Sukhi here once.

Meghan knocked on the door to Unit 7 while Katy readied the shotgun. Knocked again and then noticed the garage door was raised. She noted the stains on the garage concrete: gas and what looked like blood. The door leading into the suite was unlocked.

They entered single file, checking the downstairs suite. Toilet seat up, piss stains on the floor. Shavings and dried foam around the sink. In the bedroom, a mattress thrown on the carpet in the middle of the floor. Clothing strewn around it. A clubhouse, she thought.

Meghan rose out of the staircase into a disaster zone. Chairs had been toppled, a table overturned. Blood on the wall, more soaked into the carpet right in front of her.

"Watch the first step," she called down. "Evidence."

No one in the upstairs. Down the hall, another toilet, equally gross and masculine, beyond that a master bedroom with two twin beds and a chest of drawers.

"Clear," she said.

In the living room, Katy crouched over the coagulated blood on the carpet. Dark brown, matted with strands of hair.

Meghan bent over the bloodstain on the wall, saw a gouge in the plaster that might have been caused by a bullet. She walked herself through the damage. Blood in three locations. Probably not from the same source. Three separate incidents, with someone, probably Cam, moving deeper into the place, catching someone by surprise, shooting them, then being surprised in turn by—who?

The person whose blood was on the wall had regained their feet and left the place on their own. Meghan knelt on the carpet near the staircase and observed blood spatter on the nearby banister, less than a foot from the ground. She was no expert, but that suggested a blow dealt while the victim was on the carpet.

Cam had walked into a trap. She couldn't imagine why he'd gone there, but he'd tried to shoot his way out and been incapacitated. Maybe murdered.

There was a certain fittingness to that.

Her thoughts quickly shifted. Yes, Cameron Shaw was a killer. He'd served time, maybe not enough, and she had no idea just what he'd been up to since getting out of prison. A felon who was due for parole revocation was what Bob Sutter would have called "a low priority lowlife."

And that had been her thought, too, and the thought of everyone in the goddamn town when it came to Alexa Reed,

269

to Michael May, and yes, even to Cam. Not worth the time to notice there was trouble, much less try to alleviate it.

She put it out over dispatch, Harvinder Singh was wanted for assault and possible murder. Her guess was that Cam was already dead. But that was no excuse not to try to help him.

# NINETEEN

**T**he world swung like a naked bulb, broken.

Cam vomited into the blackness, felt gravity pull it upward. His own saliva on his brow.

He was upside down. Hanging from something. His hands were cuffed in front of him, legs bound and trussed. The flesh around his ankles felt bloody and numb. Whatever he'd been tied with was slicing into his skin.

He steadied himself, waited for his vision to focus, his eyes to adjust to the dark. He spat and tried to listen to how long it took to fall. Forever. He tried again. Heard a *pat* after less than a second.

So he wasn't far off the ground, which meant wherever he was had a low ceiling. He tried to reach up to his legs but couldn't muster the energy.

One of his eyes was swollen and his vision was blurry. He scanned through his last conscious memories. The brilliance of his plan, following the car, luring the guards away. Finding Harv alone, exactly how he wanted him. Shooting him.

When he'd killed Roger Garrick there'd been this awful feeling of completion. Finitude. He hadn't had that sense from shooting Harv. That meant he'd missed or wounded him.

He remembered Cody Hayes swinging the bat. The big man's naked form. Cody and Harv together...

Desperation filled him and suddenly he had the energy to struggle.

Cam managed to pull himself up at the waist, felt for the roof, touching cold corrugated metal. He knew the feeling all too well. A shipping container. He was in a fucking can.

He flailed with his hands at the lashings on his legs. They were cinched too tight, too expertly done, and his hands felt clumsy, groping against gravity and exhaustion. He fell back, slept...

Was woken by something cold prodding his stomach.

A too-bright light stared at him, causing him to look away. A slap to his face. He opened his eyes, blinked and took in a frown, a smile, he couldn't tell. Harv's face upside down in front of him.

"You shot me, you piece of shit," Harv said.

Cam tried to reply, had just the right thing to say—"Like you weren't going to do it to me, only lucky for you your friend was there"—but his parched tongue didn't respond to his commands. He sputtered and watched Harv, who was spinning now, splitting in two. A pain shot through his skull—Harv had struck him with the light.

"Maybe I should thank you," Harv said. "You gave me credibility. Not many of us have been shot—or done real time, which was my mistake with you. I thought you were on board."

Cam's voice came back, softer and slurred like a drunk's. "Sold me out," he said.

Harv slapped Cam's face to stop any response. "Who was it told you to kill me? Was it Marco DaSilva? He have his lawyer reach out?" Harv read Cam's face. Smiled. "Or maybe you don't even know."

"Fuck you," Cam said, his words met with another hard blow to the jaw. Blood was leaking upward into his eyes.

"Wish I could take pictures," Harv said. "Before and after. Cody might do that anyway. Me, I like to think the best revenge is just being alive."

He turned off the light, washing Cam in the same black, then striking him on the jaw, the ear. Cam cringed, unable to see the blows. A knuckle struck his temple and the black gave way to red, a blooming, searing pain that sounded like the churning of waves.

When it subsided he heard only the creak of his own body, swaying.

Harv's voice in the darkness said, "You could tell me now and they'd just shoot you. But I know you won't."

"Won't what?" he wanted to say, thinking he'd admit anything to make this stop.

"What they'll do is come in here and break your hand first. Just so you know they're serious. Then the next time, they start cutting things—use your imagination what they start with. After that your eyes. If you last that long, you'll find a way to kill yourself. Probably swallow your tongue. You really want to live through that, brother?"

Cam shivered, bit his lip to keep from sobbing. There was no reprieve from this.

"Or you could just tell me," Harv said.

"Tell. You. What?" Three syllables, spat out more than spoken.

"Who you're working with?'

"Zoe—"

A stinging slap across his face.

"No," Harv said, "who you're working with."

"Marco—"

Another slap.

"The initials you left. CPG? Who the fuck is CPG?"

It took time for him to remember. Then he laughed.

Kept laughing as Harv struck him, harder now, the blows going wild.

On the verge of passing out, he heard Harv say, "Doesn't matter. We'll get the name. I'm being honest? Even if you *had* given it to me, I'd've told Cody you were lying. Enjoy the rest of your life, you piece of shit."

Sunlight, the squeal of the door. Then back to nothing.


He didn't know how badly any of his sensory organs were mangled. His eyes were useless. Blood and other fluids seeped and crusted his nose. But he stilled himself and tried to absorb what he could about the world outside his container.

What he *didn't* hear struck him first: waves. No gulls either. This wasn't the port, nor were they on a ship. Gulps of engine noise faded in and out. The murmur of wind in tall grass. A field? Somewhere near a highway?

The container smelled of rust. What Cam thought of as Chinese dust—the smell of boxed cargo shipped across the ocean—was faint. Meaning this container had been sitting here for a while.

When a semi-trailer or truck went by, he felt its vibrations. The can was on the ground, and he'd bet there wasn't another stacked on top of it.

His eyes began to register things. The left eye swimmingly, the right more clearly. Structural faults in the container let in pockets of light. A thin bright band around the top seam of the door. A small spot below him, cast from behind his back, the odd dust mote floating through it.

Voices, too, always moving. Footsteps in what sounded like gravel. Car doors thunking shut.

Then night, darkness, human sounds dying out. An overture of crickets, feral things rustling the grass. A swoop of wind, the talons of some large bird on the roof of the container.

He fell asleep to that.

Woke to the door being pried open, no light coming in. Voices in the middle of conversation, Harv's and another.

"...he *did* shoot me, obviously, but it's not about that. There's a name he has we need."

"Hmmm." Disinterested. Familiar.

"He stupidly dropped the initials to me earlier. CPG. In the morning we'll get the rest out of him."

"The longer he's here—"

"I know, D. I get it. The absolute *second* we're done with him—"

The door closed, locked.

Much later he put a face to the second voice—it belonged to Dalton Hayes.

In the morning they broke his hand.

Uncuffed him, the chain clattering on the floor. A man he didn't know held his right forearm against the side of the container, his legs straining at their bonds. Another held his torso and pinned his left arm behind him. Cam felt the cold metal of the container wall on the back of his wrist, and clenched his fist tight, hoping it would help.

His eyes flickered open on Cody Hayes swinging something. Pain blasted up his arm as his fist collapsed, his hand turning white hot. The head of the hammer struck again. He bit through his lip and sobbed as the hammer clanged off the container, was immediately swung a third time.

Then he was released, hanging limply, the fingers useless and numb, maybe gone. Cam sobbed into darkness.

"See you tomorrow," Cody Hayes said.

# TWENTY

**W**hat am I doing? Meghan thought, spinning her patrol car around Crescent Road and back toward Harv's property.

Cam had missed court. His uncle hadn't heard from him in days. The manager of the warehouse where Cam worked, Scott Doppler, nervously told Meghan that Cam had been out sick. He hastened to add that Cam was a good worker, one of the best and most reliable. If she pushed him, Doppler would probably confess that Cam hadn't been there in weeks.

Zoe Prentice said she'd walked Cam out of jail, bought him an ice cream, and hadn't heard from him since.

"Do you have an alternate way of contacting him?"

"Afraid not," Zoe said.

"Any clue where he might be? What his plans are?" Adding, after a hesitation, "You do want him found, correct?"

"That's a dumb question, and beneath you." Zoe sighed into the phone. "Of course I want him found. If there's something within reason that I can do..."

She didn't finish. Meghan considered it, and said, "You could ask your other clients if they know. I realize this may create a—what's the term?—conflict of interest. But if he's being held by the League of Nations or the Vipers, you might be in a position to help keep him alive."

"I don't represent gangbangers," Zoe Prentice said. "Even if I did, a formal offer of cooperation should come through the prosecutor's office. But I'm sensing this is personal. Why exactly do you care, Staff Sergeant Quick?"

"He lived here, once," Meghan said.


Back through Singh's house, which had been searched and processed, barricade tape strung across the door. Meghan searched the downstairs bedrooms, found nothing.

Through the upstairs kitchen and dining nook. Plates in the sink. Beer and takeout containers, not much else. A blanket lay among the overturned furniture in the living room—not inconceivable that someone had been sleeping on the couch.

So multiple males cohabiting in the property. A hideout, temporary given the thrown-together furnishings, the mattresses on the floor. Meghan peered at the pillows on the bed, noticed what looked like hairs on the mattress. Carefully selected one and held it up.

Natural blond, different from the ones matted in the bloodstain on the carpet. This was fair and fine. Dalton and Cody Hayes had hair like that.

One of the Hayes brothers, living in her backyard. Working, apparently, with Harv and a rival gang.

She walked out to the driveway and lit a cigarette. From the apex she could look down to Crescent Road, where the burnt wreckage of the car had been.

That's how Cam had gotten inside. Burning the Honda had been a distraction.

And now he was probably dead.

Meghan drove to the station and had the guard bring Sukhi up from the holding cells. The woman came bouncing into the room, took her usual seat and drummed on the table.

"You find him?" Sukhi asked.

"Just his blood."

Sukhi played with her bottom lip, maybe weighing her options. "I mean, that's the only place Harv took me."

"He must have talked about others," Meghan said.

"Just in general terms."

"Tell me."

Sukhi stared at the ceiling. "He talked about a place called 'the barn'—he'd brought Cam there before, I think. Then there's the boat—Dalton Hayes has a yacht or something, but it's usually in storage in the winter."

"Others," Meghan said.

"I don't know any—"

"Where would they kill him?" Meghan said.

Sukhi grinned, then ran a hand over her chin. "How would I know?"

"Because you're just so very smart."

"Fuck you."

"You pay attention," Meghan said. "You notice things. And you can piece together a likely guess."

"I tell you, will I walk out of here?"

There it was, the deal, plain and simple.

"If he's alive," Meghan said. "He's dead, your ass gets nothing."

Sukhi said "No deal" and crossed her arms, but after five minutes of enduring Meghan's stare, conceded and gave her a location.

Meghan chose Katy Qiu for backup and radioed Langley RCMP as she drove out to Zero Avenue, following the route through farmland and forest that Sukhi provided.

Less an address than an area. Sukhi had indicated a string of properties running along the border between Langley and Abbotsford. Meghan had heard about tunnels stretching into Washington State, some several kilometres long. From bootlegging to the Cocaine Eighties, to the glory days of BC bud, the area had always been a hot spot for smuggling. Now it was fentanyl, precursor chemicals and guns, always guns.

Her backyard.

Katy gripped her shotgun with the barrel pointed into the roof of the car. She looked nervous. Meghan told her she'd do fine.

"Any sign of anything, we wait for backup," Meghan said. "We're just looking. You did recon in the Reserves, right?"

"I set up tents."

"Well, you probably spent time looking at those tents. That's all we're doing here."

"So we're not engaging," Katy said.

"Not unless we have to."

Meghan watched as the officer clutched the barrel to her cheek.

The properties were thick with pine trees and fallow fields. The occasional half-melted snowbank. Hard to see anything from the road. Meghan went slow, pausing at the mouth of each gravel driveway to look carefully down toward whatever buildings had been built there.

One place looked promising. A hedge of blackberry brambles obscured a century-old barn. A thick chain had been triple wound between fence posts, barring the road in. Meghan stopped the car on the shoulder and leapt over the shallow ditch, trampling the bushes but making it to the road behind the gate.

Trespassing, she thought. Waving goodbye to the moral high ground.

From behind her she heard Katy say, "Thought we were only doing recon."

"This *is* recon," Meghan said.

She walked down the path, noticing that the barn doors were wide open. A car parked next to it, something dark blue, dirty, the windows too scuzzy to see inside.

Farther down, the road dipped, continuing out into a field. Single-engine plane parts littered the grass, a once-white bucket seat now poised scarecrow-like in the middle of the field. Stuffing dribbled from its back. A gunmetal grey Airstream trailer next to it.

"Anyone in there?" Meghan called.

The trailer was locked, but a quick trek around the perimeter showed that the back window had been smashed in. A sleeping blanket lay on the floor, the ticking ripped out. An egg carton and a used coffee filter, so ancient that the grounds stood sandcastle-like inside. Something darting around the floor that turned out to be a raccoon.

The property was deserted.


Hiking back to the Interceptor, Meghan noticed a layer of gasoline scum atop the ditch water. She followed it down the shoulder of the highway. The runoff seemed to emanate from a culvert on the property across the road. She waited for a semi-trailer to rumble past before jogging over the highway to the other side.

281

Katy lumbered after her, toting the shotgun.

Here the property rose up from the road in a rocky grass-covered shelf. A pair of drainage pipes flanked a path of hard-packed dirt. A slack chain hung loose from a yellow pole staked into the side of the road, tire treads imprinted in the mud. No way to see over the hill except to walk up. Meghan did, telling Katy to wait here and watch the driveway.

At the top of the hill the ground flattened. She saw two large Quonset huts, doors shut. Beyond that several shipping containers. SUVs and pickups parked on a gravel island between the huts, the turnaround a soup of gravel, mud and rainwater.

Meghan walked to the closest container. The doors were open, tendrils of a dead rose plant snaking out of its mouth, long bent and trampled.

A bald bearded white man in jeans and a leather vest stepped from one of the huts, careful to close the door before Meghan could get closer.

"Help you with anything?" he said, some sort of Maritime accent.

"Looking for two men," Meghan said. "Harvinder Singh and Cameron Shaw."

"Uh huh." He was at least a head taller than her. Both arms sleeved out with skulls, inverted crosses, a yin-yang symbol on his bicep.

Meghan described them. The man spat and took a step toward her, trying to force her back down the trail. Meghan held her ground.

"Nah," he said, "I see anyone like that I'll tell 'em you're looking."

"Who owns this place?" she said, offering her card.

"Company sells tools. Gardening shit. I can get you a brochure."

She nodded. Kept eyeing the trailers. Only the doors of the closest one were open.

"Don't have any just now," the man said. "Brochures, I mean. Your email on that card? 'Cause I can send one to you."

"Cody Hayes," Meghan said.

The man paused, the name obviously striking a chord. "Yeah, don't know about him. I should get back to work."

"Don't let me keep you."

Meghan didn't move.

The man waited for maybe five seconds, then said, "Nobody's s'posed to be here when the owners aren't, 'cept workers."

"Are you asking me to leave?" she said.

"Guess so, yeah. Got work that won't do itself."

"Your name?"

He scoffed and, shaking his head, brought out his licence. TREECE, BRYAN R.

"Thanks, Mr. Treece. Who's your boss, and when's he or she due back?"

"Missy, I just work here," Bryan Treece said, turning away.

Missy. Meghan sighed. She'd let him have that one.

She walked back to the highway. Katy fell in behind her.

"You drive back to town," Meghan said.

"You're staying here alone?"

She nodded. "Find out who owns this place. Look up a Bryan Treece, see if he's got pals or priors. I'll talk with the Langley detachment about getting a warrant."

"What's going on in there?" Katy asked.

"Nothing good," Meghan said, taking the shotgun. "I'm pretty sure that's the place."

# TWENTY-ONE

There were two lives: The Container and What Came Before. The Container was nothing but silence and the throb of pain from his mangled hand. It was sustained by wild hopes of breaking out, diminishing and dying into thoughts of how to end this. Harv's words about swallowing his tongue would come back to him even as he planned an escape. Futile. The thought would work on him till his arms fell below his head and he'd hang, trussed up like a slab of beef, defeated.

If he told them the truth—that he'd made up CPG just to fuck with them, to give him enough time to kill Harv—they'd only scoff and ask if he really expected them to believe that. Trapped by his own cleverness, by his not being clever enough.

Tell them nothing. Let them do what they wanted.

He didn't sleep but passed out during the night. When he woke, his mouth was cracked and filled with the taste of dust. The pain in his hand was a livid throb. He tried to flex the broken hand but the pain snarled at him and he drifted out again.

Dull grey cracks of sunlight had penetrated the container. It gets worse today, he thought. Worse from here on out. Best to end it, even if that means dashing your head against the roof.

But before that, let's at least make one good try.

The sensation of swinging his torso hurt—but then everything hurt. He struggled and exhaled and contracted his abdominals and pulled himself up so that he could grab onto his jeans with his good hand, holding himself up in a jackknife position.

He couldn't sustain this for long. Worse, with his functional hand busy holding him up, he couldn't feel his leg bonds, had no sense of how to get free.

The breath he was holding burst, and he sighed and fell back, panting, swinging, choking down despair. It was over.

Everyone had seen this coming but him. From the moment he'd walked out of Kent, he'd been on track to end up here. Dying by fits and starts. Another unpleasant cargo.

He had a thought, dismissed it as impossible. Sometime later it returned, along with enough strength to try.

Again he sat up, pulling his body into a ninety-degree angle, using his good hand to cling to the leg of his pants. This time he threaded his right arm behind his right knee, pinning it to his chest. The pain in the broken hand was screaming, but he found by putting pressure on the forearm and elbow, he could hold himself in place, giving his left hand freedom to roam.

He reached and touched the ceiling, waited as his head swooned, then settled and cleared. Worked his hands over to the pulley that his legs were lashed to.

It had been done with a thick chain, wrapped around his ankles in alternating diagonals. He tugged at the chains, tensing his calves and twisting his thighs, trying to create play. His fingers crawled across the links, the chain finally terminating in a hexagonal box. A padlock.

He could work with that.

Given two hands and the proper picks and tensor tools, and his uncle's confident advice, Cam could have picked it. In his condition now, clinging to his own body to keep upright, with only what he had on him? Not possible.

Cam felt his right arm slipping. He let himself drop, then with his good hand, undid his belt. Threaded it behind one leg and around his shoulder, then tightened it, sat up, tightened it again. There was no belt hole for the tongue to fit through, but it was easy enough to wind the length of excess leather around his arm, holding the tongue in his teeth.

Upright again. Cam felt for the pulley. Bolted into the sides of the container, the bolts capped and slick with ancient grease. Impossible to work free.

How many others had tried this? Got this far and given up?

The League has done this enough to know not to leave ways out.

The thought coincided with a deep exhalation, and he felt like sinking back, then recovered by forcing himself to believe it wasn't true.

Experts? These dumb fucks? The way they panicked at the dock? Their half-assed plan to take the Vipers' shipment in the forest? Brutal, violent, smart, give them all of that. But not experts.

He'd survived seven years of prison. He'd survive this, too.

Cam tried moving the tongue of the belt into the lock but it was too wide.

Something else. *Think.*

A good padlock couldn't be jimmied open. A cheap or old one—he remembered seeing his uncle knock a padlock off his shed once, when he'd lost the key. Uncle Pete had Cam hold the lock tight while he smacked it with a mallet, just beneath the junction with the bar. Cam had no hammer and no help. He felt the padlock, twisted it against the pulley's bolt, felt no give in it.

Bending the tongue of his belt into a U, he fed it through the lock, playing out slack carefully so as to maintain his upright position. Adding his weight to the pressure on the lock's bar. Leaning back slightly so that the lock stood upside down.

No way this will work, Cam thought.

He jerked the belt down, smacking the lock against the pulley's housing. It didn't pop magically open. It didn't budge. He tried again, harder, with no result.

Lashing the belt around his right forearm, careful of the broken hand, Cam pushed the air out of his chest and crunched further, so that his head brushed the roof of the container. He played eight centimetres of belt through the loop in the lock, leaving it slack enough so that the bar relaxed away from the metal housing.

Deep breath in and out.

He let himself fall, tightening the belt, putting the weight of his falling body behind the lock, smashing its side against the pulley.

Snapping it.

The lock panged off the wall of the can like a tinny gun-shot. The chains slackened but held. Cam flailed, finding his body dropping, still entangled. If someone heard that, they'd be walking toward the container to examine it.

The chain hit the ground with an industrial rattle. Cam dropped, the leather belt suddenly snapping. He stood and stepped out of his restraints—

—and realized at once the futility of what he'd just done.

Containers don't open from the inside.

It had been a running joke with Sheedy and Tyson at the warehouse. One of them would be deep into a can, unloading a shipment, and barely notice the light go out, then the doors shut. They'd pause, realizing their predicament, then bang on the door.

Okay, that's enough, guys.

Seriously, let me out.

What'll you give us if we do?

*Anything*, he thought. *I'll give you fucking anything.*

Holding his broken hand to his chest, Cam thought of the lock rods on the outer side of the door. They'd have to be raised and then turned in their keepers to open the door. Unless Cody and Harv had left them open and merely shut the door.

He pushed, felt the metal yield—then click against the bar. It was locked, maybe not entirely, certainly too tight for him to move them.

Cam sat and felt tears form in his eyes. His great breakout thwarted by a fucking door.

There was a small hole in the back of the container where the light was coming from. A structural fault, or maybe a result of rust. He tried climbing up and working his fingers through, but cut his palm.

He walked back toward the doors, over the chains and cuffs, the small puddle of dried vomit and blood.

The lip of the right door fed over the left, so that the right always had to be opened first, once the lock rods had been turned correctly. Cam crouched down to the left. He reached out for the chain and slapped it down on the floor. Again, this time smacking it against the side of the container. Then wound part of it around his arm.

He heard footsteps and muttering, "The fuck is it now?" The lock rod turning, the door swinging back.

A figure appeared, moving inside, the bald man in the leather vest. As the man's eyes adjusted and registered the absence of a strung-up body in the hold, Cam snaked the chain around his neck and fell back, choking, thrashing, beating on the man's skull with the chain around his good fist. The man writhed. Cam sunk fingers into the man's eye sockets and slammed the man's skull hard against the floor of the can.

He'd never heard a scream like that, apart from himself, the day before.

The man shuddered. Cam's knee pressed into the man's neck, his weight on it, driving his fists into the face until the man stopped.

If anyone else was around, they'd be alerted to something going wrong inside the container.

Cam searched the man, tossing his wallet, finding a fold-up knife. He walked out into the brightness, stumbling over uneven grass.

There were other containers on either side of him, a pair of Quonset huts beyond, and what looked like a dirt road leading down. It was cold and the sky was the greasy grey of a sweat-stained pillow, the sun halfway up in the east. Behind him, to the north, lay a wide field of grass, then a treeline of evergreens.

He started down the road, thinking maybe the bald man was alone. The door of the Quonset hut was half-open. As he passed, Cam saw inside. Black plastic rain barrels, a stainless steel mash tun, translucent hosing, and a small pile of gallon jugs, the same type that he'd liberated from the port. No way this place would be left with only one guard.

As he realized this, the door to the other hut opened. Cody Hayes appeared, stooping in the doorway. He stared at Cam, eyes bulging, then darted back inside, quick for a man of his size.

Cam started running, back toward the field. A second later he heard the steady peal of automatic gunfire.

# TWENTY-TWO

The Langley detachment lent her an unmarked Explorer and brought her a Starbucks. The constables told her they'd loop back in the morning and let her know as soon as a search warrant came in.

It reminded Meghan of long nights on stakeout. Sipping coffee through a straw, not wanting to take her eyes off her target. Nights on patrol with Bob Sutter, smelling each other's farts, passing a Thermos or a gas station sandwich between them.

They'd been so close. Christ, Meghan still had keys to his place. "This line of work, Meg, it pays to make sure your partner can grab you a change of undies when you need one." All sorts of his sayings drifted through her head.

And now Bob was dead. He'd become someone different under Liz Garrick's influence. Ambitious. Corrupt. Maybe he'd realized that the job of detachment commander was filled with more failure than success, and what triumphs there were didn't amount to much. Not socially, not financially, not in terms of looking back and feeling good. There was always more you could have done.

Would Bob be out here now? Not a fucking chance. Not for Cameron Shaw.

But Meghan wished he was.

Vehicles came sporadically along the two-lane highway, mostly pickup trucks and semi-trailers. A van slowed to see if she was all right, then noticed the data terminal mounted to the dashboard and kept moving.

Meghan saw deer, a skunk. Heard a coyote at some point in the night. Something black and mangy slunk across the road, which she recognized as a black bear. Hunting for human trash, she thought. That made two of them.

Around five a white Cayenne Turbo pulled into the property, bouncing its way up the road. Meghan couldn't see inside. She'd parked the Explorer just before the turn, so that a vehicle travelling from the west wouldn't see her.

She took down the first part of the plate number but couldn't catch the rest. Radioed it to her dispatch. Meghan cracked the window slightly, the chill air keeping her from falling asleep.

She texted Trevor. *Know its late but wanted to say Cop Mom luvs u, is proud of u.*

No reply, but that only meant that he was asleep, as he should be. Trevor would read it in the morning.

Should she write something for Rhonda? *I'm sorry and I miss you. Given another chance things could be different. I'd make time for you. I swear.* She decided against it.

The sun came out and Meghan stretched, stepped out and pissed holding onto the trunk of a sapling, thankful she'd saved the napkins they'd given her with the coffee. She found a bottle of Purell in the glove box and was slathering it over her hands when she heard the gunshots.

292

Meghan radioed a ten-eighteen and gave her location. Left the Explorer with the shotgun and approached the path.

Pointing the barrel at the crest of the road, Meghan advanced slowly, knowing she'd be walking between the huts. She saw the Porsche parked on the gravel, its driver side door open. A tall man was sprinting through the field behind the containers.

The door to the hut on the left was open. She saw what looked like a meth works inside. Meghan crossed between buildings and tried the door of the other hut. Entered, saw a kitchen counter, a basin and water dispenser. A television in the corner.

At a long bench, a thin, fair-haired man sat drinking coffee. Meghan recognized him. Dalton Hayes.

"You're under arrest," she said.

"All right." Dalton Hayes gulped back the contents of his mug before standing. She proned him out and cuffed him.

There was a partition in the hut, a sliding door between rooms. Meghan opened it and heard running water. Saw Harvinder Singh standing shirtless in front of a freestanding porcelain sink, its pipes and innards disappearing into the floor. Harv's left shoulder was bandaged. A pistol balanced on the edge of the sink.

"Turn around, Mr. Singh."

He bolted, hand sweeping up the gun as Meghan fired. The sink disintegrated in a blizzard of white shards. The shotgun's recoil bruised her shoulder.

Harv was running. Meghan pursued, rushing toward the door, threading between mattresses and sleeping bags. Harv turned and fired at her, the shots pinging against the aluminum side of the hut.

Meghan crouched and aimed high, slightly over Harv's retreating head, and fired.

The man sprawled into the muck, spinning over, screaming, his hands covering his neck. And just as quickly up and running again.

Meghan trudged after him. As they passed the container, she saw a stray limb hanging out through the half-opened door. The man from yesterday, Bryan Treece. His face an odd shade of purple.

Jesus, someone had been kept in here. She'd walked past a few hours ago—

A bright ripple of gunfire strafed the door of the container and Meghan dove, pivoting, clinging to the shotgun as she inched along the side of the container. She heard footsteps, more gunfire. Controlled now. Two sets moving toward her.

"You take that side," a voice called.

Reflexively, Meghan backed away from the container, swivelling the barrel between each side of the approach. She felt her boots touch mud and realized she'd moved to where Harv had fallen.

He appeared from the left side of the container, holding the pistol in a two-handed grip. They fired almost simultaneously, Meghan's shot pattering the container door. She felt a stinging at her side, above the hip. Racked the slide. Knelt, ignoring the muck. Harv ducked back before she could draw a bead. At the same time, from the open end of the container, Cody Hayes broke right, shouldering some sort of assault rifle. She drew a bead, fired, saw the blast rip into his chest. Pivoted as Harv swung out, firing his pistol as he ran. Meghan racked, fired, felt herself hit the mud.

She was down looking up, rolled over, the shotgun out of reach. Sliding backward over the grass, looking for Harv who was still running as she worked at unsnapping her holster.

A thatch of grass a foot to her left exploded. She turned and saw Cody Hayes sitting up, a red-black crater in his right pectoral. The assault rifle propped in his lap, held in his left hand. He steadied it on his knee.

Meghan cleared her sidearm, aimed and emptied her weapon into his chest.

Cody flopped backwards onto the grass, coughed, his hold on the rifle slipping. One leg straightened before the man let out a gasp and wretched, gargled, lay still.

Ejecting her magazine, Meghan fumbled for the spare clip at her belt, finally working it free from its pouch only to drop it in the mud in front of her. Cody stared at her, his hand feebly twitching in the grass. She cleaned the magazine on her sleeve, wincing as she realized she'd taken a hit somewhere. She dropped it again.

Getting clumsy. All thumbs these days. Must be hurt.

A shadow on the grass, footfalls. Harv walking toward her.

# TWENTY-THREE

**N**o way he'd outlive Cody Hayes. No way he'd outrun him.

Cam crossed the field, not looking back. His chest and lungs felt overtaxed, his knees roared with pain at every step, and his hand—

—nothing. He felt nothing there.

The field dipped. Cam slid downward, tearing out handfuls of grass to steady his drop. No sound of gunfire. Cody must have emptied his clip. He'd need to stop and reload.

And then he'd be pursuing. Hunting him with every advantage.

Cam listened closely for sounds of footsteps, trying to still the reedy sound his throat made sucking down air. He heard no one. Thought, *it's a trap, no way in hell they'd give up.*

Then he heard a shotgun blast, the return fire of a small-calibre pistol, *pap-pap-pap*. Looked up and saw Cody Hayes retreating from him.

The cops? The Vipers? It didn't matter. This was his chance to escape.

Except—the field stretched on another three or four kilometres before it reached the trees. He was starved, body broken, unarmed and ill-equipped. If it was the cops, if they'd swarmed the place, rounded up Harv and the Hayes brothers, then the best thing to do was surrender.

Survive first, then surrender.

He started back as soon as Cody disappeared around the container. Crouched when he heard gunfire, watched as Harv, shirtless and bandaged, traded shots with someone near the can. Saw Cody slip around the other side, Harv withdraw. They were coordinating an attack against someone. A burst of automatic fire and the concussive clap of the shotgun, twice in rapid succession. Pistol shots, rolling into one perpetual growl.

He saw Harv emerge from his hiding place limping. Cam was maybe thirty yards from him. Then twenty. He saw Meghan Quick sitting up in a dirty puddle, fumbling with her pistol as Harv took aim.

Cam rushed him, knocking Harv into the side of the container, striking him in the throat with his elbow.

Harv looked annoyed, then angered as Cam's forearm cut his cheek. He swung Cam around and into the door of the container, sending him to the grass. Cam held on. Harv tumbled over, landing atop him, the weight driving out what air remained in Cam's lungs.

They were underwater. They were on fire. Cam's movements felt desperate and languid, while his opponent's were sped-up and unfathomable. Harv's fingers found his throat. Cam struggled, pawing at the man's face ineffectually. Harv released his grip and Cam breathed, then felt a roar of pain from his hand.

Harv had snagged one of his broken fingers, was pulling it backwards—farther—

—off.

The horror of seeing his digit severed sent Cam spinning, screaming, clambering across the grass. Held down by Harv, the man taking his time, pinning Cam down to the grass.

The gun went off near his ear, and his attacker's grip went slack.

Through one murky eye, Cam saw Harv tip onto his side and stare up at the cop, mud-soaked, pointing her pistol directly in his face. Harv looked at her, looked at Cam. Gazed off at the road.

Cam heard sirens.


Out and in and out again. Daylight on his face. Someone staring down into his eyes.

The feeling of being lifted, raised onto a crash trolley. Then looking up through a sedative haze at the ribbed steel roof of an ambulance. Thinking for a moment that it was yet another container and he was its cargo. Handle with care. Some damage acceptable.

Waking up in Peace Arch, catheterized, a saline drip in his arm. His right hand a bundle of gauze and bandages. A doctor talking down at him, saying the finger could possibly be re-attached, but it would be difficult and costly, and with no guarantee of success.

Too weak to move, Cam lay in a room with three other bodies, staring at the glow from the window. Everything was beige, from the blinds to the doors to the comforters on the bed. A beige existence, interrupted only with streaks of pale blue and green, the nurses and doctors.

He tried to get word of what happened. Were the Hayes brothers dead? Was he facing charges? When he asked the doctor, she shrugged. The nurses shushed him and said it could wait for later.

There was an issue with infection, and he'd need a course of antibiotics. The matter of the hand was too much for his system right now. The nurses cheerfully told him that many patients lived full and happy lives with fewer digits than ten.

On the third morning he walked down the hall and back, supervised and cheered on by a nurse. He made a second circuit at noon, this time noticing the name SINGH, H on the door at the end of the hall. A somnambulant guard in front of it. The bastard had survived.

Well, good for him. Maybe they could do it all again some time.

In the meantime, Cam's fever began to drop. He started physio, felt strength come back to his arms.

On the third day he got a visitor.

It was the blond-haired Asian kid who'd been shot in the arm. Chalk. He was dressed in a Ralph Lauren polo shirt and pre-ripped jeans. Hair slicked back and parted like a movie star. He brought Cam a box of doughnuts. Cam asked what the news was in White Rock.

"Like a ghost town now," the kid said. "Haven't seen Tito or any of them. It's, well, I think I'm gonna move away for college. I hope that's okay, bro."

Cam shrugged. As if he could stop him.

"Do me a favour, Chalk?" he asked.

The kid leaned forward, looking sheepish. "It's, uh, actually my name's Mason."

"Mason. You got a pen?"

They asked the nurse. Cam tried scribbling left-handed on a piece of Kleenex, but it tore. He dictated to Mason. He told the kid if he wanted out, he'd need to pass the note to Staff Sgt. Quick. The kid nodded and left.

Later that day Zoe Prentice called him.

"You're due back in court as soon as you're better," she said. "I've stayed the parole hearing, but I'm not sure how much I can do for you."

Cam slid off the bed. "Can you stay on the line for a second?"

He got to his feet, cradling the hospital phone, dragging himself to the nurse's desk. The receptionist looked at him with concern.

"You shouldn't be out of bed," he said.

"My lawyer's on the line," Cam told him. "Unless you get a surgeon in right fucking now, she's suing everybody, 'cluding you. So pretty please. Fix my fucking hand."

# TWENTY-FOUR

Convalescence wasn't her strong suit. After one night in the hospital, Meghan checked herself out. The wound above her hip was what the doctor described as "a deep graze." The tissue would knit as long as no strain was put on it. She preferred her own bed and food to the hospital's, and really, who was going to stop her?

Trevor drove her home in her car. He was quiet during the ride. There was admiration in the way he looked at her, but also admonishment. It came out once she was in bed, slurping through chicken soup and crushed saltines.

"You could've been killed," Trevor said. And sitting down in the easy chair he'd brought up to her room, he began to cry.

Meghan put down her bowl and stretched her arm out to caress his shoulder. He'd earned a cry, and she shared some of his feelings. But it felt too good to be alive for her to regret what had happened.

"THE BATTLE OF ZERO AVENUE," the *Peace Arch News* had called it. The *Sun* had gone with "SMALLTOWN COP TAKES ON BIG-TIME CORRUPTION." Embarrassing but not entirely inaccurate.

The Langley officers had arrived almost as soon as the shooting had ended, had been shocked by the carnage in the muck, even more to find Dalton Hayes waiting calmly on the floor of the Quonset hut amidst amphetamine production equipment and weaponry.

Harvinder Singh had been pelted with buckshot. He was now under guard in the same hospital ward as Cam.

Meghan doubted she'd ever know the true sequence of events. Cam's body showed evidence of torture. She figured he'd gone to Harv's duplex to kill him, been captured, beaten up, and somehow escaped the container. And she had come blithely walking in, just in the nick of time to save him. Or be saved by him. She hadn't yet figured out who owed whom.

Despite Trevor's protestations she was up the next day, making herself runny scrambled eggs with plastic cheese, coffee sweetened with a slug of single malt. Meghan worked on her reports, checked in at work, learned that Denny Fong had been cleared of wrongdoing for the shooting of Ivan Stepcic. Her own hearing would be in a month's time.

"That's two shooting incidents in one year for your department," the Surrey PD administrator said over the phone, chuckling to himself. "Guess things are really changing in old White Rock."


Her first day back at work, gunless, arm still in a sling, she filed her reports and went over the charges against Dalton Hayes, Harvinder Singh and Cameron Shaw. Dalton had been on the premises, but no doubt he'd produce all sorts of people, living and dead, to credit the meth-making equipment to.

Harv had shot her, so he'd be away for a while.

As to Cam—that was more problematic.

With Cody Hayes and Bryan Treece dead, it would be Cam's word against Harv's. Blood from the Crescent Road duplex had been matched to both of them. What kind of witness would a convicted killer make?

As Meghan finished the paperwork, a reed-thin kid with dyed blond hair walked through the office, escorted by Amanpreet Brar.

"Says he has a message for you," Amanpreet said.

Meghan took the paper and read.

*I only saw Harv point the gun at you.*

"Son of a bitch," she said out loud and thumped her desk, causing the blond kid to cringe. Amanpreet led him away, saying it had been a rough week for Staff Sgt. Quick.

She took off early. In front of her house was a rental car, a Saturn, parked in her usual spot.

Rhonda was sitting in the living room, drinking coffee with Trevor.

"Look who showed up," her son said, grinning.

Rhonda stood and wrapped her arms around Meghan, kissed her cheek. Then let go and said apologetically, "I'm not hurting you, am I?"

"Not a bit," Meghan said, returning the embrace.

Rhonda had let her hair go natural grey. A few new lines around her already careworn face. Still beautiful, though, and Meghan felt a surge of desire.

She kissed her. Rhonda smiled and squeezed her hand.

"Happy to see you too, ducky."

They had dinner as a family for the first time in years.

After, when Trevor had excused himself to go to a movie, with a look in his eye like Hayley Mills' in *The Parent Trap*, Rhonda opened a bottle of pinot noir. They sat on the couch, legs crossed, the way they had years ago.

"Of course I read about what happened," Rhonda said. "Simply incredible."

"It was nothing. I got lucky."

"You're very brave. You always were. But do you know how worried Trevor was?"

*Here we go*, Meghan thought.

"He asked me to come visit. See if I could change your mind."

"Quit and be a housewife."

"And be anything you want, Meg. The two of you could come live with me. My place is big enough. And maybe..." Rhonda shrugged. "Maybe away from the job, there's hope for us."

Meghan felt grateful and manipulated, but above all, too exhausted to argue. She kissed Rhonda again and told her she'd think on it.


The Garrick home looked the same as it had before the attack. Liz opened the door for Meghan, offered sincere congratulations and escorted her to the pool room. The new windows gleamed emerald green. Liz explained that she'd had to replace the surviving glass as well, to make sure they all matched.

"The casino's going through, I take it?"

Liz gave one of her enigmatic smiles. "You can't stop things like that, Meg."

"So it all worked out nicely."

"In a sense. To what do I owe this visit?"

Meghan explained what she wanted. The money she'd recovered from the Reed home, plus the proceeds from the sale, were to be used as a charitable fund for troubled White Rock youth. The funds matched by Liz, administered under the umbrella of the Roger Garrick Foundation.

Meghan had the document with her, detailing Richie Reed's arrangement with Roger Garrick. She placed it on the tea tray next to the honey and milk.

"Funny thought I had," Meghan said. "Tequila Narwal killed Michael May, and Sukhi killed Alexa. But I never learned who tied up my son."

"I imagine one of them wanted to intimidate you," Liz said.

"Could be," Meghan said. "Only, I remembered in the car the other day, Bob Sutter had a key to my place. I still have one to his. My door was locked when I got there, which is what made me think of it."

"I don't follow," Liz said. Her fingers took up the document, pulling it toward herself.

"The Bob I knew would never do that, least not on his own. Maybe if someone convinced him."

The words made no impression in Liz's perfect smile.

"Why dredge it up, Meg, with the poor man only recently in the ground?"

Meghan nodded.

"Every fucking penny gets to the people that need it," she said.

"Of course, Meg. Whatever you need to feel good about yourself."

Rhonda insisted on taking them for dinner to the Greek taverna on the beach. A tourist trap during the summer, in mid-January they were one of two occupied tables. The Costas family hovered near the kitchen, refilling their water and bringing Meghan a bottle of retsina on the house.

"I could get used to dining with a celebrity," Rhonda said.

"You're welcome to stay."

Both Rhonda and Trevor took in the meaning of the phrase.

"So you're not gonna give it a try?" Trevor asked her.

"Chicago?"

"They do have a police force," Rhonda said. "Ever see *The Untouchables*?"

Meghan broke off a forkful of warm spanakopita. "I know who I am. There's a lot I still have to do here."

"And so that's the end of discussion," Rhonda said.

Meghan wiped crumbs from her mouth. "'Less like I said, you want to stay."

"Mom, you were almost killed." Trevor's voice broke slightly.

"I love you both, to the point it hurts, but I won't have that used against me. The fact is this place is headed for trouble if there's no one looking out. And I could sure use both of you here to support me. But you have your work, Rhonda. I respect that. And Trev, it's your choice."

She continued to eat, letting them stare at her in frustration, betrayal.

"I'm going," Trevor said. "Soon as this semester's over. We talked about it already."

"Do what you have to," Meghan said. "Maybe next Christmas I'll come visit you. If things aren't too busy around here."

They'd taken separate cars to the restaurant. Trevor naturally went back with Rhonda. Meghan had twenty minutes left on the parking meter. She wandered across the train tracks to the edge of the sand.

*What a pretty fucking town*, she thought.

The water was black. Garlands of holiday lights still decorated the boardwalk. Meghan saw couples walking along it and watched them for a while. Then dried the saltwater sting out of her eyes and went home.

# TWENTY-FIVE

There was too much nerve damage to reattach the finger. A second surgeon told him the same thing. So be it. He'd manage with nine.

In a closed proceeding Cam told the judge he'd been attacked unprovoked by unknown assailants, strung up and tortured by Cody Hayes and Bryan Treece. He couldn't say who else was involved. No, he hadn't brought a gun to Harv's home. He had no idea how that car caught fire.

He was captured on video at the Reeds' old gas station, buying the jerry can of fuel. Parole revoked. On his way back to Kent to finish out his sentence.

In the pre-trial centre, while he waited for further charges to be laid, Cam saw a group of cons with long beards and tattoos. They dominated a corner of the activity room. Full-patch members of the Exiles, a few hang-arounds standing near them.

Dalton Hayes calmly sat among the bikers. He nodded at Cam as Cam passed by.

One evening before lights-out Cam was lying on his bunk, reading an Edwin Torres novel, when a solidly built South Asian man appeared in the doorway.

Cam's back was immediately against the brick, ready to kick out if need be. His body had healed up somewhat, but still felt weak. If the man tried for him, he'd strike and try to run.

Instead the man nodded a greeting, said, "Message for you from Harv. Says nothing's going down while you're inside. Says thanks for keeping quiet."

"All right."

"Also says, once he's out, you'll be hearing from him."

Cam nodded. "Tell Harv that works for me."

He didn't relax until the man had gone.

His appointment with Zoe was at nine. Ten minutes to, a corrections officer came to his cell and escorted him to the meeting room. Down a long white hallway, locked at both ends, which the guard keycarded them through.

Cam saw another co coming out of the meeting room, leading a tall redheaded man that Cam recognized from the Exiles's table. The biker didn't look at him.

Zoe was already in the room. She shook his hand, then they waited for the guard to close the door.

"Who the hell was that?" Cam asked.

"Another client," Zoe said.

It hit him, so simple he couldn't believe he hadn't seen it before. "You work for them, don't you? The Exiles."

Zoe didn't deny it. "Right now let's talk about you."

Cam sank into his chair. He could imagine what was coming. What he'd have to do to stay alive.

"Your money will be waiting when you get out," Zoe said. "My client is very pleased with your work."

"Lot of good that does me." Cam held up his hand and closed it into a fist, the nub of the middle digit only curling halfway.

"Could have been worse." Zoe opened her document case. "I'm going to tell you a fairy tale, kiddo."

"You serious?"

"Just listen," Zoe said. "Once upon a time there was a rumour that someone in the League of Nations was considering a lateral move. A partnership with the Vipers to control a new casino. A talented and beautiful lawyer was told to search out someone who could get inside the League, find out who was behind this move. Her client couldn't trust their usual contact in this matter."

"That would be Dalton Hayes," Cam said.

"This brilliant lawyer looked far and wide before finding the right person. He held up his end, not understanding that this was less an assignment than an audition. Once the dead weight was removed, what remained were opportunities."

"Kind of opportunities?"

"Rebuilding. Leadership."

"Of the League?"

"You've proven yourself," she said. "Loyal. Savvy. Able to follow orders. And you're a survivor. When you're out you could probably run things with a minimum of fuss."

"You're serious," Cam said.

"There's a health and wellbeing appeal to your sentence," she said. "It might take a while to arrange, but it's possible we could keep you from returning to prison. As to how you'd occupy yourself in the meantime..."

Zoe let a file fall on the desk. She lifted the edge, exposing a picture of Dalton Hayes.

Cam took her meaning. "Interesting story," he said

The lawyer slapped the files together and stuffed them in her case. She ran her fingers over Cam's injured hand. He noticed the buffed nails, the obscene gold watch. She patted his forehand affectionately.

"You and I are going to make an awful lot of money together," Zoe said.

On his way back to his cell Cam passed through the activity room and bought himself a Pepsi from the machine. The corner table had a card game going, Dalton Hayes playing dealer for the Exiles. The redheaded man he'd passed in the hall was sitting next to Dalton, his back to the corner. He made eye contact with Cam. His head inclined slightly in Dalton's direction.

Cam nodded. Then went back to his cell to get ready.

# ACKNOWLEDGEMENTS

**W**hite Rock and Surrey are real places. My fictional versions are drawn at times from memories or the requirements of the story. The area is on the traditional, unceded territories of the Semiahmoo First Nation and the broader territory of the Coast Salish Peoples.

All characters are fictitious, any resemblance to real people is coincidental.

For various research details I owe a debt to Kim Rossmo, Don English, David Swinson, Eve Lazarus, Aaron Chapman and the reporting of journalists who've documented the rise of gangs along the border, especially Kim Bolan at the *Vancouver Sun*.

Thanks to the following people:

Carly, first and foremost.

My mom, Linda, brothers Dan and Josh, and Kim and Mark.

Charles Demers, Naben Ruthnum, Kris Bertin, Mel Yap, Clint Burnham, Sean Cranbury, Kelly Senecal, Dennis Heaton, Gorrman Lee and Janie Chang.

All the great bookstores, especially Pulp Fiction.

My agent, Chris Casuccio at Westwood Creative Artists.

Everyone at Harbour Publishing, especially Anna Comfort O'Keefe, Derek Fairbridge and Fleur Matthewson.

Gratitude to the Canada Council for the Arts and the BC Arts Council for their support, and the Vancouver Public Library and Simon Fraser University Writer in Residence Programs.

And to you for reading this.

Sam Wiebe

# ABOUT THE AUTHOR

Sam Wiebe is the author of the Wakeland novels, one of the most authentic and acclaimed detective series in Canada. His latest, *Sunset and Jericho* (2023), was a BC bestseller for over ten weeks, and *Hell and Gone* (2021) won a silver medal from the Independent Publisher Book Awards. His work has also won the Crime Writers of Canada award and the Kobo Emerging Writers prize, and been shortlisted for the Edgar, Hammett, Shamus and City of Vancouver book prizes. He lives in New Westminster, BC.

Sign up for the newsletter at samwiebe.com.